D1539485

Praise
Drusilla Campb

LITTLE GIRL GONE

"An unflinching portrayal of life in emotional and physical captivity. Campbell has a powerfully understated voice and resists the easy path of sensationalizing the story. Instead she provides authentic drama rich with complex psychological composition. The result is a novel that is hard to read, but even harder to put down."

—*San Diego Union Tribune*

"Campbell's latest has full-blown appeal for teen readers, echoing stories of abduction in the news (a là Jaycee Dugard, and her memoir *A Stolen Life*) or popular fiction (think of Emma Donoghue's Alex Award-winning *Room*)."

—*School Library Journal*

"*Little Girl Gone* peers insightfully into the lives of people easily written off as monsters. With an economy of style, vivid details, and grace of expression, Drusilla Campbell has written a novel well worth staying up late to keep reading."

—Laurel Corona, author of *Penelope's Daughter* and *Finding Emilie*

"Campbell's powerful novel explores the depth of depravity cloaked as charity and the ability to take a leap of faith and change the direction of one's life. This compelling story will stay with you long after the book is finished."

—MonstersandCritics.com

"When is the last time you cheered out loud for a character in a novel? That's what I did as I read Drusilla Campbell's *Little Girl Gone*. The complex relationships between Campbell's richly drawn characters took me on a psychological roller coaster that tested my expectations, my values, and my heart. This story of tension and triumph is a perfect book club selection. Don't miss it!"

—Diane Chamberlain, bestselling author
of *The Secret Life of CeeCee Wilkes*

"Drusilla Campbell uses lyrical descriptions of the desert setting to make each character's loneliness more atmospheric." —*Newark Star-Ledger*

"Nobody gets to the marrow of human flaws and frailties better than Drusilla Campbell. In *Little Girl Gone*, you are immersed in the lives of people you think you'll never meet and come to care deeply about what happens to each of them. This is a compelling story that won't leave you alone even after you've turned the last page."

—Judy Reeves, author of *A Writer's Book of Days*

"Campbell writes with deceptive simplicity all the more impressive for the psychological currents simmering below the surface of a barren terrain . . . a novel that celebrates the power of friendship and the freedom to make one's own choices." —CurledUp.com

"*Little Girl Gone* is a fantastic exploration into domestic violence and the power of courage in the face of tragedy."

—BookFinds.com

THE GOOD SISTER

"Should be on everyone's book club list."

—*Publishers Weekly*

"A novel about motherhood, sisterhood, and even childhood...In a novel which examines the sometimes devastating effects of postpartum depression, Campbell has managed to humanize a woman whose actions appear to be those of a monster rather than a mother. Through her sister's eyes, we are able to understand and even empathize with Simone Duran, a woman who has failed as both a wife and mother."

—T. Greenwood, author of *The Hungry Season*

"Can you have sympathy for a woman who attempts to murder her children? The way Drusilla Campbell tells her story, yes, you can. Even more important, in this unflinching look at family relationships, postpartum depression, and the complex lives of the characters, especially the women in this book, you can come to understand how such an unthinkable act can happen. Make no mistake, *The Good Sister* is a painful story, but it is also a story that will carve away at your heart."

—Judy Reeves, author of *A Writer's Book of Days*

WILDWOOD

"The pull of family and career, the limits of friendship, and the demands of love all come to vivid life in *Wildwood*."

—Susan Vreeland, *New York Times* bestselling author of *Girl in Hyacinth Blue*

ALSO BY DRUSILLA CAMPBELL

Little Girl Gone
The Good Sister
Bone Lake
Blood Orange
The Edge of the Sky
Wildwood

WHEN SHE CAME HOME

Drusilla Campbell

GRAND CENTRAL
PUBLISHING

NEW YORK   BOSTON

This book is a work of fiction. Names, characters, places, and incidents are the product of the author's imagination or are used fictitiously. Any resemblance to actual events, locales, or persons, living or dead, is coincidental.

Copyright © 2013 by Drusilla Campbell

All rights reserved. In accordance with the U.S. Copyright Act of 1976, the scanning, uploading, and electronic sharing of any part of this book without the permission of the publisher is unlawful piracy and theft of the author's intellectual property. If you would like to use material from the book (other than for review purposes), prior written permission must be obtained by contacting the publisher at permissions@hbgusa.com. Thank you for your support of the author's rights.

Grand Central Publishing
Hachette Book Group
237 Park Avenue
New York, NY 10017

www.HachetteBookGroup.com

Printed in the United States of America

RRD-C

First Edition: April 2013
10 9 8 7 6 5 4 3 2 1

Grand Central Publishing is a division of Hachette Book Group, Inc. The Grand Central Publishing name and logo is a trademark of Hachette Book Group, Inc.

The Hachette Speakers Bureau provides a wide range of authors for speaking events. To find out more, go to www.hachettespeakersbureau.com or call (866) 376-6591.

The publisher is not responsible for websites (or their content) that are not owned by the publisher.

Library of Congress Cataloging-in-Publication Data
Campbell, Drusilla.
    When She Came Home / Drusilla Campbell.—First Edition.
        pages cm
    ISBN 978-1-4555-1035-1 (trade pbk.)
    I. Title.
    PS3603.A474W48 2013
    813'.6—dc23
                                                    2012040688

For Art, first and always

Acknowledgments

Right off, I want to thank my mother, Patricia Browne Ness. She's an amazing woman: brave, resourceful, and creative.

Rocky Campbell is as steady and dependable as his name implies. He has provided me with backbone when necessary, IT support, promotion, and advice, twenty-four/seven. Everything I know about computers and football, I learned from him.

I am indebted to Doctors Robert Slotkin and Patricia Rose for their insight as I try to understand why my characters live and act out their dramas as they do.

As always, I'm grateful to the Arrowhead Association, which honors me by letting me be a member.

The love and friendship of many people keeps me at my desk, good days and bad. I am fortunate to have in my life such bright and shining stars as Judy Reeves, Peggy Lang, Susan Challen, Betty Chase, Matt and Nikki and the three sweethearts, Margaret Green and Carole Fegley who answered all my questions about girls' soccer.

ACKNOWLEDGMENTS

It takes a particular kind of courage to be in the publishing business these days. I am grateful for the patience, loyalty, and encouragement of my agent and friend, Angela Rinaldi. My editor, Selina McLemore, has been a joy to work with. Thank you Mary Flower for teaching me the right and proper use of capital letters. Elizabeth Conner has done her design magic with the cover of *When She Came Home* and production editor Siri Silleck has turned it all into a book. Thank you, Beth de Guzman, for overseeing the whole crazy business and making it come together at the end.

While researching *When She Came Home*, I was introduced to many courageous men and women. Two I will mention here. Captain Allison Downton (USMC) and Captain Lisbeth Prifogle (USMC) shared with me their experience of day-to-day life in the Marine Corps at home and in Iraq. I have tried to honor their honesty in this book, and any errors relating to the Marine Corps are entirely my own.

My grandfather died in World War I and is buried in Baccarat, France. He left a widow and young son. My brother, Kip, was an Army medic in Vietnam. This book is a way of saying thank you to them and to all the brave men and women who risk their lives under the banner of the stars and stripes, and to the families who love them and wait for them to come home.

WHEN
SHE
CAME
HOME

Chapter 1

October 1990—Washington, DC

I t rained for three days.

This was not the soft, slow soak that twelve-year-old Frankie Byrne knew. Rain in Washington, DC, was a wall of cold liquid steel flooding the streets with rushing litter-filled water that could sweep a pedestrian off her feet if she didn't hang on to her father's hand. It swamped the Mall and ruined shoes bought especially for the meeting with President and Mrs. George Herbert Walker Bush.

Frankie loved it.

Her brother, Harry, was still in a wheelchair then, and the part of his trousers where his legs should have been was soaked. Frankie would have been in a terrible mood if she were the one who'd had her legs amputated at the knee, but Harry never complained about anything.

The limo heater blew hot air, and before they'd driven a block Frankie wanted to shed her coat—pale blue wool and, like her shoes, bought for the special occasion. She would feel more comfortable in soccer shorts or sweats and athletic shoes, but she was Brigadier General Harlan Byrne's daughter and knew what was required of her. Every night since they checked into the Hilton Hotel, she had practiced balancing a book on her head while walking across the room she and Harry shared. She wobbled on the kitten heels as if they were three-inch stilettos. He said it was the funniest thing he'd ever seen, better than *Seinfeld*.

She began to unbutton her coat. Her mother shook her head.

"We could cook a chicken in here."

"That's enough, Francine." When her father used his command voice, there was no point arguing.

She was too excited to sit still, but her parents and Harry were solemn as pallbearers. The General's back was so straight it hurt her own to look at him, but when she did she automatically tucked in her stomach and dropped her shoulders down and back an inch or two. She composed her face into an expression that she hoped matched her father's in sobriety.

More than anything she wanted the General to be proud of her, and if that meant she couldn't crack a smile from now until taps, she would manage somehow. Sitting straight and strong, her father looked magnificent in his Marine Corps dress uniform with the stars and bars polished and the Purple Heart ribbons lined up perfectly. He'd been shot twice in Vietnam, once in the leg and once in the shoulder. He rescued three of his Marines from the VC and kept them all alive in a hole in the ground until a helo found them. Another time he was hit with shrapnel; he had a five-inch scar under his shoulder blade. He'd been bitten by some kind of snake too, a death-on-speed adder, and almost died, but no one gave out medals or ribbons for a snakebite.

The General had put his life on the line for his Marines and for America and that's why he and his family had been invited to Washington. The president had declared a special day to honor the country's heroes.

Frankie had been revved up and practically manic (her mother's word) since they landed at Dulles International two days earlier. She had worn herself out enjoying all the things there were to see and do in the capital, and at night there had been adult parties where she was on her best behavior. Being Harlan Byrne's daughter, she was accustomed to meeting important people in the government and military. The year before General Powell and his wife had come to dinner. Without knowing any details, Frankie knew that her father's opinion on military matters was valued although he had long been retired.

"I'm sweating."

"Stop complaining. It's only a few more blocks."

"I can smell you," Harry taunted. "Chicken fricassee."

She aimed a kick at him and hit car upholstery where

his shins used to be. Her cheeks blazed, but he only smiled and shrugged and that made her even more ashamed.

Harry was five years older than she and ordered her around as if she were a grunt; plus he teased her, promising that if she'd do his chores he would give her half of one of his cinnamon rolls. And not always the smallest half either. There was nothing stingy about Harry. And when Frankie's life got sharky which it did whenever the General went after her for grades or table manners or not trying hard enough in sports, Harry was always there like a rock in the surf she could scramble up on and feel safe. It was Harry who told her she was a natural athlete and to be glad she was the tallest girl in the seventh grade at Arcadia School.

Harry had been accepted for Annapolis before his accident, slated to be a Marine like their father and every Byrne before him going back to the War of Independence. In the General's office there was a display case holding the medals and ribbons he had inherited from his forebears. Frankie had watched his face when he learned that Harry would never serve. Not a muscle twitched to show how much this grieved him, but Frankie knew it just about broke his heart.

Amazingly Harry had quickly adjusted to his disability. Frankie's suspicion that he was relieved to escape military duty was confirmed when he told her he had always wanted to be a pediatrician and now he could be. She was incredulous.

Until his accident he had never told anyone that his ambition was to go to Africa and work with Doctors Without Borders or to open a clinic for poor children right in San Diego. His aspirations and ambitions had been pipe dreams, subordinate to the General's determination that he would distinguish himself as a Marine Corps officer.

Harry had been breaking school rules when he took a shortcut through the parking lot at Cathedral Boys' High. It was spring and the track coach was a bear for punctuality, but Harry was a senior with girls and graduation on his mind. He wasn't paying attention and neither, as it happened, was Mr. Penniman, one of the history teachers. He'd had trouble starting his ancient VW van, had to play the clutch just so. One minute there was no one in his rearview mirror and the next there was a thump and Harry Byrne went down.

The doctors at Scripps Hospital had tried to save his legs but they were a mess, and although Harry was young, they would never mend properly. Frankie was with her parents when the doctor told them, "We're going to have to take them. At the knee." She remembered how her father's jaw set. Barely moving his lips, he said, "Do it."

For a while Frankie was angry at Harry for being late for track, for not seeing the old VW van, for never really wanting to be a Marine. He seemed like a traitor to the Byrne family, the corps, and the General in particular.

The guard at the White House gate held a black

umbrella over his head as he talked to the limo driver, then saluted the General and waved them up the circular drive to the entrance. At the entrance there were more umbrellas and Frankie's shoes got wetter, but the welcoming committee at the White House knew how to handle Harry's chair and had him inside before the rest of them.

"Welcome to my humble home," her brother whispered and swept his arm in an arc, grinning like the Wonderland cat.

Everywhere she looked there were sober-faced men in uniforms and suits, buds stuck in their ears. A Marine who looked like Bon Jovi offered her his arm, and she slipped her hand into the crook of his elbow though she was able to walk just fine in her little heels. She tried not to hear them squishing. The family was escorted down a long hall lined with paintings and mirrors framed in gold and through a wide doorway into a lovely room with windows facing the White House lawn. They were seated in the front row of about twenty comfortably padded chairs.

The room filled with other men in military uniforms from all the services. Some came alone, others had wives and children with them. Frankie hoped she didn't look as dorky and awestruck as the other kids did. After a little waiting time, a disembodied voice announced, "Ladies and gentlemen, the president of the United States," and everyone stood and there was more saluting and then the leader of the free world walked in and stood about six feet from

Frankie. She observed how pink his skin was and that he had a Band-Aid on his left thumb, as if he'd chewed on a hangnail and made it bleed.

The president called the General to the front of the room and shook his hand hard, holding it in both of his while he looked him straight in the eye. He made a speech about the General's heroism, his humility, and his service to the country since he had retired and he said the nation was grateful and proud. Through it all the General stood as still as the officer Frankie had seen the day before, guarding the tomb at Arlington National Cemetery. Composed, and in her eyes, radiant.

"Harlan Byrne," the president said, "you are a great American hero."

Everyone in the room clapped enthusiastically and then another hero came forward, but the General stayed beside President Bush. Thirty minutes later there were six men on the dais, three on either side of the president. Flash-bulbs reflected off every mirrored and polished surface in the beautiful room. Frankie wanted to be a Marine standing beside the president in a dress uniform, wanted to be covered with ribbons and medals.

At the end of the ceremony, Mrs. Bush came in wearing a wine-red dress with a lace collar and shoes with heels like Frankie's. The General introduced his family to the first couple.

The president shook Harry's hand. "We heard about

your accident, son, and Mrs. Bush and I are so very sorry. A terrible thing to happen. Terrible. I understand you've decided on a career in medicine."

"Yes, sir."

"I'm sure you'll make a wonderful doctor," Mrs. Bush said.

"Thank you, ma'am."

"Whatever he does," the president said, "he'll make you proud, General Byrne."

Frankie glanced at the General, though she did not really expect his expression to show his feelings. In Ms. Hoffman's English class she had learned the word *inscrutable*. No other word described her father as well. Without looking at Harry, she knew what he was thinking. They both knew he could win the Nobel Prize for Medicine, but the General wouldn't be as proud as if he wore the uniform of the Marine Corps.

"Mr. President, may I present my daughter, Francine?"

Mrs. Bush said something about soccer.

"Yes, ma'am," Frankie wasn't quite sure what she was agreeing to. She stood up straighter and looked right over Barbara Bush's head, out the window to where the lawn stretched away from the house and the rain fell in silver chains.

"And I understand you have a beautiful singing voice."

Mrs. Bush had a friendly way about her. Talking to her, Frankie relaxed and it seemed natural to tell her about the Bach cantata the All Souls' choir was rehearsing.

There were more questions and she must have said and done the right thing because as they all filed into the dining room for a fancy lunch, her mother whispered, "I'm very proud of you, Frankie."

The praise would have meant more coming from her father.

Chapter 2

2001 to 2007—San Diego, California

On September 11, 2001, when terrorists attacked the United States, Frankie and Rick Tennyson had been married sixteen months and had a daughter named Glory and an Irish setter named Flame. When it became clear that American forces would be going back to Iraq for the second time in ten years, she knew what she had to do.

She had Glory with her in the stroller, and the recruiter asked three times, was she sure.

She made her announcement at a family dinner.

Harry spoke first. "Shit. You're kidding, please say you're kidding."

Her mother didn't bother telling him not to swear at dinner. She sat back and covered her mouth with her table napkin as tears welled in her eyes. "What on earth possessed you?" She pushed her chair back and fled into the kitchen.

"Is this some kind of a joke, Francine? Because if it is..."
The General knew it wasn't a joke. "Why in God's name would you do such a thing?"

She had been prepared for their shock and initial upset.

"I want to serve our country, sir."

"What about your family?"

"You've got a finance degree," Rick said, sounding confused. "You work in a bank."

Her sister-in-law, Gaby, asked, "Is it final?"

"I leave for Quantico in six weeks." First there would be officer's training and then months and months of Basic, what she knew would be the most physically and psychologically grueling months of her life. "After that, I don't know where they'll send me."

"They'll send you goddamn nowhere!" the General roared.

Gaby sighed and reached for Rick's hand in sympathy.

"I can't believe you'd do this. What about our daughter?"

Everyone seated at the table looked at the baby in the high chair. Glory stopped stirring her peas into her mashed potatoes and looked back at them.

"Answer your husband, Francine. What about your daughter? I can understand a man enlisting, but a wife and mother? This is wrong. Very wrong. Unnatural."

Until the General used the word *unnatural* Frankie had not understood the depth and breadth and steel of his opposition to women serving in the Marine Corps. This was more than the shock and anger she had expected. It was worse than disapproval. As if an iron gate had dropped between them, she felt herself shut out of her father's heart.

Later Frankie and Rick put Glory to bed together as they always did, Frankie sang to her, and the baby's eyes never left her face.

Across the crib Rick interrupted. "You only got pregnant to please me. You never wanted her."

"I wanted to wait."

Rick was ten years older than she and had felt the need to hurry. Probably because of this, he had taken to fatherhood immediately; but until Glory was almost a year old Frankie had only gone through the motions. Accustomed to being good at everything she committed to, she was determined to master the skills of a good mother in much the same way she had learned to block and kick a soccer ball, by repetition and an effort of will.

She had felt foolish making conversation with a baby who didn't understand a word, but she did as all the books said she should, pointing out and naming things until her conversational skills deteriorated to the simplest sentences, just nouns and verbs with a modifier tossed in when she was inspired. She read all the recommended childcare books and followed all the prescriptions for a happy healthy baby. Eventually and without Frankie noticing how it happened —by hourly, daily increments, she supposed—the love had come. Now, like Rick and the rest of the family, she was completely smitten with Glory, who was certainly the brightest and prettiest baby who had ever lived.

"You wanted a baby and I wanted you to be happy," Frankie said. "I love her now. Isn't that what matters?"

Glory followed the conversation, her sleepy eyes looking back and forth between her mother and father.

"Anyway, I'm doing it for her."

"That is such a load of crap." Glory's eyes opened wider. "How can you even say it? You should be gagging on the words."

"Rick, there were children on those planes. Glory could have been one of them."

He exhaled in disgust.

Rick was doing fast and furious sit-ups on the far side of the bed, his toes tucked under the chest of drawers. He jumped to his feet and faced her. The tendons in his neck stood out like the roots of an old tree.

"Just tell me why."

"Don't poke your finger at me."

"I want to hear the truth. No more bullshit."

"I'm not lying."

"Frankie, don't you know yourself better than that? Have you so little insight?"

He used his condescending, I've-lived-longer-and-know-more-than-you voice, and her desire to cooperate froze.

"I told you. I'm doing it for her."

"The hell you are. You're doing it because you're a twenty-five-year-old woman who's still trying to get her father to love her."

13

On the soccer field if someone elbowed Frankie out of the referee's line of sight, she waited for the right moment and got her back. In games and life, the impulse to retaliate came to her as naturally as breathing. But this was Rick and part of her understood his anger and even sympathized with it. If their positions had been reversed, she too would be confused and heated; however, she would eventually accept his decision to serve and defend because she had been raised to believe that this was what military families did when the country was threatened.

"It would be different," she said from the closet doorway, "if it were you who wanted to go."

"But it's not me, Frankie. It's you, the mother of my daughter."

"I'm a woman, so I don't get to do what my conscience tells me? There has to be some deep dark Freudian explanation?"

"Shall we pursue that idea? Do you think you're up for that conversation?"

She ignored his challenge. "This war is about who we are as a nation."

"Stop." He held up his hand. "If we're going to talk about this, you have to do one thing for me. Stop the spin. Stick to the truth. You enlisted because you're the General's daughter and you'll do anything, even leave your family to fight in some godforsaken desert, just to hear him say you're a good girl and give you that look."

"What look?"

"The one he gets on his face when he starts talking about his father and his uncle and grandfather. All the bully Byrnes who risked their lives so America can be free." He looked disgusted. "If you knew how tired I get of listening to that crap."

His vehemence stung her. "I thought you loved my father. He loves you."

Rick laughed. "But he'd love me so much more if I were a Marine."

They had always talked in the dark. It had been their way from the beginning.

"What are Glory and I supposed to do without you?"

He was calmer than he had been, more hurt than angry. But this was harder to bear. She wanted so much for him to understand.

"On the plane that hit the Pentagon there were a bunch of kids on a National Geographic field trip. And there were two little girls. Sisters. I imagine I'm their mother and I know they're going to die and I can't help them."

He rested his index finger on her mouth. "Just stop. It isn't your fault those children died and it's not your job to save the world."

"Your folks live in Massachusetts, Rick. We've flown in and out of Boston ourselves."

"There are dozens of flights every day."

"But it could have been us. We could have been at your

15

folks and had Glory with us...." She sagged under the weight of the images. "It can't happen again. Ever."

War was men's business and the General knew how to call in favors. Though he could not undo her enlistment, he made sure that after officers' training and the Basic School, his daughter was separated from her unit and posted to the small finance office at the Marine Corps Recruitment Depot in San Diego, about twenty minutes from Ocean Beach. Most nights she was home from the shop in time to fix dinner. She became a fixture at the MCRD, and every day it rankled, it gnawed, it galled her that while her friends were in Iraq and Afghanistan, she was a paper pusher in her hometown.

Glory was just finishing first grade when the opportunity arose for a ten-month deployment in Iraq, what the Marine Corps called Temporary Additional Duty. Frankie would be posted to a Forward Operating Base as part of a joint effort to win the hearts and minds of the Iraqi people. She told herself, she told Rick and her father, that the TAD was only ten months.

"I have to do this."

Rick looked grim and clenched his jaw. The General stopped talking to her.

Chapter 3

October 2008—San Diego, California

Frankie had been home from Iraq for almost two months, back at the MCRD, a captain now and adjutant to the chief financial officer, Colonel Walter Olvedo. She and Olvedo were meeting in his office on the day the call came from Glory's school. Frankie's phone vibrated against her thigh but she didn't touch it.

The situation in the office had reached near critical, and she and the colonel had been trying to have this meeting for weeks. The surge announced by the president had created problems for the previously insignificant San Diego Office of Financial Affairs. It had tripled in size and now handled not only payroll for the MCRD but other bases in southern California as well. Also—and this was new—a number of sensitive classified matters came across Frankie's desk. Seven of the nine young Marines in the office had inadequate clearances and insufficient financial training to deal with these and were inclined to be careless unless Frankie rode them hard and constantly. Olvedo had sent a dozen messages up the pipeline requesting more qualified personnel, but with everything that was going on in Iraq and Afghanistan, no one had time for anything as far from the line of fire as Frankie's shop.

"Is that your phone buzzing, Captain?" Olvedo had heavy black brows that made him look cross most of the time despite his pleasant and easygoing disposition. "It sounds like a killer bee."

Olvedo's wife had once been a career Marine but after their third child was born she left the service to go back to school to become a teacher. His mother-in-law lived with them and helped out with childcare. He knew Frankie couldn't ignore a call from Arcadia School.

"We're done here." He waved his hand toward the office door. "Do what you have to do."

Thirty minutes later she was hurrying across the parking lot to her Nissan.

"Captain Tennyson, please, wait up. Please."

At the car she turned to see a young man in chinos and a blue blazer hurrying toward her.

"I'm glad I caught you," he said, panting a little. He handed her a card.

"You work for Senator Belasco?"

"I've been trying to reach you for the last three days."

He added in the tone of a parent to a willful child, "You haven't returned my calls."

"If I wanted to talk to you, I would have called back."

"Then you did get my messages."

"I'm in a hurry, Mr. Westcott." She unlocked the Nissan and threw her tote across to the passenger seat. "I don't have time for you or your boss."

"There are things you don't know, Captain."

"I'm late for a meeting at my daughter's school."

"Have you been following the hearings, Captain?"

Senator Susan Belasco's investigation into allegations of criminal wrongdoing by the private contracting firm Global Sword and Saber Security Services, G4S, had been front-page news for the last several weeks.

"I have nothing to say to the committee."

"A boy was killed at Three Fountain Square. He was ten years old."

"Don't call me again." She slammed the car door and revved the engine as she shifted into reverse, muttering as she backed up. "Move your toes, you son of a bitch."

Taking the back road out of Mission Valley, she used her cell phone to call her therapist, Alice White. As expected, she got her voice mail. Frankie's situation could not honestly be called an emergency so she hung up without leaving a message. What good was a therapist if she never picked up her phone?

The Arcadia School secretary had sounded vaguely

accusatory, or maybe Frankie had imagined that. Lately she felt like everyone was trying to pick a fight or poke a finger at her. Dr. White said stress made it hard to read people and situations correctly.

Walking fast across the asphalt parking lot to the school entrance, her breath fluttered at the base of her throat and she wished she were wearing her service uniform, not the utility camouflage that was blousy and comfortable as pajamas. More officially dressed, she would not feel so much like a schoolgirl about to be called on the carpet for kicking a soccer ball through a school window.

Arcadia School had grown within her experience from a small private primary school to a complex of buildings and grounds spread over two blocks of prime San Diego real estate. She had a cloudy recollection of walking this hall for the first time when she was younger than Glory, excited and scared and proudly self-conscious in her new school uniform. The waxed floors still rippled with reflected light from fluorescent bars in the ceiling and the mural in the foyer next to the office depicting generations of Arcadia schoolgirls tossing up handfuls of posies with Native Americans, Father Serra, and Cabrillo's ship in the background was as hokey as it had been that first day. She had gone on to be one of the stars in Arcadia's constellation. Class valedictorian, a National Merit Scholar, president of the senior choir. She had played serious basketball and captained Arcadia's soccer team at two national championships.

At the office door she inhaled, wiped her palms on the thighs of her pants, set her hand against the doorplate, and pushed.

The office was exactly as she remembered it: a long, crowded, and disorderly room. Across from where she stood, a wall of windows was covered by slatted blinds drawn up to irregular heights. She had to look away to keep from ordering someone to even them up.

Below the level of the counter, she pressed two fingers against her wrist. Her pulse hammered. What was she afraid of? This was a school and she had spent ten months in Iraq, for godsake.

Frankie had read the standard issue pamphlets on stress the Marine Corps provided. She knew that readjusting after deployment took time and was always a challenge, greater for some than others. Her deployment had been fairly typical, even uneventful. The General had been through much worse in Vietnam and adjusted to being home without making a fuss and so would she. Her wide goalkeeper's hands made fists hard and tight enough to punch a hole in the counter as she waited for someone to notice her.

A gray-haired woman looked at Frankie in her cammies and then over her shoulder at the door as if she expected an invasion to follow. "You're Captain Tennyson. Of course you are. I'm Dory Maddox, the head secretary. I'm sure you don't remember me. I started here when you were in the senior school."

Arcadia was divided into the lower school for girls in kindergarten to third grade and upper school for grades four through eight. Senior school was high school.

"I have an appointment, ma'am."

The parentheses at the corners of Dory's mouth tightened, hinting displeasure, and Frankie realized she should have tried to make a little polite conversation. She had been deployed less than a year, but in that time she had forgotten the rules of polite behavior; and not only were her expectations frequently unreasonable, she was often abrupt and unintentionally rude.

Her therapist's calm voice came into her head. "It's hard to readjust but little by little, you'll feel more comfortable in your skin." After months with all her senses pumped, no one expected her to switch them off like a light at bedtime. No one except Frankie.

At the far end of the Arcadia office, a door opened and Frankie recognized Trelawny Scott, still wearing her black hair pulled into a tight chignon, still peering at the world from behind round Jackie O glasses. Years ago, Scott had taught biology to Frankie's ninth-grade class. Today she looked smaller and thinner than Frankie remembered her, but still formidable. Her palm was dry and cool when they shook hands.

"Look at you! A captain in the Marine Corps. I'm sure the general is very proud of you."

Scott's well-meant ebullience embarrassed Frankie though she knew it was meant to put her at ease.

"There's a marvelous photo of you in one of the trophy cases. Have you seen it, Frankie? Making that famous save? I don't care how much that coach argued, the ball never made it over the line. It's perfectly clear in the picture."

"Speaking for myself, ma'am, I never had any doubt about it."

"Frankie, you were never one for doubts! I imagine Glory will be just like you."

"You know my daughter?"

"Oh, my yes. I should have explained. I'm headmistress of the lower school now. I took over from Miss Winslow six months ago." She opened her office door wider. "Come in and sit down. You already know Glory's teacher, Ms. Peters, of course."

Frankie stopped in the doorway. *Trapped.*

She had learned in the Marine Corps to avoid dead-end spaces. Like right now: no matter how much the headmistress was trying to cover it up, Frankie smelled an ambush up the road.

Chapter 4

Ms. Peters was short and slight, a schoolgirl with a drill sergeant grip.

"And this is Dr. Wilson, the school's psychologist."

Wilson had a beige and forgettable face, silver hair buzzed close against his skull.

Frankie forced a smile. Her teeth felt huge, like the ceramic plates that fitted into her flak vest.

You can walk out any time you want to.

She could load and fire an M16 A4 rifle and a .45 pistol with sharpshooter accuracy. In Basic she was near the top in leadership and fitness points. But sit in a school office, exchange pleasantries, and then hear the truth about her daughter, truth that had to be bad because why else would she be called to a last-minute meeting? She would rather lie facedown in swamp water.

"We got to know Rick while you were away, Frankie," Scott said. "In case you were ever worried about Glory—"

In case?

Of course she had worried about her daughter. In the morning when she brushed her teeth, she hoped Rick was reminding Glory to do the same and teaching her to floss. Looking at the piles of French fries and khaki-colored string beans in the mess, she worried that Glory wasn't getting enough fresh vegetables. But like all the other mothers she had met in the service, Frankie had learned to put thoughts of her daughter off to the side of her mind so she could get on with the job, but she was never far away. Like the memory of rain in the midst of a sandstorm, some days Glory was all that kept Frankie upright.

"—your husband was a pleasure to deal with. Such a wonderful father."

"Yes, ma'am." Her voice broke and she cleared her throat.

Major Olvedo and her therapist had both urged her to see a throat specialist about her persistent hoarseness. She stalled, afraid of hearing that in Iraq she had inhaled chemicals that had permanently damaged her vocal folds. Once she had been a singer and a public speaker; now there were times when it hurt to speak.

"But we do prefer to conference with both parents," Wilson said.

"He would have. Come." Actually she hadn't thought to call Rick. The summons from the school had been a surprise, and she had not been thinking clearly. "He had a meeting."

Dr. Wilson said, "These things happen, of course."

What kind of things? Are we still talking about Rick?

The more she needed to stay focused, the more ragged and drifty her thoughts became. At the same time—and this was crazy-making—she was hyper-vigilant and aware of the details of her environment as if her life depended on it. Since sitting down she had mentally measured the size of the office, roughly sixteen feet square, and noted a closed closet door. At least she thought it was a closet. It bothered her that she did not know for sure. It might be an exit. Or an entrance someone could barge through without warning. The wall of windows opening onto the empty green playing field made her nervous.

Scott picked up a file and opened it.

"I'll get right to the point, Frankie. We're worried about Glory and we thought it would be better to talk about this now instead of waiting until ... well, we don't want it to get any worse."

Worse. Frankie nodded. *Worse* meant it—whatever "it" was—was already bad. Did Rick know? Had he told her? Had she forgotten?

The smell of wet grass came through the office windows. Automated arcs of water caught the light and danced before Frankie's eyes like rain. There should be a rainbow somewhere but she couldn't see it.

Behind her oversize glasses Scott's brows came together, and Frankie realized she was expected to say something. She managed another nod and a hugely inappropriate, bulletproof smile.

Scott said, "I'll let Ms. Peters explain."

"Glory's a darling little girl, Captain Tennyson. Really smart and she seems to love school. She reads very well and just shines academically." It was obvious that Glory's teacher wanted to appear nonthreatening, the kind of woman to whom a parent would trust her eight-year-old daughter.

She blinked too much.

"Really, I wish all my girls were as smart as Glory."

"I don't think you invited me here for the good news. What exactly is the problem? As you see it?"

Ms. Peters recoiled a little, and Frankie realized that she had asked the question in her command voice that sounded peremptory and rude in the context of a parent-teacher conference. *Cut the crap and get to the point.*

"Well." The teacher looked at Scott who nodded for her to continue. "She's having problems on the playground. With the other girls."

"What kind of problems?"

"She's very aggressive, Captain." The psychologist had a beige voice to match his looks. "We have a video."

Adrenaline shot through her. "You've been taking pictures of my daughter? You've been surveilling her?"

"It's nothing to be alarmed about, Frankie. We've been doing it for years," Scott said. "Playground observations are a wonderful diagnostic tool."

"Did I give you permission to diagnose my daughter? Did I sign something?" Her throat stung. "Did my husband?"

"The school is perfectly within its rights," Dr. Wilson said. "There's been no invasion of privacy. A wide angle camera is mounted—"

"The point is," Ms. Peters interrupted, "there have been complaints, and then I saw the video and—"

"What kind of complaints? Complaints from whom?"

"Glory has a terrible temper." The teacher's chin lifted. "As I'm sure you know."

No, Frankie did not know that.

"Your daughter has a strong personality." Wilson spoke with a determined pleasantness. "And a need to demonstrate her power."

"She's eight years old. What kind of power are we talking about?"

"She has threatened one of the girls in her class."

Frankie remembered that she had a bottle of water in her tote, popped the top, and drank. The tepid water soothed her throat and bought a little time to steady her nerves.

Glory was a Marine Corps child, the granddaughter of a celebrated hero. At bedtime she whispered fairy tales to stuffed bunnies and bears and a plush chartreuse snake, but during the day she got real and why shouldn't she?

Frankie said, "She's strong and assertive. I think these are positive traits, Dr. Wilson."

"Under most circumstances, I would agree with you."

"But?"

He leaned in, resting his hands on his knees. She became aware of how close he was to her, right on the edge

28

of her personal space. That awareness was something she had brought home from Iraq, along with a self-protecting need to control the space around her. She wanted to pull back, but knew Wilson might interpret that as a sign of weakness. Or maybe civilians ignored such things. She didn't know what was normal anymore.

He said, "At eight it's common for little boys to act out aggressively. Girls, on the other hand—"

"Just tell me what she did."

"She threatened to shoot another student," Ms. Peters blurted, her eyes darting from Scott to Wilson and back to Scott. "She said she was going to bring a gun to school and shoot her."

"Who? What's her name?"

"Colette."

"I've never heard of her."

"It's all on the video," Scott said. "Colette and some of the girls were on the picnic table and Glory said something and then Colette and—"

"There's no audio track?"

"But it is clear that Colette did nothing to deserve—"

"How do you know that? If you don't have audio, you can't tell much of anything."

"Colette told us."

"And you believe her?"

"I'm sorry, Frankie." Scott removed her glasses and folded them neatly on the desk in front of her. "When we questioned Glory she admitted making the threat."

"And she absolutely wouldn't apologize. She felt no remorse at all."

"She was provoked."

"If she just flared up and knew it was wrong and said she was sorry but—"

"Colette must have started it. I know my daughter."

"Captain, children change. You've been away for almost a year."

Frankie glared at the psychologist. "If she were a boy you know this wouldn't be a big deal."

"Boys or girls, a school must always take any talk of guns very seriously." Scott lowered her voice. "I'm sorry to have to ask this, Frankie, but you'll understand how concerned we are."

"Ask what?"

"Are there weapons in your home?"

Of course there were weapons in her home. Frankie was a Marine. And she'd been raised in a house with handguns and rifles. "With due respect, ma'am, I don't think that's any of your business. As I recall the Second Amendment hasn't been repealed."

"We need to know—"

"If we let our daughter play with guns?" She took another gulp of water.

"I wonder if you've considered this." Dr. Wilson held his hands before him, fingers spread, tapping the pads together. "There is a condition known as SPTSD. Are you familiar with it?"

"What does the 'S' stand for?"

"Psychologists have observed that in military families when a loved one returns from Iraq or Afghanistan, sometimes a member of the family takes on his, or her, symptoms of PTSD. Hence secondary PTSD."

"You're saying I'm contagious."

"What Dr. Wilson means is that having you gone and now back has been challenging for Glory. In the same way you may be having some trouble adjusting, so is she."

"Dr. Scott, this conversation is not about me. But for the record, I don't have PTSD. And this blanket assumption that everyone who comes back from the fight is mentally damaged is, frankly, an insult to the armed forces of this country."

No one had a response to that.

Dr. Wilson said, "Perhaps we should reschedule our meeting for another time when the father can be here."

"I don't think that will be necessary," Scott said. "I'm sure Captain Tennyson will want to speak with her husband about this and to Glory as well, of course. But I don't expect we have a significant problem here. Frankie, you were a spirited little girl as I remember, and no doubt Glory has inherited some of that from you. Here at Arcadia we haven't had as much experience dealing with the children of military personnel as the public schools have, but that doesn't mean we aren't aware of the realities. And certainly we only want the best for Glory."

She went on talking from the bottom of a well, being

kind and empathic, assuring Frankie that whatever challenges Glory was currently facing, they were manageable and the school had the resources to help her. Frankie barely heard what she said but she let her gentle tones float up and then sink back and around her, soothing as a cascade of cool water.

Frankie looked at Ms. Peters. For Glory's sake she wanted and needed the young teacher's approval.

"There's nothing wrong with Glory," she said. "She's a good girl."

"That's right," Ms. Peters said. "She *is* a good girl, and that's why I wanted to have a conference with you. So we could stop this before something happened. It's not right for an eight-year-old girl to talk about guns and shooting people."

Chapter 5

In the school parking lot Frankie tried to reach her therapist again and got the message machine yet another time.
Frustrated, she wanted to kick a hole in the side of her car
but she imagined Scott, Wilson, and Peters at a window,
shaking their heads, tut-tutting as they watched her, like
entomologists observing bug behavior.

If Dr. White would just pick up her damn phone.

She wished her friend Domino had a cell phone. Or a
house or apartment, somewhere Frankie could go and talk
to her. Domino was the only person who understood what
Frankie was going through.

They had met on a Saturday at the free children's clinic
Harry and Gaby operated on Abbott Street in Ocean
Beach. Frankie had been home from Iraq three weeks and
volunteering at the check-in desk; Glory was with her.
Domino had brought her daughter, Candace, in for a pre-
school checkup. What Frankie recalled most clearly from
that first meeting was Candace's dark hair pulled back

from her forehead in intricate entwined French braids with red ribbons twisted through them. To Frankie this time-consuming effort spoke of a mother's love and concern.

They had been the final patients of the day and the atmosphere in the clinic was relaxed and unhurried. While Candace and Glory colored and whispered and giggled, Frankie and Domino talked, and though they had almost nothing in common apart from their daughters and military service, they liked each other right away. Frankie didn't have to explain why being home was difficult. There was nothing to explain or make excuses for.

Domino—Dominique—was the daughter of a small-town pharmacist, a good Lutheran girl from Kansas who wore her hair and skirts long and went to church twice on Sunday. She and her siblings had been raised in a strict congregation in which the life of a woman was pegged down by three words: *Kirk*, *Kinder*, and *Kuche*. Church, children, and kitchen. Looking at her mother, Domino had seen her future and rebelled. She and Jason, her high-school boyfriend, married on the run and joined the Army together. When Candace was born Domino's mother took over the job of raising her.

Candace was almost eight now, but apart from informal home schooling, she had no education. This year Domino was determined to enroll her, but it would not be easy. Mother and daughter lived in their van, moving from the Walmart lot to Costco to, sometimes, the narrow, deserted streets behind the sports arena. A counselor at Veterans'

Villa was trying to find them a room somewhere but, so far, no luck.

The day they met Rick was at meetings in Las Vegas and wouldn't return until Sunday night. Mothers and daughters had eaten hamburgers for dinner. Domino insisted on paying for herself and Candace, but afterward when they walked down the street to the Korean-owned doughnut and ice cream shop on Newport, she let Frankie treat them all to sundaes. Afterward they walked on to the park, and while the girls worked off their sugar highs, Frankie and Domino sat at a picnic table and talked through the warm August twilight into the dark. They had been meeting and talking every few days since then.

Frankie told Domino the truth: about her mood swings, her anger and problems with concentration, the way her mind drifted out of reality in the middle of a conversation, one thought interrupting and squabbling with another. When Domino recommended that she see a psychologist, Frankie paid more attention than if the suggestion had come from Rick or Harry. Even so, she didn't consider it seriously at first. Frankie was a Marine brat and knew how the system worked. Although psychotherapy (emphasis on the *psycho*) was supposed to be confidential, this was a condition she did not believe existed at any but the highest levels of the military. At the MCRD gossip was a form of entertainment. By one avenue or another, word that she had sought help at Balboa would eventually reach her office there and then the General. It had taken more than

Domino's prodding to get her into therapy. It had taken a visit to the supermarket on the Friday before Labor Day weekend.

The day had begun badly.

At breakfast Rick was sullenly quiet as he scrambled eggs, still resentful that Frankie had left him alone with the television the night before so she could talk to Domino on the phone for an hour. He had grumbled and Frankie defended her right to choose any friend she wanted, even a woman with no home who had to borrow a phone and worked at a fast-food restaurant. The way Rick put it, Frankie preferred a homeless woman's company over his, and in a way he was right.

That morning Glory didn't want her eggs, and Rick, normally a paragon of parenting, threw her plate into the sink. Glory cried. He made a guilty fuss apologizing, as if a father didn't have every right to lose his temper. The General had certainly yelled at Frankie a few thousand times. Weepy and plaintive afterward, Glory begged to stay home but Frankie put her foot down.

"School's your job. You go whether you want to or not."

She practically had to shove her daughter out of the car in front of Arcadia School.

By the time Frankie got to the MCRD, her nerves were shredding, and she lost her temper three times before noon.

Glory was morosely uncommunicative when Frankie picked her up at the curb in front of the school that afternoon. Waiting, she stood apart from the other girls, chewing the end of her corn-colored ponytail, her expression a thundercloud on the hot Indian summer day. She slung her backpack over the seat back.

"Whoa, easy there, tiger." Frankie forced a lilt into her voice, a lightheartedness she did not feel. She looked at Glory more closely. "You okay? Have you been crying? Why were you crying?"

"I am so hot. I'm gonna die. They oughta close school when it gets this hot. Back East they have snow days, we oughta have heat days."

"You know it's always like this in September. And they can't close school. You only started back last week."

"When's it gonna rain?" Glory flapped her skirt up and down in front of the air-conditioning vent. "I'm gonna die if it doesn't rain soon."

"Stop being dramatic, Glory. Believe me, this heat is nothing to complain about."

Frankie had landed in Kuwait in midwinter when it was cold and the air cracked like dry twigs. She remembered thinking what would become a theme running through every day's thoughts: when will it rain?

I'm going to die if it doesn't rain soon.

Her lips, the corners of her eyes, and inside her nose had cracked and bled in the dry frigid air. She begged Rick to send economy-size jars of petroleum jelly, but this made the condition worse. The sand stuck to it, made a crust. Gradually the days had warmed and at first the heat was a welcome relief; but by the time she left Baghdad in early August, the thermometer often read one hundred fifteen or twenty degrees in the middle of the day and no one, not even the Iraqis, was comfortable. Regardless of the temperature, on community visits she wore her cammies with the sleeves buttoned at the wrist and tucked into her boots, Kevlar and helmet, sometimes gloves and goggles. Under all this she sweat and no matter how much water she drank, she was always thirsty. She longed for water. She thought about water all the time and in every form from ocean waves to rain. The more water she drank, the more she sweat.

Her body stopped feeling like her own.

In the car Glory said, "Are you even listening to me? Do you even care how I feel?"

"I'm listening and of course I care."

In Iraq the wind was worse than any southern California Santa Ana, stronger and steadier, hot and dead dry. It came with a hollow roar or a whine or the banshee's scream, thirty or forty or fifty or sixty miles an hour.

The wind was part of the everywhere noise. The thuppa-thuppa of helos and the engines of vans and trucks and tanks and Humvees, sometimes gunfire, explosions, horn blasts, yelling, always yelling: silence was a luxury in Iraq. For the first few weeks the constant noise at Forward Operating Base Redline gave Frankie a headache that made her eyes cross.

The air stank of motor oil and other things. Outdoors

there was no escaping the constant, eye-watering reek of burning garbage and sewage, sometimes the chemical tang of explosives, sometimes death.

And sand. Sand was everywhere, indoors and out, in the offices and gym, the mess and even the showers. At night it found its way between her sheets and scraped her skin like an emery board. Sand was infinite in its variety. There was the kind of sand that was all hard grit and stung like BBs when it blew in her face. Moon dust was sand as fine as baby powder that clogged her nostrils and caked her lips and caught in her eyelashes. Her boots sank deep in the heavy sand that made walking a hundred feet feel like a mile-long, uphill trek. Like walking through molasses. Wind lifted the sand and carried it across the desert. It hid the sky and turned the day orange or muddy brown. Fine and coarse, bearing grit and insects and fragments of litter, a sandstorm was a bombardment that might last an hour, sometimes a day or more.

Heat. Wind. Noise. Stink. Sand. They blended into one sensation that she felt in her ears and her eyes, up inside her nose and at the back of her throat. Even her gums felt dry.

"Mom, watch out! You just ran a red light, what's wrong with you?"

Half in the car, half in Iraq.

She had been one of several female Marines involved in an operation intended to empower Iraqi women and enroll their communities in rebuilding the nation that Saddam, sanctions, and generations of war had destroyed. For most of her deployment she was the only female Marine officer on FOB Redline. Her particular assignment was the rebuilding of a school destroyed by mortar fire during Operation Iraqi Freedom.

From the beginning she had fought a sense of isolation, of having been forgotten by the corps. Living in prefab housing called a can, a room large enough for a bed, a locker, and a table for a television and DVD player, given no official team and no clear orders and lucky to have a female interpreter, she worked with more soldiers than Marines.

Despite the downside she had been proud of her mission and willing to put up with anything so that the school might be built. Though she wore a flak jacket and Kevlar helmet, carried a rifle and traveled in convoy, Frankie thought of her work rebuilding the school as diplomacy with the potential to create a solidarity that might hold up where politics failed.

"Where are we going? Why aren't we going home?"

"We have to stop at Vons. There's nothing in the refrigerator."

Food did not interest Frankie; she'd lost weight in Iraq and more since she'd come home. But her family had to eat and while Rick enjoyed cooking, he hated marketing so the job fell to her. Mostly she went to the Exchange, but it wasn't always convenient.

Four-thirty on the Friday before Labor Day wasn't the

worst time to shop at the huge Vons on Midway, but it was up there in the top ten. Frankie and Glory got to the checkout stands and there was a line at every one.

"We'll never get out of here." Glory moaned dramatically.

Frankie clearly remembered the faces of the three people standing ahead of them in line that day. Two men and a fat woman with a child banging his tiny shoes against the metal cart.

"Can I go to the car?" Glory draped herself across their heaped grocery cart. "I'm exhausted."

"Show some backbone." Frankie heard the General's voice.

The woman in front of Frankie wore blue jeans stretched tight across broad hips and pushed a cart full of pasta and cheese and varieties of frozen potatoes. The child in the cart swung his tubby legs, clanged his heels, and stared at Frankie with round blue eyes.

She stuck out her tongue.

"Mom!"

The boy burst into tears.

"Oh. My. God. Why did you do that?"

She didn't know.

The child was inconsolable.

She said, "Your kid's got a set of lungs on him," and felt Glory making herself small beside her.

The mother turned. Frankie felt like sticking her tongue out at *her* too. Instead she jerked the shopping cart forward and back, forward and back. "Tick-tock, tick-tock." Like a metronome.

"Can I go to the car?"

"Would it kill you, Glory, to keep me company?"

The boy's cries descended to the whimpery level. Occasionally he glanced furtively at Frankie as the woman unloaded food onto the checkout belt. She pulled cards out of her wallet and shuffled through them once, twice, a third time.

Frankie called out to the checker, "How much longer is this going to take?"

"I'm sorry, ma'am." The checker looked barely older than Glory but she wore a wedding ring. "You can check your items in the self-serve line, if you wish. There's never anyone there."

"That's because it's effing impossible to operate the damn machines."

Glory tugged on Frankie's sleeve. "You're in uniform, Mom." She knew what was expected of a Marine in uniform even if it was just cammies. "We can wait, it's okay."

"Are you telling me what to do?"

Glory snatched up a *People* magazine and buried her head in it.

"I'm not going to buy that so don't ask me. Put it away and stand over here."

"No."

The shopper's card was declined.

"For godsake, just give her the goddamn groceries. I'll pay for them."

"Mom!"

Frankie knew she was humiliating her daughter. She even knew that later in the day she would regret all this. She should not make a scene while in uniform—under no circumstances should she berate this woman—but she couldn't stop herself. She felt the terrifying headlong rush of being on a bike going downhill, feet off the pedals, bouncing into potholes and over bumps, so far out of control that she could only surrender to the disaster she knew was coming.

In line behind her someone grumbled a few words, someone else laughed. She didn't hear the comments, but she knew that she was being criticized or ridiculed for giving voice to what all of them in the line were feeling.

"You're happy standing here?"

"That's it," Glory said. "I'm walking."

Frankie grabbed her. Above the elbow Glory's arm was tender as a satin pouf.

"You're hurting me."

"Don't. Move."

A week later Frankie had her first appointment with Dr. Alice White, a private practitioner. They spoke of nothing important: family information, the terms of her enlistment in the corps. Frankie imagined the psychologist like a rock climber probing for a handhold, and she thought of what she would tell Domino, that psychotherapy was a waste of time and money; but on Thursday of the second week, she heard herself admitting, "I got a little out of control the other day. At Vons."

"How did that feel?"

Frankie stared at her hands. *It felt free.*

Her hands were big and her fingers were long. In Basic School one of the stupid-ass guys had told her she could jerk off an elephant. She had fists like a man. Standing in the supermarket she knew that if she wanted to, she could knock over the magazine rack or send the Big Red chewing gum and Snickers bars flying. She liked that thought. She liked the image of M&M's lofting in all directions like little multicolor grenades. Sitting in Dr. White's office, she remembered the sticky rubbery feel of the cart's handle against her palms as she jerked it out of line.

"Therapy only works if you talk to me, Frankie. If you can't say how it felt to lose control, tell me what happened."

"I dumped the cart. On its nose."

Two hundred dollars' worth of groceries spilled across the floor of Vons. Steaks and sausages and chicken thighs, cheese and bagels and a package of tortillas and cans of beans and soup, a carton of organic milk that split and splashed and a flat of eggs that broke.

"It'll be a long time before I go there again." Frankie knew she should be ashamed of herself, but she could not muster the requisite guilt, not when it had felt so good.

"Did you write about it in your journal?"

Dr. White had been talking about journal writing since Frankie's first visit. Keeping a diary had never much interested her. Not since she was ten years old and someone gave her a five-year diary with a lock. Fearing that her mother or brother would read what she wrote, she hid the key so well that for several weeks she couldn't find it herself, and by the time it turned up, she had lost interest in keeping a diary.

"Writing your experiences and feelings can objectify them. Give you distance. It's an opportunity to understand our lives from a fresh perspective."

"It won't work for me," Frankie said.

"You're so resistant. Where does that come from, I wonder?"

Frankie hated the question and for the moment disliked her therapist.

"Do me a favor and just try it for a while. Humor me, okay? I'd like you to write in it every day for, say, a month. Give it a chance."

Frankie had said she would do it, but she forgot her promise as soon as she left the office that day. Almost six weeks later she still hadn't bought a journal.

Chapter 6

In the lot at Arcadia School, she sat in her car and tried Dr. White's number for the third time. This time she answered. Words tumbled out of Frankie: *closed doors, too many windows, Ms. Peters, Colette, guns and threats.*

"What I'm supposed to do about Glory? Have you heard of that condition, secondary PTSD?"

"I have."

"Are you saying she got it from me?"

"I can't say, one way or another, Frankie. I don't know Glory."

"Great. Can you say anything? Anything at all?"

"Where are you?" Dr. White could not be goaded into a fight. Frankie didn't know if she liked this about her.

"I'm still at the school. In the parking lot."

"Well, stay where you are for twenty minutes. You shouldn't be driving right now."

"I have to get Glory from extended care. I'm already late."

"Focus on your breathing—"

"I told you on Monday, that meditation stuff doesn't work for me. My mind jumps around too much."

"When it jumps, just come back to the breath. This isn't meditation, Frankie, it's very basic stress management."

"I'm not stressed. I mean, I am, but I wouldn't be if it weren't for this school . . . stuff." She had learned to swear in the Marine Corps. Now that she was home she had to watch her mouth all the time. *Shit.*

"Mindful breathing works. Just try it."

The problem with cell phones was she couldn't slam down the receiver.

"Have you gone to the PTSD group at Veterans' Villa yet?"

"You only told me about it last week."

"It meets every night."

She might go if she wasn't too tired or busy or if she didn't forget.

"The man who runs it is named Dekker. I heard him speak at a conference last month. He's a good man, Frankie, and he knows what he's talking about."

"I'm already seeing you twice a week."

"Dekker has skills I lack. And he's experienced in ways I'm not. One of his groups would be something special for you. It would give you a chance to talk to other soldiers and Marines who're maybe going through the same thing you are."

"There's nothing wrong with me." She was tired. She

47

was angry at Glory's damn teacher. It would all pass. Coming home was never easy.

"Please try it, Frankie. And mindful breathing too."

And journaling. *And standing on my head in a bucket of ice water.*

"Yeah. Okay." She would force herself to follow directions. Maybe then she wouldn't have to sit in a room full of shipwrecked soldiers, sailors, and Marines talking about Iraq. She didn't want to talk or think about Iraq. She wanted to wipe Iraq out of her mind.

As soon as Glory got in the car, she started in on Frankie. "You forgot me, I know you forgot me. I waited *forever.* Why can't I ride the blue van?"

"I didn't forget you. And I'm sorry you had to wait but there were things I had to do and there was nowhere else for you to go."

"I rode the blue van last year."

But now Frankie was home and she wanted to be the one Glory saw waiting for her at the end of the school day.

"Did you have any trouble, Glory?"

"What are you talking about? What kind of trouble?"

"I don't know, I just asked the question."

"Why are you mad at me?"

"Should I be? I'm not."

"I can tell you're mad. You sound mad."

"You're the one who sounds like she's mad, Glory. Are you? Mad at me?"

48

Glory looked out the side window, gnawing on a hangnail.

"Don't chew your fingernails."

Dramatically Glory sat on her hand.

All at once Frankie felt very tired. "It's been a long day, Glory."

"You always say that."

Because every day is long.

"I wanna find Candace and Domino and get some ice cream."

"I don't know where they're parked."

"Candace says sometimes they stay up by All Souls. Can't we at least go see if they're up there?" To Glory, the idea of living in a van that never stayed in one place for more than a day had a kind of gypsy romance with no connection to violence or poverty. "You could call Domino."

"You know she doesn't have a phone." She called Frankie when she could borrow one.

Glory's sullen lower lip would trip a train.

"The church is on the way home. We go right by it. Could we just check?"

But the van wasn't parked at All Souls. Across the lot the back door to the parish hall opened and eight or ten animated men and women exited. Frankie and Glory watched them go to their cars, still talking and calling to each other.

"Stay and do your homework. I'll go in and see if Martha's around. She might know where they are."

Frankie had known Martha Wainright since she came to All Souls as a young priest, fresh from the seminary. She had married Rick and Frankie and it was she who had given her Dr. White's name and number. On occasions when Domino and Candace parked in the church lot, she let them shower in the parish hall facilities.

In the hall the gray folding chairs were arranged in irregular clusters. A podium stood at one end with a large, clean, whiteboard behind it. Through the kitchen pass-through Frankie saw Martha struggling to dump a coffee urn into the sink. She was small, a pretty woman in her forties. The clerical collar looked large on her.

"Let me do that." Frankie took the cumbersome urn from her. She rinsed it and set it upside down on the drain board. "Have you got a minute, Martha?"

"Actually, Frankie, I was going to call you. You saved me the effort." The priest began to fold and stack chairs. "I was going to ask when you're coming back to the choir. To tell you the truth, it's beginning to sound a little shrieky. We really need a strong alto to balance all those sopranos."

"I can't yet. I brought some kind of laryngitis back from Iraq. I wouldn't add much to the choir at this point."

"Maybe you should see a doctor."

"Harry says it's tension." Tension, stress: it was like having one of those musical worms in her brain. She kept hearing the same thing, repeating over and over wherever she went.

"How is your brother? I see Gaby at eight a.m. sometimes, but I think he worships St. Mattress on Sundays."

It was a tired old joke, but Frankie laughed anyway.

"He works hard," she said.

"Oh, Frankie, I know he does. I don't begrudge him his Sunday mornings, and I'm sure God doesn't either. Can you believe the crap he has to put up with just so he and Gaby can do something worthwhile? I was in the drugstore the other day and someone wanted me to sign a petition saying the clinic had become a public nuisance." Martha grabbed the back of a chair and pulled the seat up with more force than was necessary. "What in the world have they got against a children's clinic?"

"Ocean Beach's changed."

"It sure has," the priest said. "It used to be the one place in San Diego where you didn't have to be rich to live near the water. Now Mrs. Greenwoody and her committee want to turn it into La Jolla."

"I volunteer at the clinic on Saturdays and there're always protesters out front. Harry even gets hate mail."

They talked about this as they finished the job. Martha rolled the whiteboard to the side of the room.

"Glory's plaguing me to find Domino. Have you seen her around?"

"Not for a couple of days. She said her husband's in town."

"I was afraid of that."

Jason had never accepted the divorce and stalked his wife and daughter from Kansas to San Diego. According to Domino he suffered from a mood disorder exacerbated by his years in the service, and his moods swung from manic to depressed to angry at himself or the world or Domino in particular. The last time they were together he had grabbed her so hard his fingers left deep red bruises on her upper arm. He threatened to do worse if she and Domino didn't return with him to Kansas.

Frankie leaned against a table at the back of the parish hall and stared at the toes of her boots.

"Frankie, you didn't drop in to help move furniture or talk about Domino. I appreciate your help, but I wonder what else is on your mind."

"I'm seeing Dr. White on Mondays and Thursdays." She considered telling Martha about the meeting at Arcadia School and decided not to. She wasn't sure why. "She wants me to keep a journal and she says I should meditate. It seems pointless."

"You don't believe in meditation? What about prayer?"

"Are they the same?"

"Sometimes."

"I can't shut my mind down for long enough to do either one."

"Have you spoken to her about meds?"

Medication meant that Iraq had made her sick. As the General might say, it meant that she *didn't have the guts for it.*

"I'm not depressed. I'm just sort of . . ."

Not here sometimes. Too much here at others.

"She wants me to go to a support group at Veterans' Villa."

"You might see Domino there."

"I know group therapy helps some people, but you know my family. I was raised to keep my feelings to myself. Can you imagine the General in group therapy? And besides, nothing much happened to me compared to those guys—"

"Which guys are you talking about, Frankie?"

"The guys who go to support groups."

Martha looked mildly amused. Frankie resisted the impulse to take offense.

"Okay, I'm having a few adjustment problems. That's normal, right? If I came home from the Suck all jolly you'd *know* I was crazy."

"No one's talking about crazy."

"Don't you read the paper? Every Marine with a headache has PTSD. It's insulting. My mind wanders and sometimes I lose my temper, but basically I'm okay."

As she heard herself say the words, she realized that she did not truly believe them. No matter how she tried to dismiss it as not really important and certainly not symptomatic, the memory of letting everything go at the supermarket was as vivid in her mind as any memory could be. The experience had left her shaken and frightened, but at the same time, exhilarated. She had let herself go to the limit and beyond and at that moment had felt more fully alive than she had in months.

Chapter 7

M aryanne Byrne had seen it all before.

Post-traumatic stress disorder, PTSD, shell shock, battle fatigue, nerves: the name changed with every war but the suffering did not. Going back to the Peloponnesian Wars, there wasn't a wife or mother or girlfriend who didn't know what it was.

The General had brought it home after his last tour in Vietnam. For months it had poisoned his days and torn up his nights. Eventually the symptoms moderated but he had been forever changed. Afterward it was as if a crack ran through Harlan Byrne's personality. On one side he was the dreamboat she had fallen in love with, the father of her children, the man she trusted and admired. On the other he was unsure of himself, a moody and volatile stranger, rigid, unpredictably mean, and forbiddingly silent. For years after his return from Vietnam, she didn't know from day to day, or sometimes hour to hour, which side of the crack he would be standing on. He had refused to get help for what they were calling battle fatigue in those days. A trip to a psychologist at Balboa Hospital would have been noted in his service record. The book on Harlan Byrne would have gotten a black mark in permanent ink.

And now there was Frankie, home from the Middle East with the same brokenness.

Maryanne was as much dreading the General's seventy-fifth birthday party as she was happy for it. If he was in a funk—as he might be on such a momentous occasion—he would try to make himself feel better by drinking too much; and if that happened, he would almost certainly take off on the nearest target, which would, inevitably, be Frankie. He could always find a way to get at her.

Maryanne had been perilously close to thirty when she met Lieutenant Colonel Harlan Byrne. At the end of the sixties it was just becoming an accepted thing to marry "late," but it was a trend she never wanted to be part of. Too old to be caught up in the sixties rock 'n' roll free-for-all, and not impressed by Germaine Greer or radical feminism, she had been on her own for eight years teaching sixth grade on Chicago's south side and had her fill of liberation. A Norwegian girl from a family of Rockefeller Republicans, she yearned to be a wife and mother and set her heart on a strong man, a big house, and children; but after her twenty-eighth birthday, her confidence that all this would happen began to fracture like an egg too long on the boil. She moved to San Diego. It was wartime and there were plenty of eligible men there.

For a smart, pretty girl, poised, athletic, and brimming with bright conversation, it had been like fishing in a well-stocked pond. Maryanne threw back the small fry until, at a dinner dance, she met Harlan, his ribbons, stars, and bars aglow with possibility. He had a brash boyish sweetness in those days. He was courageous and sure of himself, and he looked stunning in his Marine Corps uniform. Before she met him, if Maryanne had been asked how she felt about the war in Vietnam, she would have said that it was a waste of life and treasure. By the time she and Harlan were a couple and she had gone into debt for a wardrobe suitable for the girlfriend and then fiancée of a Marine Corps lieutenant colonel, she could argue persuasively in support of the war as essential to American influence abroad and security at home. Dominos, etc.

They had been married less than a year when he went back to Vietnam, leaving her alone in military housing with baby Harry. If anyone thought making the world a safer, freer place was the way to get rich, they didn't know anything about the Marine Corps. As a young married woman she had remodeled out-of-style clothes and economized on food and utilities long before it was the green thing to do. It had taken five years of going without before she had enough money in a special fund to afford the Mission-style table that extended to seat sixteen, the chairs, and matching sideboard. Looking at it now as she set an extra place for dinner—her mother's silver, her mother-in-law's Wedgwood and Spode—she still felt proud of the self-discipline it had taken to bring the beautiful furnishings into their life. She came from thrifty stock. Her parents had saved and invested all their lives in anticipation of a time when they would need a chunk of money. They had happily paid for Harry's years at Cathedral Boys' School and Frankie's at Arcadia and left their daughter a comfortable inheritance.

Some of which had helped Harry through med school. He would be at his father's birthday party, of course. Maryanne looked forward to that. It was always a special occasion when she had her son on his own. Gaby, his French-Canadian wife, was on one of her extended fundraising trips, soliciting money for the kids' clinic. Despite her liberal politics, Harlan loved his daughter-in-law and, in his own begrudging way, he respected her and let her know it. Maryanne wondered how it felt to be Frankie, watching her father give Gaby the approval she had longed for since childhood.

Sergeant Major Bunny Bunson, USMC Retired, had called that morning and invited himself to the party. Luckily Maryanne had bought a large rib roast. Bunny was a gormandizer.

Bunny had been the General's closest friend since their first tour. Maryanne had never liked him. Too opinionated and showy for her taste. A strutter. At almost seventy he was still a compulsive bodybuilder and wore his shirts tucked in, military style, to emphasize his trim waist and broad shoulders. He shaved his head to hide the truth that his hair was white, and Maryanne suspected a cosmetic surgeon had firmed his jawline with a scalpel and needle and thread.

She first met Bunny when she'd been dating Harlan only a few weeks. In his terse, always correct way, he had just declared that he loved her. She remembered him telling her that she was the prettiest girl at the party, saying he was so proud his brass buttons might pop. It was 1969 and Maryanne had been told that she looked like Jean Shrimpton, the British model who was in all the style magazines, so she dressed the part in Carnaby Street mode. That night she wore an extremely short black dress with a white ruffled front like an old-fashioned men's dress shirt and patent leather shoes that her roommate called "French hooker heels." Her blond hair was shoulder length and ironed dead straight.

She and Harlan were talking with some other officers and their dates when Bunny swooped down upon them and enveloped her in a hug that was an inch too tight, a second too long. She didn't like the amused, appraising look in his eyes when he pulled away.

He said, "So this is the one," and nodded, grinning at Harlan. "Gol' dang it, I wish I'd gotten there first!"

Maryanne remembered being insulted by the way he put his compliment, and thinking how grateful she was that he had not *gotten there first*. Bunny Bunson might have soured her on the Marine Corps altogether.

But he was Harlan's friend and over the years he had become a fixture in their lives. There had been girlfriends and two ex-wives, but none lasted long enough to make much of an impression on Maryanne. After retirement he bought a house on a lake in the Cascades and vanished for a while, saying he would fish and hunt until he thought of something better to do. She wasn't exactly sure what had tempted him away from the slaughter of fish and deer, but she thought it was a consultant job of some kind with the corps or DOD. He rarely stayed in one place very long. He kept an apartment in DC and one in Oceanside. Once she'd asked Harlan what Bunny's job was. His answer had been vague, and she wondered if her husband knew for sure.

Anyway, tonight he was in San Diego and like it or not, he was coming to dinner.

Chapter 8

In Frankie's memory, family parties all ran to a similar pattern.

They began, as her father's birthday did, with the necessary social lubrication—martinis, whiskey sours, Manhattans, the lethal cocktails of her parents' youth—served from a bar that took up half of one wall in the den, a room full of easy chairs, books, and memorabilia. In military circles, alcohol was the drug of choice; and while Frankie could not remember ever seeing her mother finish a drink, the General always had two of something, wine with dinner, and milk punch at bedtime.

On the evening of the party, one day after Frankie's meeting at Arcadia School, Glory ran through her grandparents' house like the healthiest, happiest, and best-adjusted kid in three counties, though only a few hours earlier, she had been reluctant to go to school and complained first of a stomachache and then a headache. For a moment Frankie had been tempted to send her across the street to her grandmother for a mental health day, but the impulse passed quickly when she thought of explaining this to her mother and the General. She had not yet spoken to Glory about the incident at school, nor had Frankie told Rick anything about it. She dreaded both conversations and until she figured out how to begin and get through them, she convinced herself it was better not to try.

It was a thin excuse and all day she'd been fretting, feeling both dishonest and cowardly.

In the den her godfather was tending bar. Bunny grinned at her from across the room, his front teeth shining like a clean sink.

Frankie's throat tightened.

She kissed her mother's cheek and then the General's and handed him an expensive bottle of champagne. "This is for you two later."

"And I made *this* for you." Bunny handed Frankie a sugar-crusted cocktail glass. "Sidecar. Your favorite, right?"

In college, yes, maybe. These days she preferred a shot of Johnnie Walker up, but she thanked Bunny, took the clown drink, and stepped back into the corner of the room behind a big wing chair. One sip of the cocktail and she set the glass on a bookshelf. After the week she'd had, she needed to be in close control of herself. Her brother arrived, apologized for being late, and launched into a story about the clinic's latest problems with Mrs. Greenwoody and her Build a Better Ocean Beach committee.

Frankie listened, her attention barely engaged. She

wasn't exactly hiding in the corner behind the chair, but she was safely out of the conversational line of fire. She turned her head as if she were following the conversation and occasionally nodded as if she were interested. Her focus drifted like a net cast between Iraq and San Diego, childhood and the present. When she was young and the upholstery was a serviceable blue-and-white striped cotton, the corner behind the chair had been a good hideout if the General was angry and looking for a target.

In the den the television was on and set to PBS, the *NewsHour*. Frankie's mother preferred this channel, and the General tolerated it so long as she did not complain when he swore at the onscreen guests and commentators. At a family gathering the television was always on and, like an opinionated guest who knew the scoop from inside the beltway, it often determined the course of the conversation. That night Senator Susan Belasco was being interviewed. Over the murmur of conversation, Frankie heard the words *Global Sword and Saber Security Services . . . bodyguards for top officials . . . a secret army over there. . . .*

Her attention jerked away from the screen and dilated to a pinprick as she counted the points and lines in the wing chair's plush beige herringbone.

"You okay, goddaughter?"

She wished Bunny would just call her Frankie or Francine like everyone else.

"Drink up. You look like you need to relax a little."

And Bunny was a ridiculous name for a grown man.

"You think too much, goddaughter."

What was he now? A mind reader?

Maryanne called them in to dinner.

For Frankie family gatherings were an ordeal of dancing around the General's mood, dipping and pirouetting and trying to make herself agreeable. In contrast Harry always seemed to have a great time. The accident that crippled the General's plans for his son's military career had liberated Harry. These days he laughed and argued and was as outspoken as if the General's approval meant not much to him, either way.

"Gaby sends her love." Harry's wife was not only a pediatrician but held an MBA from Boston University. It was she who managed the finances and did most of the fundraising for the clinic. "She said to tell you that she wouldn't have missed your birthday, but she's got an amazing opportunity to talk to some really big donors in show business. She's eating lobster and filet mignon tonight."

"Love Gaby, hate lobster." The General walked around the table, filling wineglasses with a heady cabernet. He put a drop in Glory's water glass, tinting it pale pink. "Might as well eat a cockroach."

"She's seeing some television folks tomorrow morning. Did you know that shows like *American Idol* give grants to not-for-profits? They're talking about funding mobile clinics so we wouldn't be limited to Ocean Beach."

"The BBOB would be glad to hear that." Rick helped himself to a thick slice of rare prime rib from the platter.

He put a smaller piece on Glory's plate. "The dreaded Veronica Greenwoody was in my office yesterday, trying to get me to sign one of their petitions."

"Who's Greenwoody?" Bunny asked.

"Local developer," Harry said. "She lives out on Sunset Cliffs in a house full of cats and buckets of cash. She and the BBOB want the poor out of Ocean Beach so they can build McMansions and make a fortune."

Rick did not disagree although he too was a real estate developer. He favored controlled growth, and despite having built a large home across the street from the General and Maryanne, most of his projects were modestly sized and styled residences.

Harry said, "Greenwoody's been fighting us for three years but we haven't moved and we're not planning to."

"I don't think they actually begrudge care for the children," Rick said. "I meet with them from to time, to stay on top of things, and they're not monsters. Except her, of course."

"She's a Godzilla, right, Daddy?"

Everyone at the table laughed at Glory's precocity.

Frankie took some meat, the smallest slice she could find on the platter. Salad was what she really wanted, but this was the General's birthday and his favorite kind of meal: rare beef, potatoes, and peas.

"You've got to admit, Harry, this town could use a little cleanup." Frankie felt Rick looking at her as he spoke and knew that he wanted her to say something supportive. "It's getting pretty hard to avoid the homeless. Frankie's even got a friend who sleeps in her car."

Why was he talking about Domino now? Either he was angry or rubbing sticks together, but starting flash fires at the dinner table wasn't Rick's style. He'd grown up in a big Boston family where cooperation and good manners were praised virtues. If he and his brothers wanted to fight, they were told to "do it in the basement and don't forget to wash up before dinner."

"Her name's Domino," Glory said. "And they don't live in a car, Daddy. They have a cool van with shelves for stuff. Her daughter? Candace? She's almost eight and she's never been to school but she's a really good reader cuz Domino's taught her how. She's my best friend."

The General looked up from his roast beef. "Your best friend lives in a car?" The General's cheeks were rosy in the candlelight. "You go to the best school in the city and your friend sleeps in a car?"

"A van, Grandpa. And it's really a good idea. Domino works at Jack in the Box and she parks behind so she doesn't have to get a babysitter."

"God Almighty."

"Right now her and her mom are hiding out from Jason, he's Candace's father and he's really mean sometimes." Glory was matter-of-fact, as if violent fathers were something she knew all about.

Frankie spoke up. "Glory, it's not polite to talk about Domino and Candace when they aren't here."

"And they never will be," the General said.

"I know Domino," Harry said. "She's plenty smart and she's a good mother."

"In a van?"

"Don't be a snob, Dad," Harry said. "It's un-American."

Emboldened by her brother's support, Frankie said, "Domino served in Iraq, sir."

"Then she's got benefits coming, Francine."

"Benefits aren't always easy to get," Harry said. "The VA can run you ragged, Dad. You had it easier in your day."

"I'm not saying anything against Domino," Rick said. "I don't even know her, but some of the homeless are genuinely creepy. A woman who works with me, my assistant, owns a house on the flats—"

"Her name's Melanie," Glory said. "She's my other best friend. Her house is next to the beach and one time me and Daddy were there and we saw this man do a dirty thing right in the yard." She looked at her father. "It was gross huh?"

"Yes, it was, sweetheart."

"Can't we talk about something more pleasant?" Maryanne asked. "Taxes, maybe?"

Harry laughed.

Glory said, "Melanie's got a Jacuzzi in her backyard but she can't use it anymore cus of the creeps."

Rick raised his glass. "I rest my argument."

"Creeps?" Frankie said. "You don't call people who are less fortunate than you are *creeps*, Glory."

"That's what Melanie calls them."

"I don't care—"

"We're thinking about getting a Jacuzzi," Maryanne said, smoothing the way onto a different topic. Should they have it installed in the backyard or the bathroom? How much did Rick think it would cost? Would it really help the General's pinched vertebrae?

Glory dropped her fork on her plate and made a face. "I don't like pink meat."

"Yes, you do," Rick said.

"She doesn't have to eat it," Frankie said, still ticked off at Rick for bringing up Domino when he must have known that it would upset the General. "Rare meat isn't everyone's taste."

Now it was Bunny's turn to change the subject, which Frankie wouldn't have minded except that he turned the floodlights on her. "How much more time you got?"

"Too long," she said.

"Don't complain at this table. I never wanted you to enlist in the first place." After six years the General still never missed a chance to remind her of his opposition. "And I absolutely did not approve of you taking TAD so you could go over there where you didn't belong. But since you did, you might as well reenlist and take advantage of the experience."

"That's not going to happen," Maryanne said quickly.

Bunny was amused. "She doesn't want to sit behind a desk processing pay vouchers 'til she's forty. She's your daughter, my friend, and she'd die of boredom. Right, Frankie?"

Frankie felt defensive on behalf of her shop. "If it weren't for the finance office, no one would get paid and the Marine Corps would grind to a dead stop, believe me."

"You're right there. Money makes it all happen." Bunny rubbed his index finger and thumb together.

Frankie clenched her fists on her lap and thought about punching her godfather in the jaw. In the time before she went to officers' school at Quantico, she had worked out every day, loving especially the boxing lessons she'd taken at her gym. By the time she got to Virginia she was in the best physical shape of her life. Since then she had stayed fit and could still do some damage. If she wanted to.

For a moment she was distracted, imagining the riot that would ensue if she did actually punch her godfather.

Glory showed Rick her plate. "Is this enough?" She'd eaten half of what he'd cut up. "*Now* can I go watch a video?"

"I'll go upstairs with her." Frankie wanted to get away from the table as much as Glory.

"She doesn't need help, Francine. When you were gone, off playing war"—the General couldn't let the topic go—"the girl practically lived in our guest room. She could start a video blindfolded. Isn't that right, L'il Dynamite?"

"You'll tell me when it's time for cake, okay, Grandpa?"

"And you'll come down and sing to me. You can sit on my lap and help blow out the candles."

"I'm too big for laps."

"How old are you, anyway?" His gruffness vanished as he played at being astonished. "Maybe five? You look about five. I bet you can't even spell."

"I can too."

"Can you spell *loquacious?*"

"Grandpa, that's not fair."

"How 'bout *ostentatious?*"

"I'm in the third grade not college." Glory punched the General's shoulder gently, then hugged him, squeezing tight, and Frankie felt a sharp flash of envy.

"I'll get you settled."

"I don't need settling."

Rick said, "Go with your mother, Glory."

"You come, Daddy." She tugged on his hand.

Harry came around the table. He was so accustomed to his prosthetics that his gait looked no more awkward than if he had a mild charley horse. "You're with me, kid."

Glory didn't object. She was crazy about her uncle Harry.

In the moments of silence after Harry and Glory left the table, the murmur of the television talking to itself in the den reached the dining room.

"I thought I'd shut that damn thing off," Maryanne said and excused herself to do so.

Conversation turned to the Belasco hearings. Bunny had a few dozen opinions. As he talked he ate and gestured with his fork, stabbing the air as if he were inflicting wounds on the senator.

Rick said, "What I don't understand is why we need these special security outfits in the first place. How'd the military get along without them before?"

"Iraq's a whole new kind of war."

"I'm aware of that, Bunny. And you don't have to tell me that most of the contractors do routine stuff like food service and construction, sanitation." Rick sounded irritable. "But some of those guys are just mercenaries."

Frankie had met a couple of G4S employees back in the spring when they came through FOB Redline for a few days. Several of them shared an apartment not far from the Green Zone where they made their own beer. The idea of making beer in Baghdad had amused everyone. One man, a Brit with special service experience, had told her he was making more money than he'd ever seen in his life, but he wanted to make clear that the paycheck came at a cost. Whereas Marines never left anyone behind even if it meant returning to the scene of a battle days, weeks, or even years later, the Brit knew that if he were kidnapped or wounded, he was on his own.

"*Mercenary* is a word I don't like." Bunny put his fork on the edge of his plate, lining it up precisely parallel with the knife. "You say the word—*mercenary*—and you think about killers for hire, assassins, or something, right?" He raised his fork again. "But the guys who work for G4S, they just want to get the job done, same as Marines."

"Whatever they do, they make a whole lot of money,"

Harry said, resuming his seat at the table. "Some of those guys are pulling down two-fifty K a year."

"There's nothing wrong with making money when you fight the enemies of democracy," Bunny said. "It's either we hire contractors or we bring back the draft. That's what it comes down to. Manpower. This country can't fight a war with a volunteer army."

"Would that be so bad? The draft, I mean? Why not national service for everyone over the age of eighteen, male and female? Even a gimp like me can do paperwork."

"Never going to happen, Harry. Nation hasn't got the stomach for it."

"This G4S thing." The General spoke up for the first time. "Americans should be grateful for the help they're giving us over there instead of wasting a truckload of tax-payers' money to investigate them. They risk their lives same as any fighting man."

"Amen, brother."

"Mind you"—the General raised his glass for emphasis, sloshing the wine dangerously close to the rim—"if G4S has broken any laws they have to be called on it. But the Senate should keep its nose out of it. That Belasco woman's been against the war from the start, and now all she wants to do is make trouble."

"And she's going to get a lot of people up to testify and half of them won't know what they're talking about. She sure as hell doesn't. The woman's stone-cold ignorant about what it takes to win a war and she'll sit up there lording herself over a lot of good men who, if the truth is told, are doing more for this country's interests than she is." Bunny looked at Frankie. "What do you think? About G4S?"

The blood rushed to her cheeks. "I don't have an opinion."

"Of course you have an opinion," her father said. "Good God, Francine, you were over there for almost a year. How can you not have an opinion? What did you do? Stay in your rack the whole time? 'Wake me when it's over'?"

Frankie's mother laid a hand on his wrist.

Harry said, "Leave her alone, Dad."

"I can't ask my daughter a question? It's my goddamned birthday! Bunny go ahead and have that last slice of meat, you know you want it. Francine, give me your glass." He raised the wine bottle and when she shook her head, he refilled his own.

"That's enough wine, Harlan." Frankie's mother swiped up his glass and shoved her chair back. "Bunny, I don't know what your cholesterol numbers are, but I'm sure you don't need any more prime rib. You all just stay here and try to be civil to one another while I see about dessert."

Frankie could not sit still, and her palms prickled with anxiety, as if she'd grabbed hold of a thistle. She knew that family occasions didn't have to be fraught. Rick and his brothers didn't always get along, and his sister nursed a permanent grievance, claiming no one paid attention to

72

her opinions. Sometimes his father drank too much or his mother got her feelings hurt because no one asked for a second helping. But the affection they all felt for each other was there at the table, no matter what. No one was judged too harshly; they teased but they didn't insult. When Rick's family got together, no one was bullied.

The General's birthday cake was a many-layered splendor of raspberries, chocolate, and cream.

Frankie went upstairs to get Glory. In the empty guest room the television was on, a Pixar movie about cars boinging from laugh to laugh. She checked the bathroom and then walked down the hall, glancing into the rooms that had once been hers and Harry's but had long been given over to an office for the General and a little room that her mother called her bolt-hole. She found Glory in the General's office, standing in front of his towering gun cabinet.

"Cake time."

"Did Grandpa kill people when he went to war?"

"Everyone's waiting downstairs. We're ready to sing 'Happy Birthday.' "

"Did he? Kill people?"

"We can talk about this, Glory, but now isn't the time."

There would never be a right time to talk about killing and threatening people with guns, but if ever there was a teachable moment, this might be it. Still Frankie could not begin. She wanted more than anything to be the mother

Glory needed and deserved, but at that moment the task was beyond her mothering skills. She felt a leaden certainty that no matter what she said, she'd get it wrong.

"Grandpa won't cut his cake without you. You should see how gorgeous it is."

"I don't care about cake. How come I ask you stuff and you don't answer?"

"Another time, Glory. It's been a long night."

"Well, did he?"

"Your grandfather was a hero in Vietnam. You know that. He saved the lives of his Marines."

"So that means he did kill people. What about you? Did you shoot anyone?"

"No."

Not exactly.

"But you had a gun, right? Why didn't you shoot it?"

"I wasn't that kind of Marine."

Glory's blue-green eyes seemed to turn a darker, harder shade when she was thinking.

"Did you see anyone get shot?"

She couldn't talk about this to an eight-year-old, she couldn't talk about it to anyone. She had built a wall in her mind so she wouldn't even have to *think* about it.

"We're going to sing and eat some dessert and then we're going home. We're not going to talk about guns and shooting."

Glory crossed her arms over her chest and stuck out her pillowy lower lip. "I know about free speech, Mom."

74

"Sorry to disappoint you, Tiger, but there's no free speech for eight-year-olds."

"I can ask any question I want and you can't stop me. It says so in the Constitution."

Downstairs the doorbell rang. Frankie heard voices from the entry.

"It's Melanie," Glory cried. Shoving past her mother, she flew down the hall. From the top of the stairs Frankie watched her tumble into Melanie's arms and hug her emphatically.

Melanie extricated herself, laughed, and shook back her long sheet of blond hair, almost the same shade as Glory's. "I feel so bad busting in on you all like this." She had a sweet high voice to match her schoolgirl hair. "Richard told me he wanted these papers signed and in the mail tonight."

"Can she have some cake, Grandmommy? Can she?"

Richard.

Frankie's mother, standing just behind Melanie with her hand on the doorknob, looked up at the stairs and caught Frankie's eye. Her head tilted slightly in a way that asked a question Frankie could not answer.

Chapter 9

Melanie had declined the invitation to join the family for dessert. After her departure and a plate of cake and ice cream, Glory collapsed in whiny exhaustion and only Rick could comfort her, saying to Harry as he held her on his lap that some days an eight-year-old was just a taller version of a four-year-old. For a minute Frankie felt like a stranger in the family. In the time she had been deployed Rick had learned how to be a single parent and required no help from her.

At home he carried Glory upstairs, and she did not stir except to tighten her arms about his neck. Following behind them Frankie reached for the banister to steady herself, staggered by a wave of soul-sapping weariness. Jared Wentcott, the conference at Arcadia, and her father's baiting: it was more than she knew how to handle. And the worst of it had been those moments upstairs, confronted by the fierce little girl she and Rick had made.

She had failed to do the right thing, to be the mother she wanted to be.

She sank to the stairs and sat with her head in her hands, her fingers pressed hard against her closed eyes.

At Three Fountain Square she had failed to be the Marine she wanted to be. So little had been asked of her. All she had to do was force open the door of the Humvee and step out. But she had done nothing.

Lions and bears and two or three different floppy-eared dogs, a pony the color of Pepto-Bismol, Zee-Zee the chartreuse cobra, and more creatures whose names Frankie did not know were arranged in a protective wall around Glory. Frankie's impulse was to clear the bed and give her room to uncurl like a blossom from a tight bud. She had once tried to do this but the results were unhappy. Glory had awakened in the darkness without her protectors, screaming for Daddy, her eyes alight with a nightmare she could not remember.

Frankie didn't think she had ever screamed for her daddy in that way. But then she hadn't ever had a "daddy." Her father had been either "the General" or "Sir" for as far back as she could remember, a formidable and sometimes frightening figure. Even so her memories of childhood were mostly happy. Eight had been a year of wonders, of falling into bed exhausted at the end of every day and being asleep before her head touched the pillow. It was a time of bikes and Rollerblades and Boogie-boarding, sleepovers and learning to sail and horseback ride, of finding that she was strong and naturally adept at a lot of things, that when she made a suggestion, the other girls agreed and went along with her. Somewhere around age eight she had begun to sense that she was a leader.

She could not remember ever being afraid at Glory's age.

And then, without warning, an experience leapt out of memory to contradict her. The General had gone on a Canadian fishing trip and been away ten days. At eight she had only a map-gazing knowledge of where Canada was, even less of British Columbia and a lake called Ruination. She looked the word up and the meaning raised the hair on her arms when she realized that the General had gone to a place named for destruction and death. He might never come back from Ruination. In this way she had first understood that her demanding, powerful, and awe-inspiring father could die. And, therefore, so could she.

Children died all the time.

Glory shifted under her patchwork comforter. "Hi, Mommy." In half sleep, her voice was whispery and moist. "Sing the blackbird song, okay?"

"I can't, honey."

"Please?"

"It hurts my throat."

Bye, bye, Blackbird.

Frankie and Rick lay in the dark, neither of them ready to sleep. Through the window the fog reflected and dispersed the city's light, illuminating the room with an ashy glow.

"It's not really dark in here," she said. "Maybe we should get blackout curtains."

"I like being able to see you."

"In the desert, if there's cloud cover, the darkness is so thick sometimes you can be looking right down at your feet and not see them. You just put one foot in front of the other and hope you're going in the right direction."

"Hard to believe."

Rick rolled onto his side, his face a few inches from hers. She wondered what would happen if she leaned in and kissed him. Would she regret it like the last time and the time before, like every time they had been intimate—and there were not that many—since she came back from Iraq? If she kissed him now would he think she wanted him to make love to her when it was the last thing she desired? She tried to believe her therapist's promise that someday she would want him to touch her again.

"In the Middle East most of the heavy construction is done at night because of the heat. They use those big white-bright lights. I knew this Marine from OT. She was stuck in Bahrain and lived in a condo twenty stories up, brand-new and mostly empty. Right next door they were building another high-rise. At night it was so bright in her apartment, she bought rugs in the souk and hung them over the windows."

"I don't think you need to go that far."

"An Indian family lived in the apartment next to hers. She could hear him beating the wife, but she wasn't allowed to do anything. She told her CO and he said she should get a headset. Listen to music or something."

"Frankie, honey—"

Smothering under the comforter's feather weight, she kicked it away and sat up, slumped on the edge of the bed, digging her toes into the thick carpet. "It's bizarre, how you can be surrounded by people and still be lonely. At FOB Redline sometimes, I felt like I lived at the bottom of a big hole. I'd get up and do my job and that was good, a lot of the work was good. But at the end of the day I went back in my hole. If it weren't for Fatima—"

"You never mentioned her before."

Frankie shrugged. "My interpreter." *My friend.*

"Tell me about her," he said, stroking her back through the T-shirt she slept in.

But Fatima meant talking about Three Fountain Square. She shivered and shifted away from his hand.

"Please, talk to me."

"I'm too wired."

"How can you be wired? You never sleep. You should be falling-down exhausted."

"Let me be the way I am, Rick. Just try to understand."

"I'm trying, baby, I really am. But you've got to see how hard you make it. You know, Frankie, we were lonely too. Do you ever think about that? Glory and I were a family while you were gone, but not the family either of us wanted.

I know, I know, we're military and deployment comes with the package. Okay, I've got that. But does that mean we can't miss you and want you back? Frankie, you're home now. How come it feels like you're still gone?"

"I'm a Marine, Rick."

He pressed the heels of his hands against his eyes. "Have you got any idea how sick I am of hearing those words? *I'm a Marine.* Like it's some kind of sacred calling? You're my wife, Frankie. You're Glory's mother. Swear to God, I think nothing means as much to you as the almighty Marine Corps."

"I love you both more than anything."

"Then why don't we feel it?"

She didn't know how to answer. She wanted to get in the car and drive away, stop somewhere, and begin her life all over again where no one expected anything of her.

"Just tell me one thing. Do you want to go back?"

She closed her eyes. "No."

"Then what is it you *do* want?"

To forget Iraq and what she'd seen there, to forget the sand and heat and parched air. The mistakes, all the fucking mistakes that were made every day. The missteps and oversights and, despite everyone's best efforts, the failures again and again. She wanted to love Rick and for Glory to laugh and tell moron jokes as she once had. She wanted to sing her daughter to sleep again.

Her voice broke like kindling. "I don't know."

She waited for his breathing to become deep and

regular, the sign that he had gone wherever he went in sleep, the faraway place that kept him until morning, scarcely moving while she tossed beside him. This night he stayed awake and they lay so far apart she felt the wind howl between them.

"Glory's having trouble in school." She spoke into the darkness, giving him an abbreviated account of the school conference.

"She threatened that girl? She admitted it? Why didn't you tell me this before?"

"They're making a big deal out of nothing." She punched her pillow into a backrest. "She's got spirit. What do you expect? She's the General's granddaughter."

"Frankie, she's *my* daughter. If she's having trouble in school I want to know about it. She and I were on our own for almost a year. I know this little girl. She doesn't go around threatening people for no reason."

His comment felt like an attack, she had to retaliate. "What about Melanie? Does she know her too? Glory's crazy about Melanie."

"Frankie, I needed a babysitter when you were gone. Mel's young and maternal—"

"And I'm not."

"I didn't say that. But Glory needed someone and they bonded. I don't know why you aren't happy about that."

"Use your imagination, *Richard*."

"She took care of Glory."

"What about you? Did she take care of you too?"

Chapter 10

M uch later she ran a bath, steamy and deep. Against her skin, the water was silk, the stuff of dreams in Iraq. Half asleep, she laid her head back against the tiles. Through the bathroom window, open above the back garden, the last of the mock orange smelled sickeningly sweet. The fragrance brought back a memory of another sweet-smelling flower, this one growing along a mud brick wall.

Soldiers and Marines, guns and fear and adrenaline: any way they mixed, the combination could be incendiary; but it was known, if only grudgingly acknowledged, that having women along often tamped down a volatile situation. This was not strictly what Frankie had signed on for; she was supposed to be building a school, but during her time in Iraq she learned that when it came to day-to-day military operations, there was a lot of improvising, and it was her job to go with it. The military preferred that women work in teams of two because a secure search required one to search and one to cover; but there were sometimes no female soldiers available and on this day, Frankie was on her own with Fatima.

A native of Mosul, Fatima had been sent to live with her aunt and uncle in Pittsburgh when she was ten. She was teaching at a small college in Ohio when President George Bush declared victory in Iraq. She had returned to her homeland, hoping like many other expatriated Iraqis, to help rebuild the country. Between then and the time Frankie knew her, Fatima had been in two explosions and one mortar attack. As testament to her experiences, the right side of her face bore a stretch of smooth shiny skin where she had been branded by the end of a metal can exploding from an IED buried in a trash pile at the side of the road. Fatima lived on FOB Redline with her mother and two brothers in one of a few dozen derelict trailers. Beyond this section of the base lay the tents of the sanitation and maintenance contractors, most of whom came from Africa or Asia. Officers and enlisted men and women never entered those areas.

Fatima had told Frankie that if her family were not with her at Redline, they would probably be killed because of her work with the coalition.

"I am ugly now. No man will want me. But my mother and brothers, they think I am beautiful because I keep them safe."

On the day Frankie remembered, she and Fatima had accompanied soldiers on a routine investigation of an Iraqi compound where there was rumored to be a weapons cache. Garbage and junk was piled up outside the wall surrounding a house and several outbuildings. The kind of crazy-ass litter that made Marines and soldiers breathe double time because it could conceal any kind of explosive device. The house was in the middle of a small community where every building was constructed of the same dun-colored bricks that had been used in that part of the world for thousands of years.

The military vehicles, two trucks and an unarmored Humvee, were ordered to park in the street outside the wall, facing away from the compound, and a guard was set. Exiting the Humvee Frankie inhaled the familiar smell of Iraq: dust and trash, spices and the ripe smell of meat, burning garbage, and open drains.

Within the walls the courtyard was spacious and remarkably clear of trash. Growing from a stout pot was a bright yellow-flowered vine that smelled in the heat like the mock orange back home. Somehow it had managed to thrive in the ferocious sun and spilled up and over the wall voluptuously, a cascade of yellow. Frankie wanted to stroke her fingertip along the curve of its petals, knew they would feel silky. Like water.

The house had windows secured by iron bars and a flat roof where the family probably slept during the hottest weeks of the year. When snipers were in place up there, Guardian Angels with M-16s, Frankie, Fatima, and the rest of the convoy entered the courtyard. At one end three black-haired boys in blue jeans and rubber sandals were kicking a soccer ball. As the soldiers entered, the ball scooted out of control and stopped right in front of Frankie. She paused, sized up the distance between herself and the boys, and kicked it back to them with the inside of her left foot, a nice solid hit. They stared at her. Six feet tall in size eleven boots, fully armed and wearing a helmet, goggles, and body armor, Frankie was sure they didn't know she was a woman.

A soldier, with Fatima just behind him and to one side, knocked on the door of the house. Frankie followed with the Army CO, Major Whittaker. She wondered why a major had come on this patrol when a lower-ranking officer would have served as well. Realizing this might be more than a routine investigation, the knot in her stomach tightened.

Even in full gear it was plain how bowlegged Whittaker was. The soldiers called him Major Cowboy behind his back and he obviously enjoyed the nickname and encouraged it by wearing a cowboy hat to cover his bald head when he wasn't helmeted. He came from New Mexico and claimed to feel more comfortable riding than walking.

After almost a minute the door was opened by a man wearing a long, loose-fitting cotton dishdasha and sandals. Standing in the open door he said nothing until he had put on sunglasses, a pair of Ray-Bans. The first thing Frankie thought was that this might be a signal to someone. Automatically she looked back over her shoulder. Her face was hot and a pulse beat under her cheekbone. Fatima stepped forward and explained why the Army had come. The man's eyes were hidden behind his glasses, and Frankie was glad not to see the expression in them.

The soldiers secured the interior of the house, then Frankie and Fatima followed. The main room was large and full of furniture, lamps, and suitcases as if the residents were prepared to leave at any time. On the walls were ornately framed adages from, Frankie presumed, the Koran. Looking around her she was distinctly conscious of having invaded someone's private space and thought of her own home and how she would feel if Iraqi soldiers insisted on searching it. When she had thoughts like this, she wondered if she belonged in Iraq. She would never know if such things occurred to other Marines. She would never ask for fear of revealing something vulnerable and exploitable in herself.

Three women swathed in black abayas huddled on a couch, holding hands and wailing as if the end of the world had come. Major Whittaker tried to talk to them but they were too terrified to listen or respond. Soldiers searched the house and outbuildings and found no weapons cache. No need for Major Whittaker after all. The soccer players were brought inside and interrogated with Fatima interpreting. In the end it was decided that they were no more than they seemed, children playing ball. As Fatima questioned them, they stared at the glossy swathe of scar tissue on her cheek, but if she noticed or cared about their scrutiny, she hid it well.

When the soldiers ignored the crying women, the noise subsided; but if anyone approached them, they resumed their wailing. Frankie thought she knew how to settle them once and for all.

"Just so you know, sir," she said to the major, "I'm removing my helmet."

"Don't do that, Tennyson. We're not secure here."

"Sir, I'm taking it off now."

As she lifted the Kevlar helmet from her head, her thick Nordic-blond braid tumbled to the middle of her back. The silence in the room was as shocking as it was sudden. Then the women began chattering to Fatima, and the youngest of them laughed, covering her mouth. Frankie looked at Major Whittaker. He wanted to smile, she could tell.

Frankie and Fatima, followed by a couple of young soldiers hanging back at a discreet distance, took the women into a small side room and a search revealed they were concealing guns under their voluminous black robes. Small arms, but more than they were legally permitted for self-protection though they asserted repeatedly that this was their only purpose. All but the allowed number were confiscated.

As Frankie and the soldiers were getting back in their vehicles, she heard one soldier say to another, "Jesus, that Scarface is an ugly bitch."

For the last two and a half hours, since the Iraqi man stood in the door and put on his sunglasses, Frankie's nerves had been pulled tight like a slingshot, waiting for a target to let go on.

"You watch your mouth, soldier." She was several inches taller than the young man and broader in the shoulders. It flew across her mind that she had grown up being bullied by an expert and that if she wanted to, she could make this kid wet his pants. Even with her farmer's-daughter braid hanging out the back of her helmet, she knew she was formidable. "I never want to hear you speak that name again, do you understand me? She's seen more action than you'll ever have the guts for."

Major Whittaker stepped behind the soldier. "Captain Tennyson." He had piercing steel eyes. "Time to mount up."

Back at FOB Redline he told her she had almost crossed the line.

"You gotta lasso that temper, Captain."

"Yes, sir."

"And how come you didn't know? They all call her Scarface. That's just the way it is."

"It was disrespectful, sir. She's part of the team."

"Yeah? Well, she's an interpreter. She lives with it. So can you."

"She's my friend."

He raised one eyebrow. "She's an Iraqi. Think again, Captain."

After that she felt closer to Fatima than before, more protective. One night as they watched a video in her quarters, Frankie made a promise.

"When this is over, I'll see you get back to the States. And your family. All of you. You'll be safe there."

Chapter 11

Frankie parked the Nissan in a quiet residential neighborhood a block from Arcadia School.

Before breakfast and during Glory had recited a litany of aches and pains and excellent reasons to go to her grandparents' house across the street instead of school. She was a good student, and it was probably true that she could miss a few days with no serious consequences, but in Frankie's school days, the only excuse for absence was something broken or a fever above ninety-nine degrees. She told Glory to haul her butt into the car. Glory had slumped against the passenger door ever since, silent and sulking, clutching her backpack to her chest like body armor.

She parked under a Brazilian pepper tree so old and twisted that it must have been growing in that square of soil before the lots and streets of Mission Hills were surveyed or houses built. It had broken and buckled the sidewalk, bored beneath the asphalt, and lifted it like veins on the back of a hand.

"Why'd you stop here?" Since Frankie's breakdown in the supermarket, Glory had a way of looking at her as if she expected a bad surprise.

"We need to talk."

"Now?"

"Are you going to be okay today? Will you be nice to Colette? No threats?"

"How do you know about Colette?" Glory's question was more an accusation.

"I know what happened in the playground." Having said too much, Frankie had to say more. She blazed ahead, one size eleven boot after another. "I know that you threatened her. Ms. Peters told me."

"Her! She hates me."

"Why do you say that?"

Pouting, Glory kicked her toes into the dashboard. "If she died, I'd be glad." Her anger at the teacher sucked the oxygen from the air.

Frankie rolled down the car windows. In front yards and gardens up and down the street, hoses and sprinklers were at work. She took a deep breath. Until she went to the Middle East, she hadn't known that damp green air was a luxury.

Awake at three a.m. the night before, she left the bed and went downstairs to the computer in Rick's office. Wrapped in a blanket, she'd gone online and input *bullying*. She had learned that the best advice for parents was to *listen*.

"Ms. Peters loves Colette, Colette's her favorite." Tears pooled in Glory's eyes and floated against her lower lids, but she was the General's granddaughter and knew she wasn't allowed to go soft like a bad apple. "Why are we just sitting here?"

"Can you pretend to like Colette? Would that help?"

"Mommy! You don't get it. She doesn't *care* if I like her."

Colette cared about something, though. Frankie didn't need her therapist or the Internet to tell her that. Probably attention. And power, definitely power. But there was no point explaining this to Glory.

"What does she say to you?"

Glory muttered something.

"I didn't hear you."

She whipped around and yelled, "She says I stink."

It was so ridiculous that for a second, Frankie didn't take it seriously. Then she remembered her own elementary school experiences and wondered if girls still used the insult word *cooties*, or if all the little bugs had died off with her generation. *Big Foot's got cooties in her big booty.* Where had they come up with that? Who said it first and passed it on until half the fifth graders were chanting it?

"Colette says I don't wipe my butt but I do, Mommy. I'm really careful. Only—" She cut off her words and stared out the car window. "Can I go now? I'll get in trouble if I'm late." She tried to open the door but Frankie had engaged the security lock. She flung herself back into the seat corner and stared straight ahead.

"I'm not letting you out of the car until—"

"Okay, okay." Now the tears spilled. "I didn't mean to do it but I had a stomachache and when I went to the bathroom I had to use a lot of paper because, you know, and that made the toilet get plugged up and overflow. I didn't mean to do it. I didn't do it on purpose."

"Is that what this is about?" Frankie leaned across the console and held her daughter's damp cheeks between her hands. "A plugged-up toilet?"

Glory sniffled and nodded.

"Oh, my sweetheart, my girl."

"After, at recess, Colette called me stinky pants and now she says it every day. If I try to talk to her, she holds her nose. I got so mad I told her I'd shoot her." Her eyes shimmered like blue-green turquoise at the bottom of a clear pool. "I wasn't kidding either."

"You were so mad."

"I wanted to shoot her with one of Grandpa's guns."

Frankie heard in Glory's voice how misery got mixed up with fear and excitement when she talked about guns. It was the same in any battle, any skirmish, any run-in with the enemy, the thrill and terror of the power that came with guns. Frankie wasn't immune. The truth was she liked wearing a sidearm.

"You do know that there's only one way to handle a mean girl?"

Glory's square little shoulders drooped as if she knew her mother's advice wouldn't help.

"You have to ignore her."

"It's not just her, it's her friends too. They all say it."

"You're a stinky pants, Glory." Frankie waited for a reaction. "Stinky, pinky, rinky-dinky."

"Don't be dumb."

"Stinky pants, full of ants, stands on the table and does a dance."

"That's disgusting." And dumb, but kind of funny.

In the distance Frankie heard the first bell.

"Dumb and disgusting, but just words. When Colette and her gang say mean things, I want you to think rinky-dinky, stinky-pinky. And when you look at them, I want you to see their faces like big old toilet bowls."

"Mom, that is so gross."

"Exactly. You're going to want to laugh when you see those toilet bowls and it's going to be hard not to. When Colette says 'stink' you're going to think *stinky-pinky toilet bowl* and you're going to want to laugh, but you have to promise you'll try not to. They're going to ask you what you're smiling about, but you can't tell them. Even if they beg you, you have to keep the picture of those rinky-dinky-stinky toilet bowls locked up in your imagination like the guns in Grandpa's cabinet."

"It won't work."

"Oh, yeah, it will." Frankie sounded more confident than she felt. "It's like learning to kick a soccer ball, Glory. You have to practice and practice and then one day you make a goal." She leaned across the console again and kissed her damp forehead. "But that isn't all you have to do. And the next part is the hardest of all."

"What?"

"I want you to walk away from them and not look back."

"What if I can't do it?"

"Oh, you can do it. You're a girl who can do anything if you set your mind to it. You just have to do it and do it and then one day it'll be so natural, you won't have to think about it at all."

"How do you know? How can you be sure?"

In front of the parked Nissan a yellow cat ambled across the street as if it owned the right of way. There had been a few cats hanging around FOB Redline. When she was new to the place and green, Frankie bent to stroke one and a hundred fleas leapt for her hand. Was that what cooties were? Fleas?

"It happened to me."

"No way."

"When I was in the fifth grade I was almost five feet eight. Taller than the teacher."

The petite little girls at Arcadia School had pointed at her big feet and whispered about her behind their tiny hands, giggling: *Bigfoot.*

Maryanne's advice had been self-control. "Bite your tongue, make it bleed if you have to."

Once Frankie had done exactly that and been sent to the nurse's office, where she held the tip of her bleeding tongue in a piece of gauze for ten minutes.

"Did they stop saying that stuff?" Glory asked.

"Eventually. Mostly I got tougher and so will you."

A block away, the second bell rang, a note more insistent.

"Glory, I know something you don't."

In the bright sunlit car her daughter's pupils had contracted to black dots.

"Girls like Colette would wash out of the Basic School in the first week."

"Mom, not everyone wants to be a Marine."

"Yes, they do. They just don't admit it."

Thirty minutes later Frankie surrendered to tears in her therapist's office. Mortified, she grabbed a fistful of tissues from the box beside the couch and wiped her eyes. It was good to have a neutral space where she could vent, but under any circumstances, crying left her exposed, undefended.

Dr. White's office was on Herschel Street in a mixed-use bank building, nicely anonymous. Anyone seeing her go in might think she was visiting a dentist or making arrangements for a new will. At just eight thirty in the morning, the marine layer was low and heavy over La Jolla, shrouding the palm trees and three- and four-story buildings in damp gray wool. From the couch where she sat Frankie could look down four floors and across the street to the microbrewery on the corner. In the outdoor patio a man in white pants and shirt and wearing a headset held a conversation while hosing down the flagstones. Stores up and down the block were still closed but the bagel shop next to the brewery restaurant did a brisk business. As Frankie watched, a woman in a bright orange blazer, pencil-slim brown trousers and torturous heels, double-parked and ran in, leaving her Mustang convertible's caution lights blinking.

An irrational anger tightened her chest. Frankie despised the woman for her entitled behavior. *Stop the world! Drive around my snazzy black car. I want, I need a cup of coffee, I deserve a double latte immediately.*

She became aware of her therapist speaking to her.

"Frankie, where do you go when your mind drifts?"

"What? Nowhere. Anywhere. Mostly Iraq."

"Just now. What were you thinking about?"

"A woman getting coffee across the street."

What was the point of talking about this? Frankie's therapy was going nowhere. But it was embarrassing to sit in silence. She had to say something so she told White about her conversation with Glory.

"For someone who didn't know what to say, that was quite a pep talk."

"Was it okay? I didn't make everything worse?"

"I wouldn't say so, Frankie. What you read online was correct. Listening is the most important thing you or any parent can do. In almost any situation, Glory feels angry and hurt and she's confused. She needs to know that these feelings are absolutely normal and acceptable under the circumstances. Girl-on-girl bullying is different than what goes on between boys. For the most part, boys are refreshingly direct. Girls on the other hand are sneaky so that when a girl like Glory gets picked on, it comes out of nowhere and like this business of calling her stinky, it's so out of left field she has no way to defend herself. By now she might half believe that she *is* stinky."

"She and Colette were friends last year."

"I'm not surprised. And next year they might be friends again."

"She's never setting foot in my house."

"Oh, Frankie, you'll change your mind. To make Glory happy."

"I almost took her out of school. If I'd had to listen to her teacher for another five— Glory would never fire a gun or hurt anyone. Never."

"I'm sure you're right. But when she was looking around for some way to defend herself, she spoke in the language of power she's heard all her life. Coming from a family steeped in the culture of the military, her response seems completely understandable."

Frankie wanted to throw her arms around her therapist.

"Do you think that toilet bowl stuff will work?"

White smiled. "We can call it creative visualization and see what happens."

They were quiet again but now the silence felt comfortable.

"For the record, Frankie, there's not much you can do about bullying. If you want to, take her out of school for a few days to relieve the pressure. Most important, though, just keep on listening and let her be as angry as she needs to be. Part of the problem is that most girls aren't allowed to express their anger when it happens. Feminism has brought us a long way, but by and large girls are still expected to suppress negative feelings. They turn them into something else, most often shame. They put themselves in the wrong for *being* bullied and then for feeling angry about it."

Frankie talked about her own experience in the fifth grade.

"I imagine you took your anger out on a soccer ball."

Frankie thought back to the hours she had spent kicking a soccer ball into the net from every angle, begging her brother to take her to the batting cages, shooting baskets until the daylight was gone and her mother called her in from the driveway. If there was something to kick or hit or throw, she wanted to do it.

"The anger you're getting from Glory now? All that sullen, resentful, belligerent eight-year-old behavior? You may have to resign yourself to being a soccer ball for a while."

Waiting at the timed ramp onto the freeway, Frankie's hands began to stutter on the steering wheel, and when a motorcycle paused a second too long at the green light and the driver gunned the engine, she thought her eardrums would explode. She wanted to ram her car into its rear tire and shove it off the road into a ditch, to turn it over as she had the shopping cart. Slamming her foot down on the accelerator, she laid on the horn and screamed in the closed car. The long muscles in her thighs twitched as she swerved around the bike, missing it by inches, and burned into the traffic lanes, cutting off other cars to reach the middle lane, speeding up to eighty as she headed south to the MCRD. Where the road went under the Pacific Coast Highway, she laid on her horn again and screams tore her throat.

She had lied to her therapist about road rage during her first visit, saying it had never happened to her. The truth was that she was angry at someone or something pretty much all the time. Drivers, Colette, Melanie, Ms. Peters, Rick: these were the targets that first came to mind, but there were others.

Chapter 12

Frankie had a headache the size of an exercise ball by the time she got to the shop. Four Tylenol and a triple latte later, if anyone spoke out of turn she would pick up a printer and throw it at them.

"What's wrong with you, Tennyson?" Olvedo asked when she slammed a file drawer and the whole cabinet shook. "You trying to get my attention?"

"No, sir."

She attended two meetings with senior officers whose sole function appeared to be the creation of elaborate electronic spreadsheets for her to fill in and then route across the nation and world to nameless entities whose functions in the enterprise of war were unknown to her. The surge meant huge amounts of money were going to individuals and companies she had never heard of. And for this she had gotten a one-hundred-thousand-dollar education at Stanford University. For this she had survived the Basic

School and scored near the top in leadership and highest in physical fitness.

By lunchtime her head still throbbed too much for a run on one of the MCRD gym's treadmills and her legs were still adrenaline-shocked from that morning's motorcycle moment. But she knew she needed either exercise or a change of scene if she was to make it through the second half of the day, so she drove to a nearby mall where she bought a passion fruit and mango smoothie with two scoops of protein powder at Jamba Juice, carried her drink to an outside table under a shady overhang, and pulled up a second chair as a footrest. She sucked up a mouthful of mango and passion fruit, tilted her head back a little, and let it slide, numbingly cold, down the back of her sore throat.

That morning her therapist had again recommended that she should make an appointment with a throat specialist.

"Harry might be right and it's stress. Then again, if there is..."

"I'm not making it up, you know."

"I didn't say you were."

"Isn't that what *psychosomatic* means?"

"I didn't use that term." White's laugh was light and bubbly. "You really shouldn't put words in my mouth, Frankie."

Frankie had looked at her watch and seen that she would have to hit all the green lights between Herschel and the MCRD if she was going to be on time that morning. No wonder she had lost her temper with the motorcyclist.

Dr. White had talked about the mind-body connection. "A headache isn't always just a headache, and a sore throat may be the body's way of getting you to look at something you wouldn't want to consider otherwise. Something emotional."

What would Frankie prefer? That her croaky voice be caused by inhaling noxious fumes in Iraq or by some kind of message from her subconscious? She wasn't even sure she believed the mind and body were connected that way. As her therapist described it, they were like roommates incapable of asking or stating anything directly. It was an absurd concept.

She put her smoothie down when she saw Bunny's dark blue BMW sedan cruise by. A beep of the horn let her know she had not only been seen, but looked for, and there was nowhere she could go to avoid him.

She watched him park the car and then lope across the lot toward her, his bald head gleaming in the light. He scraped a metal chair across the concrete and sat down.

"The kid in your office, the one with the pimples, he told me you were here."

"Remind me to have him court-martialed."

"You're mad at me," Bunny said, looking down-at-the-mouth. "I thought so the other night."

"I really don't want to talk, Bunny."

"Yeah, I know how you feel."

No. You don't know anything about me. I am the far side of the moon to you, Bunny. I am the red wastes of Mars.

He crossed his ankle across the opposite knee. To Frankie it seemed he was flaunting his relaxation to accentuate her tension. "I know what's happening to you, Frankie, but you've got to stop thinking about it, shut it down. Tell yourself you were never at Three Fountain Square and neither was G4S."

"Go away, Bunny."

As he shot the cuffs of his crisp blue-and-white shirt, the diamonds encircling the face of his watch flashed in her eyes.

"Wow." Impulsively, she held his wrist. "Aren't you scared someone'll cut off your arm to get that thing?"

"Let 'em try."

"I guess it's not a Timex, huh?"

"Chanel. Three hundred and twenty-five diamonds."

He did not bother to conceal his pride in the big watch with all its dials and sparkle. But he had not worn it to the General's birthday party, which Frankie thought was tellingly strange. Under most circumstances, Bunny was the kind of man who enjoyed attracting attention to his possessions: a grotesquely valuable watch, smart clothes, a new car every year.

"I heard something about your old interpreter," he said.

The sun beat down on Frankie's back and shoulders. At the nape of her neck she felt the pinch of her cells giving up their moisture.

"She's in Syria. Damascus." He smiled, showing all his teeth.

Frankie had promised she would help Fatima get back to Pittsburgh, her family with her. She often talked about what they would do when they lived there, safe from reprisals. She wanted to open a deli and got particular pleasure telling Frankie about the menu and design of the place. Stuck in a Humvee, waiting for the road ahead to be cleared, Frankie had become caught up in Fatima's dream and sometimes the deli was all they talked about. Recipes for hummus: was it best to use dried or canned chickpeas, would American customers be able to tell the difference? Lamb kebabs: to marinate or not and for how long? Parsley, flat or curly?

"It was a promise you knew you couldn't keep," Bunny said.

"I would have gone to the General."

Bunny shook his head in the maddeningly paternalistic way he knew—*he knew*—exasperated her.

"How did she get to Damascus? Where did the money come from?"

"These things get done, Frankie."

"Meaning?"

"Whatever you want it to mean."

"Is her family with her?"

He nodded.

"Can you get her address?"

"I don't think you want to write her any letters. She's got her life, you've got yours. Best leave that alone."

Frankie watched the traffic on Rosecranz, measuring her breaths as her therapist had counseled her.

Fatima the interpreter with the scarred face would be an easy target to identify. In a torn and violent country like Syria where everyone carried resentments that were age-old, virulent, and deep, she was in almost as much danger as in Iraq. And even if she somehow escaped reprisals, her brothers were sure to be infected by the fever of political and sectarian conflict that was a fact of daily life. There would never be a deli in Pittsburgh or anywhere else.

Bunny said, "Someone from Belasco's committee's going to ask you to testify."

"Who told them I have anything to say?"

"Use your brain, Marine." His bushy eyebrows veed with irritation. "You couldn't keep your mouth shut about Three Fountain. You talked to that chaplain and then you went to Culligan."

"How do you know? That day, when you came to Redline, I never told you who I talked to."

But she *had* described the incident to him. Hard to believe that just a few months ago, she had still trusted her godfather. "How do you or anyone else know I went to Culligan?"

"Doesn't matter." He waved her question away, diamonds strobing. "The point is that Senator Belasco's after you. You'll be front-page news, Frankie. Is that what you want?"

She stared at him for a long moment. "Who are you, Bunny?"

"I'm your godfather," he said, beaming innocently. "And it's my job to look out for you. Belasco's handing out subpoenas to anyone who ever complained about G4S. She's going to ask you what you think you saw."

"What I *did* see. I saw a murder."

Bunny winced. "If you testify against the military—"

"It *wasn't* the Marines or the Army." She forced the words out, her throat pinching shut as she spoke. "It was Global Sword and Saber Security Services. G4S."

"Your father and I believe—"

"The General doesn't believe in murder."

"Frankie, sometimes there's a bad apple and I agree it should be tossed. But the way Belasco wants to do it, she's gonna throw out the whole bushel basket and nuke the orchard. A bad apple, Frankie. That's all that guy was."

"So you admit it happened."

"I don't admit anything. How can I? I wasn't there."

"But I was. I saw it all through binoculars."

"You'd never been under fire, Frankie. You were frightened."

Frightened? Afterward yes, but at the time she had never felt more intensely alive.

"I saw him. Later."

It seemed to Frankie that she heard a click as Bunny came to attention.

"I was in the airport in Kuwait, going home." She had been in a line to buy coffee and seen the G4S contractor leaning against a wall with a cell phone pressed to his ear. He looked right at her.

"You imagined it, Frankie."

She would never forget his face. In a land of mahogany skin and black hair, the contractor was alarmingly fair. White-blond hair, a milky face despite the desert sun. "And he was short. He was built like a tree stump."

Bunny sighed and rolled his neck from left to right. "Okay, let's look at this thing another way. Suppose Belasco asks you to testify and you do it. Senator Delaware is on the committee and we all know he supports the contractors one hundred fifty percent. He's gonna ask you questions and make chop suey out of your answers. You say the shooter looks like a tree stump and Delaware's going to laugh 'til he busts. I guarantee he'll make you out to be a hysterical female who had no business being in Iraq in the first place. He'll talk you in circles until you admit yourself that you should have stayed home with your husband and daughter." He ran his hand back from his forehead over the crown of his head as if he still had hair to groom. "You'll humiliate the corps, Frankie. And the General with you. You won't mean to, honey, but it'll happen."

It was too easy to imagine.

"Whatever happened in Baghdad, you were hurt by it. I know that and if I could undo it, I would. But isn't that enough? Do you want to spread the hurt around? Believe me, Jesus, I'm thinking of you and your family."

She imagined herself standing at attention before the congressional committee, in uniform of course, her hand on her heart. The perfume and aftershave body smell of the overheated hearing room. The reporters in the well between the witness table and the senators' podium, the microphones, the light reflecting off eyeglasses, wristwatches, camera lenses. She would not have to turn around to feel the eyes of the crowd in the room watching her. By a small stretch of her imagination she saw her father at home in his den, his attention riveted to the television screen as she swore to tell the truth.

Bunny was right. The risk was too great and the chance of doing good by testifying was almost infinitesimally small. Iraq teetered on the edge of a flat world. Blood was blood and dead was dead. Forever. She would not humiliate the corps or herself, and she would never, under any circumstances, do anything that would hurt her father.

Chapter 13

That night it was after eight when Frankie left the MCRD and walked to her car. The early dark was oddly quiet but she heard the rustle of hidden life in the huge palm trees. She didn't want to know what kind of life, but there was no way to pretend it wasn't up there skittering around. In the half quiet darkness, she heard the scrape of tiny claws from nest to nest, up and down the shingled trunk. From a power line a crow as black as ink watched her and she was tempted to call up to it, tell it to go away, leave her alone. Carrion crows were everywhere in Iraq.

She called Rick and told him she was going to the support group at Veterans' Villa. He knew this was a big step for her and he said twice how proud he was. She wished he would not praise her. She wasn't doing anything worthy and she did not intend to participate in the group. If Domino wasn't there, she wouldn't even hang around.

She parked in front of a hiring agency whose blue neon sign outlined a coyly posed nude and crossed the street. At the entrance to Veterans' Villa a notice directed her to a "closed" support group at the end of an arcade open on one side to a center patio. At the round tables the umbrellas had been drawn down and strapped and the chairs were tipped forward, balanced on two legs. In a corner two women sat on a bench talking quietly. As she passed near them they looked up briefly, took in her boots and cammies, and resumed their conversation. At the door Frankie put her hand on the knob and paused. She knew the women were watching, making up stories in their minds as to why she was there, fitting them into the lines and spaces of their own histories.

The long, narrow room was floored in vinyl, a gray marble design that could not conceal the wear of hundreds of pairs of boots. The walls were a similar nondescript color, but she smelled fresh paint. At one corner there was a bulletin board with nothing posted on it. Opposite a line of windows faced the street where Frankie's car was parked. Off-white plastic vertical blinds laid stripes of blue neon across a dozen metal folding chairs arranged in the approximation of a circle. Faces turned and a dozen pairs of eyes stared at her.

She didn't see Domino. One man, tall and very thin, raised his hand and beckoned her to join the group.

"Sorry. I must have the wrong room."

She ducked back and closed the door. For a moment she stood, leaning against the building while she waited for her pulse to stop racing. She hurried along the covered walkway, out, and across the street. Fumbling for her keys, she looked up the street and saw Domino's van parked just inside an alley, almost out of sight. It hadn't been there when Frankie went inside.

Domino had a pillow rolled between her neck and the car's door. Frankie knocked on the window, startling her. Domino pressed a finger against her lips for quiet and carefully opened the van door and stepped out into the street. The door clicked softly as she closed it.

"Candy's asleep," she said. "We spent the whole day at the beach. She's beat."

"I've been looking all over for you." Frankie hugged her. "And Glory's been driving me bat-shit asking when she'll see Candace again. Are you guys okay?"

"Been better." Domino rubbed her upper arms.

"Let's sit in my car. It's chilly out here. We'll be able to see the van." They walked back to the Nissan and got in. Frankie turned on the heat. Domino faced her directly. Her right temple was bruised and swollen up into her hairline.

"Son of a bitch."

Domino half smiled. "Easy, girl, don't get your panties in a bind."

"Did Jason do that? Have you seen a doctor?"

"What you don't know about real life would fill an encyclopedia." Domino laughed darkly. "There's nothing I can do about this except live with it."

Frankie had been bruised and battered playing soccer,

but there was always a doctor or EMT on the sidelines to check out any injury. She felt embarrassed and ridiculously pampered.

"How'd he find you?"

"I don't know. Luck. Perseverance. Whatever. He showed up at Jack in the Box the other night and started in, making a scene, threatening me."

"Tell me you called the police. A restraining order—"

"Frankie, a piece of paper from a judge won't stop him if he wants to see me."

"How did you ever hook up with a guy like that?"

"You don't know him. You don't know what he was like back in the day. In high school he was so incredibly gorgeous and sexy. And such a gentleman. There was a kind of elegance in him." She shook her head as if she did not quite believe her own memory. "All the other guys were always trying to see how far they could get but he got me by just being sweet and mannerly. You know how it is."

Actually Frankie didn't know. Tall and big boned, with hands that could grab a soccer ball out of the air and heave it halfway down the field, she just wasn't the kind of woman men hit on. Even on FOB Redline, where men vastly outnumbered women, the men of the Marine Corps had been generally respectful, soldiers a bit less so. There had been plenty of innuendo from both sides, of course. All the women got that and to survive life in the service they learned to ignore most of it. Some of the officers knew she was the General's daughter and challenged her to prove she was worthy of respect. This was how the game was played, being male or female made little difference. She earned respect by following orders, working hard, and by not asking or expecting favors on account of being a woman or a Byrne. It helped that leadership came naturally to her. Ironically her biggest problem had been other women. Many distrusted her at first, but she had played sports all her life and this was an advantage. She knew how to lead, but she was essentially a team player and when called upon to do so, she could follow. In time most of the women she'd met in the service came around to liking her well enough.

Unlike Frankie, Domino had been a sexual target all her life, starting at age ten with the older brother of her best friend. When it happened she hit him in the shin with a Rollerblade and he never troubled her again. But he paid her back by telling tales, giving her a rep she did not deserve but never entirely lived down. It was not surprising that she attracted attention, for she was beautiful in a dark-eyed, tangle-haired way. A very unlikely Lutheran from Kansas, Frankie always thought.

"If I call the police, they'll find out Jason has a record and almost for sure, he'll go to jail. Jail's bad for him. It messes with his head. He's always worse after they lock him up."

Until she met Domino Frankie had thought that

divorce meant the end of love. Now she understood that sometimes it just meant survival.

"I wish you'd let me give you some money so you and Candace could get a place."

"I told you, I don't want to be indebted. Not to you or anyone."

"It'd be a loan. And if you don't pay me back, I promise I'll send Guido after you. Think what a difference a couple of thousand dollars would make in your life. You could move somewhere Jason wouldn't find you, where the cost of living isn't so ridiculously high."

"I'm not giving away what I want. Candace is going to grow up living near the beach."

Frankie could not comprehend Domino's resistance to help, the need she had to stand alone and go her own way, never mind how hard.

"Friends help each other."

"If you don't shut up, I'm outa here." She sounded like she meant it.

The moment was briefly awkward but it passed.

"I went into the meeting," Frankie said. "For about two seconds. I thought you'd be there."

"Usually, yeah, but with Jason around, I didn't want to leave Candy asleep in the van. There's a guy inside, though, a friend of mine. I'm waiting for him."

"What kind of friend?"

Domino laughed. "What're you, my mother? He's as old as my dad. He knows a woman who rents out rooms. She's picky though, wants to check me out. We're going over to meet her."

"So late? You really trust this guy? Does he have a phone you can borrow? Use it to call me."

"I know men, Frankie. Dekker's cool. Jason's the one I have to worry about."

Chapter 14

Glory said, "But what if I don't want to play soccer?"

"It's just an idea, honey."

Frankie watched as her daughter clomped noisily to the top of the aluminum tip-and-roll bleachers set up at the edge of the soccer field. At the far end a pair of well-dressed women turned to see who was making so much noise. Frankie supposed they were mothers come to watch their daughters practice. She smiled and lifted her hand in greeting.

"Just because you were some kind of superstar—"

"That's not the point. This isn't about me."

Glory made an *oh yeah* kind of sound and leaned against the bleacher back, her arms folded across her chest. Down on the field Gina Calvello was putting the senior school team, twenty or so girls in white tees and blue shorts, through speed drills. Gina had been in her last year at Arcadia when Frankie, only a sixth grader, had begun practicing with the senior school team. Gina and

118

her friends had resented her and for weeks made her life miserable until even they had to admit that she was just as good at the game as most of them despite her youth. Earlier in the week while Frankie was waiting for Glory after school, she'd seen Gina. They had reminisced a bit and Gina invited her to watch the team practice.

"She's mean," Glory said.

"Gina?"

"She's a lesbian."

"Glory! Where do you get that stuff?"

She shrugged.

"Maybe she is, maybe she isn't. But it's none of your business." When had every conversation with Glory become a challenge? "Is that what you and your friends talk about? Sex?"

"I don't have any friends. I just heard someone say it."

"Do you even know what it means?"

"No. Sorta."

Frankie took a deep breath. "Do you want me to explain?"

Glory made a face, squinting her eyes and wrinkling her nose. "Gross, Mom."

She was, after all, only eight.

On the far end of the bleachers the two mothers were joined by another and a moment later two more. Each new arrival glanced up at Frankie and Glory. One of them could come up and introduced herself. Would it happen if she were not wearing camouflage fatigues?

"Can we go now?"

"We just got here."

"They're looking at you," Glory said.

"They see the uniform, not me."

"You're wearing cammies! You look like you just got out of bed."

"You know I work in these, we all do."

"They can tell you're a Marine."

"So? What's wrong with that?"

Glory sighed and rolled her eyes.

If this was what raising an eight-year-old was like, how would Frankie manage a teenager? Life was going too fast for her. She was like one of the girls on the field, sprinting as though her life depended on it.

"I'm bored."

"Watch what's going on. You might enjoy it."

"They're not playing a game."

"Not yet, but they will."

"I told you—"

"If you don't want to play soccer, is there another sport that interests you? Basketball, maybe?"

"I'm not a giant like you, Mom."

"What about volleyball then? Ginn says they've got a good team here."

"I don't want to play on a team."

"It's fun. You learn to cooperate—"

"I already know how."

"—and it's a great way to make friends."

"Is this about Colette? Is this about that?"

"Dad and I want you to have a good time in school, Glory. That's all it's about."

"I wanna surf. Isn't that a sport?"

"What about softball? I used to love— What's the matter?"

Glory had dropped her head to her knees and appeared to be making herself as small as possible.

"It's her."

Three girls Glory's age paraded in front of the bleachers, walking in the direction of the gathered mothers. The dark-haired girl in the middle was talking and the other two were listening. Frankie knew immediately that this was Colette.

"*Now* can we go?"

"It's your right to sit up here and watch the practice. Just act like you don't see them."

"Colette's sister's one of the forwards. Her name's Solange, but they call her Solli."

"Is that why you don't want to play?"

The three girls sat several seats higher than the mothers. The two on the outside leaned toward Colette, two fair heads and the dark one in the middle. Frankie heard them laughing.

"Ignore them." Saying this, making it sound easy, Frankie knew it was anything but. The gossipy girls and their well-dressed mothers made her feel oversized and plain, just as she had felt when she was Glory's age, before she found her place in sports and music and study. She wanted to leave the soccer field almost as much as Glory, but it would look like a retreat, as if they'd been intimidated into leaving. Frankie wouldn't give the girls and their mothers that satisfaction. So they were stuck.

"They aren't going to run us out of here, Glory. Just talk to me as if we're the only people here. Act like you're having a good time."

"As if."

"Don't knock it, Glory. Learning to pretend is one of the secrets of life. When I was in Iraq, in the beginning especially, we'd go out in convoy and I was really scared but I acted as if I wasn't. Tried to anyway. Sometimes I even managed to convince myself."

She had Glory's attention now and to prolong the moment, she could tell her more about Iraq. But was it appropriate—even if she smoothed the edges of her experience, sanded the rough spots, and left out the craziness—to tell Iraq war stories to an eight-year-old? In the end her instinct to protect Glory won out at the price of losing the moment.

"We're going to sit here and pretend we're having a good time. You aren't, I know. But why share that with them? It's not their business. They don't matter, Glory."

"They're talking about you too, you know."

"I know."

And she could guess what they were saying.

Frankie only half believed the civilians who said they

opposed the Iraqi war, but fell all over themselves supporting the troops. It was the politically correct position to take, just as its opposite had been during the Vietnam years. She knew that the mothers in the bleachers took one look at a woman in uniform, cammies or dress, it didn't matter, and made assumptions about the kind of person wearing it. None of them good.

She asked, "What do you think they're saying?"

"You know."

"Tell me, honey." She nudged her gently. "I'm a Marine. I can take it."

"Colette says you have to be stupid to want to fight in a war."

"Honey, no one *wants* to fight. But sometimes it has to happen."

"She says Marines are stupid."

This made Frankie laugh. "You want to know a secret?"

Glory nodded tentatively.

"One or two of them are."

They stayed another twenty minutes, pretending to enjoy themselves, and after a while they did—as much as was possible for an unhappy eight-year-old and her mother, deep in enemy territory. Frankie pointed out what Gina and her coaching assistants were doing, explained the purpose of the drills. The girls divided into teams for a practice game.

"That's Solli. The one with the bandage on her leg."

"She's too aggressive," Frankie said when she had

watched a few moments. "You make errors if you're all the time pushing, pushing, pushing. She doesn't have any sense of strategy and she's a ball hog."

When they were leaving Gina jogged off the field and walked them to the parking lot. Frankie mentioned Solli.

Gina waited to answer until Glory was in the car. "Solli's a pain in the ass and her mother's worse. Remember how much fun soccer was, back in the day? It's not that way now. You wouldn't believe the level of competition and the mothers are in it up to the roots of their perfectly colored hair."

"I thought Glory'd want to play but she's not interested at all."

"How old is she? Third grade, right? If she hasn't been playing for at least two years already, she'll never catch up."

"But she needs something to kick or hit."

"Don't we all?" Gina laughed. "My niece is into kickboxing. Ten years old and you don't want to mess with her."

Chapter 15

A few nights later Frankie and Rick left Glory with the General and Maryanne so they could have a night out together. At dinner Frankie described Glory's visit to a gym to observe a kickboxing class made up of elementary school girls, all doing their best to look and sound fierce. Glory had been interested enough to give it a try, six classes to start with. Over hamburgers and microbrew beers, the laughter came easily and their quick back-and-forth conversation felt familiar and comforting. There were times during the evening when Frankie felt almost normal.

But after the movie, walking back to their car three flights down in the parking garage, she broke out in a sweat in the echoing stairwell. She worried who might be coming up or down the stairs, and each of her senses sprang to alert. Rick wanted to talk about the parts of the movie that had moved him and didn't notice how uncomfortable she was. He stopped on a landing to make a point.

"When the guy got left on the platform, when his

brother took off? That long, slow shot of the train pulling out of the station? It was amazing, the way it sustained." She didn't answer him. "You didn't see it, did you? You were asleep."

"I wasn't."

"I teared up," he said. "I really felt for that guy."

"It was sad, yeah." She started down the stairs. He pulled her back.

"You didn't even see it."

A security door clanged, one floor up.

"Can't we talk about this in the car? I don't like this place."

At the sound of footsteps and murmuring voices, Frankie held her breath and stepped back into the corner of the landing.

"Honey, what's the matter?"

She dropped to a crouch and Rick, suddenly aware of what was happening to her, jerked her up into his arms and held her. Frankie had the sensation of ants crawling across her back, a thousand legs, thin as hairs.

"Breathe, baby. In and out, feel my breath. Follow my breath."

A second later a pair of men with friendly faces came down the stairs, talking animatedly. They smiled when they saw the couple embracing in the privacy of the stairwell, said hello, and passed. Another security door clanged on the lower level and in the stairwell it was quiet again; but Rick didn't let go of her.

He pressed his cheek against her hair. "Breathe with me, stay with me, Frankie. You're safe."

Driving home on Washington Street she tried to make conversation but the earlier mood had evaporated. She saw the sign for Jack in the Box ahead on the right.

"Turn here," she said impulsively. "Let's see if Domino's working. You can meet her."

"It's late."

"You're always saying you want to meet her. Come on, it won't take long. I promise." She pointed at a parking place and was out of the car before he pulled on the emergency brake. "I'll be right back."

Inside there was no one in line and the manager was the only person working. His moist brown eyes had seen everything and been disappointed by most of it.

"Not here. Flu or sumthin." He was beyond curiosity. "She better get well fast. I been takin' her shift at night and it's killing me."

"Has anyone else been asking about her? Besides me?"

"Ex-husband. Shows up every couple nights."

"What do you tell him?"

"She lives in her van. What else is there?"

Frankie's throat ached.

"You wanna order something?"

"A small Coke."

When she opened the car door, Rick had reclined his seat back and was listening to classical music with his eyes shut.

"She's not here."

"Well, that's too bad." He jerked the seat upright, turned the key in the ignition, and jammed the car into reverse. "I'd like to meet her since she seems to be the most important person in your life."

"I hate it when you're sarcastic."

"I'm trying to understand what it is between you and this woman, this woman who *lives in her van*."

"Why is that so important to you, Rick? Why does that bug you so much? She came back from Iraq and she was a little fucked up, not a lot, but considering she'd been raped once and—" She stopped. "Don't look so shocked. It happens all the time."

He shifted back into park and turned off the engine.

"Not all the time, Rick. That was an exaggeration. But it's there, it's always there."

On FOB Redline she never walked to the showers alone at night or took the shortcut to the mess, and like most of the female officers, she did nothing to emphasize her femininity. Even now, working at the MCRD, she didn't wear makeup; and though her hair was still long, she kept it pulled back, braided and clipped down. She was vigilant, always.

Like a prey animal.

"Domino's five feet three and weighs a hundred and twenty pounds. I'm six feet and as strong as most men. Rape wasn't a big worry for me, but I stayed alert."

Like a wide-eyed gazelle in lion country.

"And now?"

"I can't just turn it off, Rick."

"In stairwells."

"Everywhere."

Constantly.

There was no way to make Rick understand how war exhausted the senses. The smell of an alien spice, the taste of sand, sunlight glinting off a piece of junk in the road ahead. The noise and the heat, always the heat. War exhausted the senses as it focused them to a pinpoint laser. Domino understood this. Frankie didn't have to sit in a car and explain it to her.

"If she and I had met before the war, maybe we wouldn't have been friends, not the same anyway. Now we have the girls in common, that's important. But what makes us friends is..."

She wanted him to understand, but these days the right words were rarely there when she needed them.

"It's crazy over there, Rick." No one safe at home could ever understand that. "It's insane."

During her ten months in Iraq Frankie had been in the Green Zone only once, with Fatima, to be interviewed for an armed forces radio program about reconstruction efforts, specifically the school the Army and Marine Corps were rebuilding in a community on the edge of Baghdad, a few miles from Redline. After months on the base a visit to the

Green Zone seemed like a vacation, and even though they would be gone less than a day, Frankie had been excited.

She was used to the look of the city from the ground, but viewed from above, evidence of years of violence spread to the horizon in every direction. Baghdad was a vastness of biscuit-colored rubble, many streets lined with immense concrete blast walls, rights-of-way obstructed by checkpoints and rolls of concertina razor wire. Darting children played and scavenged among the ruins of bombed-out vehicles, and Frankie would not let herself imagine what their day-to-day lives might be like. The fear, the confusion, and the anger they must feel. She had joined the Marine Corps because of her empathy with the children who were victims of war. At the same time, coalition forces of which she was a part were contributing to the misery of the boys and girls in the ruins. It was a moral conundrum that twisted her mind into knots. She left it alone most of the time.

And yet, in the midst of war, the ordinary chores had to be done. Below and to the west Frankie saw laundry laid out on the roof of a building that had escaped damage. In the midst of the blasted-out scene, a stippled mélange of black and brown and tan and white, she glimpsed a scrap of brilliant tropical turquoise. Perhaps a headscarf, a relic of peacetime. To Frankie's eyes it was like seeing a pool of clear water, Lake Tahoe on a summer day.

The Green Zone had once been a riverfront compound, embraced on two sides by the syrupy caramel-colored Tigris River. The Americans and their allies had expanded the elite area to include the convention center and Hotel Al-Rasheed and surrounded the entirety with blast walls almost twenty feet high, surmounted by coiled razor wire.

The driver of the white GMC Suburban that picked them up at the helipad was an Army corporal named Ansten from Yakima, Washington, with yellow hair and eyes the shade of washed-out denim. In the vehicle the air-conditioning was cranked so high that Frankie was actually chilly. Ansten was a talker and nothing, including a direct request from a Marine Corps captain, could silence his ebullient chatter for long. He seemed to regard himself as the Green Zone's official tour guide. The car stereo played classic rock.

Over the vocals of "Sugar Shack" Ansten told her they were listening to Freedom Radio, 107.7. "On the FM dial, ma'am."

In front of the Republican Palace, the headquarters of the Coalition Provisional Authority, their Suburban proceeded at a crawl under the scrutiny of heavily armed military guards. Frankie and Fatima gazed at the palace like tourists.

Fatima said in her slightly accented English, "When I was very young, before my parents sent me to live in Pittsburgh, the enclave was only for the rich and powerful. My mother told me that there were no stray dogs here, no trash. Not even a cat without a home."

Further along the road Frankie saw three men in white shirts and ties talking together at a shaded shuttle stop, anonymous behind expensive sunglasses, pistols strapped to their thighs. Several signs identified restaurants serving Chinese food. Burger King welcomed them to Baghdad. A young man with a clipboard stood under its awning wearing a T-shirt that asked "Who's Your Baghdaddy?"

Suddenly Frankie was ravenous for a fast-food hamburger. "After the interview we'll come back here."

"Whatever you want, Captain," Ansten said. "We got everything here. You like salsa, there's dance classes two nights a week. Bible studies too. It's Little America, you know? There's booze and cafés and just about anything you want if you got the cash. You can even go to movies in Mr. Bad's palace. What about that, huh?"

Checkpoint Three, the main entrance to the Green Zone from the city of Baghdad, was directly in front of the convention center where the broadcast studios were located. Hesco barriers—containers the size of Volkswagens filled with rock and dirt—created a protective wall shielding soldiers at the checkpoint. Concrete slabs blocked off what had once been an eight-lane expressway. What Frankie thought must once have been a grandly impressive entrance to the convention center was now lined with dead trees where flocks of crows perched and observed. Trash of all kinds was everywhere—scrap metal, punctured tires cooked by the sun, plastic bags, and candy wrappers on the ground or caught in the barbed ringlets of wire. Between the S curves of concertina wire, extending back from the checkpoint, hundreds of Iraqis waited in line to pass into the Green Zone.

"Did you ever see anything so crazy in your life? It's the same every day." Corporal Ansten pointed at the lines of people making their way through the checkpoint into the zone. "They all want something, ma'am." He had never acknowledged Fatima. "They come for a job or information or they got something to report. And the reason it takes so long is, they gotta show double ID and they get frisked two, three times. Plus there's sniffer dogs and Iraqis aren't crazy for dogs. Can you believe that? Man's best friend but they don't care for them." Pointing at the blast wall marking the perimeter of the zone, his tone became serious. "Can't keep the rockets out though. We get hit almost every day. And it don't matter how high the wall is, if a guy can get in with a bomb stuck up his—"

"We get the picture, Corporal."

"Hang around long enough, you'll see stuff in the zone like you never expected. This place is cray-zee."

Frankie thought about telling Corporal Ansten that his irrepressible opinions were out of line, but he was harmless and not a discipline problem for her so she let it go. And, anyway, he was right about the zone. It had a Disney-gone-terribly-wrong quality that managed to be simultaneously funny and disturbing. No wonder some called it, derisively, the Emerald City. It made her halfway nostalgic for the overall cruddiness of Redline, which at least looked like what it was.

Corporal Ansten dropped them off outside the convention center. "This is as far as I go, ma'am. I'll be here

133

when you get done." He added, "In case you're nervous on account of what I said about attacks? The broadcast center's the safest place around. Right in the middle of the building. It'd take a nuke to blow the radio off the air."

The interview had gone well. Asked about the relationship between a Marine Corps officer and her interpreter, Fatima replied that trust was the essential ingredient. When Frankie remembered the interview later, these were the words that hurt.

Now Fatima was in Damascus and Frankie was home, except that she wasn't completely. A big part of her was still back in the crazy.

Chapter 16

In a brilliant blue sky, the autumn sun was warm at eight a.m. on Saturday when Frankie and Glory walked down the hill and into what Ocean Beach called its downtown. Crossing the boulevard, she reached for her daughter's hand, but Glory pulled away.

"I'm not a baby, Mom." These were almost her first words that morning. She would not talk about what was going on at school and she was noncommittal about kickboxing. There were many ways to say "get out of my face." "I'm not a baby" was one of them.

The Ocean Beach business district smelled like breakfast: toasting bread, warming muffins, frying bacon and ham, sizzling griddles, coffee. Edging the sidewalk, paving stones inscribed with names—memorials and tributes to friends, pets, and loved ones—made entertaining reading for those waiting in the lines outside the diners. Ocean Beach was between tourist seasons now, and the customers were probably locals, happy to have their streets and sidewalks to themselves for a while. Frankie stopped in at the Moonglow, a coffee bar that had refused to shut down despite the competition of a Starbucks across the street, and got a cappuccino for herself and cocoa for Glory.

In the next block, Murray, the owner of Trashy Cans, a local head shop that had done a rousing business since the mid-sixties, was dragging out a rack of neon-colored T-shirts as Frankie and Glory passed. Murray had inherited the business from his father, a flamboyant hippie with hair to the middle of his back, and he and Frankie had known each other as neighborhood kids who congregated on the pier to smoke pot during long summer twilights. Standing with the bright T-shirts between them, they spent a few minutes catching up on the high points of their lives while Glory read the inscriptions on the sidewalk stones.

There had been a time when Frankie knew the names of everyone who owned a shop along Newport, and if she misbehaved in plain sight, word was certain to reach her mother before she got home, and then there would be hell to pay because she wasn't just anyone, she was Francine Byrne, the General's daughter. Rick and Mrs. Greenwoody could object and argue about the community's homeless population and, by extension, the kids' clinic, but Frankie did not want to change grungy old Newport Avenue with its resale shops and nearly antique stores, the cafés and head shops, surf shops, and tattoo parlors. The Korean-owned doughnut shop on the corner where she could still buy Glory an ice cream cone for under a dollar was one of the places that told Frankie she was home even if she no longer had much to say to Murray and recognized only a few of the names tiled in the sidewalk border.

At the beach end of Newport the public parking lot was full of cars. Surfers were coming up from the water in their wet suits speckled with sand, boards under their arms, their hair still plastered to their heads. Others prepared to go out, pulling on their black neoprene suits, shielded from public view behind the open doors of their cars.

"Melanie says Daddy should learn to surf. She says it would relax him."

Melanie should jump off the pier and forget to come up.

They turned the corner onto Abbott Street.

The clinic was at the end of the block, separated from the corner by an old beach hotel, newly painted and refurbished with natty red canvas awnings at the windows, cement benches with a beach view bookended by Italianate pots full of ferns and blue marguerite daisies. Farther down the street, a few people were lined up on the sidewalk outside the clinic, but across the pavement on the sandy side of a low wall, between two orange plastic cones, a long line had formed. Glory was quick to notice a black-and-white parked in midblock with two officers in the front seat.

"How come the police are here?"

"For security. Same as always."

"What kind of security?"

"You know there are some people in town who don't want the clinic to stay open. They might cause trouble."

"Like what? Like shooting?"

"Not shooting. Honey, all these people want is a vaccination or a flu shot." They could not afford a weapon if they did want one.

"Melanie says homeless guys give her the creeps."

"That's her opinion, it doesn't mean you have to agree."

"Me and her were watching the news one night—"

"She and I," Frankie corrected automatically. "Where was Daddy?"

"At work. I was sleeping over with Melanie and we saw this thing on TV about suicide bombers." Glory's blue-green eyes searched Frankie's face. "Do you know about those, Mommy?"

It was an important question, an important moment. Somewhere Frankie had read that children opened up to their parents when they were ready, not when it was convenient.

"I do."

"Did you ever see one?"

"I never did, Glory." But she had seen the ruin of an ancient city, its schools and homes and marketplaces. She had seen eight-year-old kids throwing rocks at a donkey dying at the edge of the road. And she had seen everything that happened at Three Fountain Square.

Glory asked, "Why would anybody want to get blown up on purpose?"

"Some people think that's the way to get to heaven faster."

"That's so dumb."

Frankie's throat hurt and she didn't want to be having this conversation in the middle of a crowded street, but Glory had chosen the moment.

"People believe all kinds of things, Glory."

"Melanie goes to a church where if you're in a family when you're alive you get to be in the same family in heaven too. She said she wished I was in her family so we could be in heaven together."

Melanie, always Melanie.

"Do you believe that, Mommy? About heaven?"

"I don't."

"What about Daddy?"

"You'll have to ask him." She smoothed Glory's hair back from her forehead, thinking hard for the right words. "It doesn't matter what anyone tells you, even if they sound absolutely sure they're right. No one knows anything about heaven. The people who say they do, really, they're mostly hoping." She put her arms around her daughter and held her close, resting her chin on the crown of her head in the fluster of cowlicks and curls.

"But if you're dead you know. Those suicide bombers, they know."

"Yeah. I guess they do."

"In the war, did you think you were going to die?"

At the beginning she had been frightened all the time, but she pretended she wasn't and sometimes managed to fool herself.

"Are you scared now?"

"No. Why do you ask that?"

Glory shrugged as if to say, *Let's drop the subject.* She picked a bud off the marguerite plant and began to pull it apart like an artichoke until she reached the heart and let it drop to the sidewalk.

"I want to go home. What if someone from school sees me? Maybe they'll think I'm homeless. What if they say I am and someone believes them?"

Frankie stepped back, looking at her daughter in her glittery T-shirt and cropped denims from the Gap, and she almost laughed at the idea that anyone would mistake her for a girl without a home.

"Listen to me, Glory. If people tell lies about you, call them liars and then ignore them. If they say mean things to you, think stinky-dinky and ignore them. I'm not saying you can't be mad. You have a right to be furious. But be smart. Go ahead and scream or cry when you're on your own or with me or Daddy. Don't give them the satisfaction of seeing how they can get to you. Don't make them that important, Glory. Learn to walk away."

"You never walk away from Grandpa."

"What do you mean?"

"He says mean things to you."

A note sounded in Frankie, a waspy buzzing that was unmistakably a warning. "It's not the same thing, Glory. He's my father."

This conversation was over.

Chapter 17

There were children of all ages and descriptions waiting to enter the clinic, which did not officially open until nine, but as soon as Frankie and Glory passed the square front window, Marisol, a short dark-haired woman in cartoon-patterned scrubs, let them in. Behind the desk Frankie found her name tag in a cluttered drawer. Marisol handed her a blue smock, she slipped it on, and pinned the name tag to the collar. She glanced out the window.

"It's going to be busy around here. More than usual, I think."

"Middle of the week folks just wander in whenever, but even if you haven't got a job, there's something about a Saturday...." Marisol pursed her lips and exhaled. "I'm guessin' it's gonna be a nut house. I've just got a feeling."

Cray-zee

The clinic's waiting room was an area roughly twenty by fifteen feet with one large plateglass window facing across Abbott Street to the beach. A rainbow of plastic chairs with contoured seats lined two walls. Wherever there was space on the pale yellow walls, posters illustrated basic health information about good nutrition, dental health, obesity, and childhood vaccinations. The children's area was in front of the window: chairs and a low table on which were big boxes of drawing paper, crayons, and pencils. On the floor stacked plastic bins were full of toys and books.

For the busy Saturday clinic Harry and Gaby employed a total of three nurses, a physician's assistant, and a lab technician who could do a quick screen of blood and urine samples. Two retired internists helped out and a handful of other volunteers advised the parents of children being treated about local housing and employment resources. Sometimes this help was rejected but more often than not the clients seemed grateful, for the attention if nothing else.

Frankie hoped to see Domino and Candace that day. She had promised herself that she would get Harry to look at the bruise on Domino's forehead whether or not she wanted the attention. Midmorning there was a tussle in the children's corner over a particular red crayon, but generally the boys and girls were well behaved through the long wait to be seen. They demonstrated a touching stoicism with regard to their bug bites and stomachaches. At odd times different staff members came up front to speak to Frankie and to report on how Glory was behaving. She was being allowed to watch Marisol give shots and occasionally swab the puncture points with alcohol—wearing gloves, of course, and closely supervised. This was surely a violation of some kind of law but no one seemed concerned.

After lunch the clinic treated a twelve-year-old boy whose home tattoo oozed infection.

A two-year-old with a dog bite.

Several cases of pink eye.

Head lice, fleas, runny noses.

A dozen tetanus shots.

Four babies with earaches.

A disoriented teenaged girl wandered in without a parent or guardian, her clothes stinking, her hair matted.

On the street a trio of protesters appeared with placards saying variations of "get the homeless out of OB." A scuffle between the police and several men and women yelling insults at the clinic patients lined up on the beach brought another black-and-white to the scene, but in the end the demonstrators dispersed. A man threw a bottle, shattering it. The police went after him and the protesters reappeared, taunting the old drunk. Those waiting in line observed the dramas but kept their distance. They had brought their children to the clinic to be seen by a nurse or doctor and not to cause trouble.

Late in the afternoon Domino and Candace came through the door. Domino wore a flag-patterned bandanna headband, but it wasn't enough to control her thick, dark hair or completely cover what remained of her bruise. Like her mother Candace wore jeans and a tee, rubber-soled flip-flops on her feet. As always her dark hair had been tamed into a complicated French braid.

With a delighted cry Glory leapt up and she and Candace grabbed hands and jumped up and down, shrieking, the classic greeting of eight-year-old best friends. In another moment they were at the table whispering and coloring earnestly, their heads—one fair, one dark—almost touching.

"I'll take a break." Frankie asked Mirasol to cover the desk. "We'll be outside on the wall."

Arno, the security guard, had left early for a dentist appointment, but the cops in the cruiser were still parked nearby.

"Show me your forehead."

Domino removed her sunglasses and lifted the fold of her bandanna. The bruise had faded to a jaundiced yellow. "Almost back to my own gorgeous self."

"What happened about the room you went to look at?"

"Way too small."

Frankie laughed. "Dom, you live in a Dodge Caravan. There's nothing smaller than that."

"Shows what you know. It was the size of a closet and it felt like a jail cell. One pissy little window looked onto the next-door wall. And the bathroom was down the hall with rules on the door. Even Dekker said I shouldn't take it."

Domino had grown up in a white house with yellow trim and shutters, a mile outside Scanlon, Kansas, population roughly five thousand. It had two stories and a dormered attic, and sat at the end of a gravel road on a gentle rise overlooking a meadow and a broad shallow creek. From Domino's bedroom window she could see the steeple of the Lutheran church where her family worshipped several times a week. She could see the main street where her father operated the only pharmacy for miles, the high school where she met Jason, and beyond that, the road out of town.

"You know you can't live in the van indefinitely. You need an address for school."

"Yeahyeahyeah."

"Unless." Frankie held up her hand, anticipating Domino's objection. "Don't say no. Just think about this. You can use our address on Newport. That way Candace could at least start school."

"No."

"But people use each other's addresses all the time. She deserves..."

"Don't tell me what she deserves. No one knows better than me what my daughter deserves. It's not going to kill her if she misses a few more weeks of school. I work with her. We go to the library almost every day. She's learning her times tables."

Frankie wanted to argue the point, but knew better.

Though Domino had an attitude that told the world she feared nothing and no one, in the weeks since they'd met, Frankie had seen through this façade; and while she did not doubt her friend's courage, she knew she had a constellation of anxieties around Candace that she was too proud to show.

"I can't break the law, Frankie. I can't do anything that'll give the welfare people a reason to say I'm not a fit mother."

"What about your job? I was there the other night and the boss said you were sick. Is that so?"

"It was Candy. She's got some kind of stomach bug. She gets them all the time. I didn't want to leave her alone." Nervously she looked up and down the street. "Did the boss tell you Jason's been hanging out at Jack's, bugging him almost every night? If it doesn't stop, he says he'll have to fire me. He says he's not a marriage counselor. The thing is, I can't even buy gas if I lose my job."

"Priest Martha might let you park at the church."

"Yeah, for a day or two but eventually someone would complain. Maybe report us. I just can't take the chance." Child protective services would leap at the opportunity to put Candace into foster care until Domino found them a home. Once in the system it would be hard to get her out. "I'll go back with Jason if I have to."

"Don't even think about it, Domino."

"If we were together I could keep him on his meds and

146

he'd be okay. It's when he goes off, like now, he gets crazy. And he's on disability, Frankie. He could support—"

Something moved at the edge of Frankie's peripheral vision. She glimpsed a running shape, a raised arm, and then, suddenly, there was an explosion of shattering glass and the screams of children.

Chapter 18

Candace had been hit and lay on the floor next to the children's table, blood streaming into her eye from a gash at her hairline. Whimpering, she smeared it away with the back of her hand. Domino dropped to her knees beside her. A rock the size of a grapefruit lay nearby with a piece of paper taped around it.

Frankie heard the raucous crows spreading the excitement, pegged to the power lines like black rags. Her head spun and she did not recognize the man in a white coat who bent to pick up a girl with blood running down the side of her face. She heard someone say, "She'll be okay, Domino. We'll have her fixed up in no time."

A blond girl clung to Frankie, which seemed odd, a blond child in Iraq. Though she didn't know who she was, it felt right to hold her and tell her she was safe, that her mother would come soon.

The man in white spoke to a man in uniform. A policeman, not a soldier or Marine, which to Frankie was another odd thing. So much oddity, nothing was quite right in this place.

A woman in a smock covered with comic book pictures took the blond girl away from Frankie. Another woman crouched before her. She had some kind of accent.

"Who am I, Frankie? Say my name."

She tried and almost had it. She was ashamed of her confusion. She looked down at her big capable hands and they seemed to belong to someone else. She directed them to stop trembling, but nothing happened. Her mind and body didn't seem to be connected.

"I am Gaby." The woman held out her hand, palm up, and Frankie took the pill she offered and water from a paper cup. "Do you need to lie down?"

"I'll be okay." She wondered why she said that. She didn't believe it.

She sat with her back against the wall and gradually her mind came back to itself. Besides Glory and Candace, there had been four children, a teenaged boy, and three adults in the waiting room when the glass broke. None had been injured. Glory had just stepped away from the table to get two paper cups of water from the cooler.

"Not even a scrape," Harry said later. "But she's had a shock—you both have." He paused to make sure Frankie was listening. "There's likely to be some kind of delayed emotional reaction. Nervousness, anxiety, something like that."

"I'm fine now."

"Maybe. Just be aware and take it easy, okay?"

An officer asked her to describe what she'd seen from the corner of her eye. A man or a woman, young or old, was he or she alone? She didn't know. There had been motion and then crashing glass. Cries and screams and yelling, door-slam, siren-whine, panic, and then she had heard the children crying and it was a sound that cut into her sanity like a sharpened saw. What followed was an off-center, more-than-real time when her body was one place and her mind another. She didn't tell the police about that.

"Until I knew she was okay, I wasn't thinking about anything except Glory."

She organized the cleanup. Creating order out of confusion calmed her mind. She hoisted Glory up onto the reception counter where she could watch the work, clutching a stuffed bear she had dug out of the toy box. Frankie and other volunteers picked up the large pieces of glass and dropped them into a trashcan someone had dragged in from outside. Marisol told her there had been a note attached to the rock. *HOMELESS OUT OF OB.* Frankie drove a heavy-duty vacuum across the utility carpeting as furiously as if it were a tank. Rick said her name twice before she looked up and saw him lifting Glory from the counter.

"It's time to go home."

Before she left she gave Marisol three twenty-dollar bills and asked her to shove them into Domino's purse, deep into the side pocket where she kept her keys.

At home Glory was amped. She couldn't stop telling the story—*she had just been getting a drink, standing at the cooler and not doing anything when a rock, practically a boulder, came through the window and hit Candace in the head and there was crying and screaming and glass everywhere.*

Rick showed his concern. He listened to everything she said and asked questions, but not once did he look at Frankie. She began to dread the time when Glory would go to bed, leaving them alone together.

After dinner Glory was sent upstairs to have a bath and change into her pajamas. She came downstairs in her pink robe and Rick wrapped her in a blanket and held her on his lap as they sat on the deck, watching the orange sun melt along the horizon of the sea. As always they watched for the green flash that was supposedly visible for a second as the sun set. As usual they didn't see it.

At bedtime Glory had arranged her bed with at least half of it covered with stuffed animals, including, Frankie noted, the hand-me-down bear she had latched on to at the clinic.

"Mommy, I don't want to go to Uncle Harry's clinic anymore. Daddy says I don't have to."

"Let's talk about it tomorrow, Glory. We'll work something out."

"But when will I ever get to play with Candace? Do you think she's okay? She was really really bleeding."

"Uncle Harry took good care of her."

Glory lay back. She pulled the comforter up under her

151

chin and folded her arms across the top of it. "He's a good doctor. Remember that time I had to have stitches?"

"I was in Iraq." Glory had proudly shown her the injury on Skype.

"I was riding my bike down the hill and my feet went off the pedals and I started getting all wobbly and when I fell I hit my foot on the sprinkler thingee in front of Mr. Davies's house." She reached for Zee-Zee the snake and smoothed its cobra head against her cheek. "I didn't cry but there was lotsa blood."

Frankie struggled to steady her voice. "I should have been here, Glory."

Her own mother had always been in the bleachers, the audience, the pew at Frankie's soccer games, her debates and choir solos, so predictably loyal that she was virtually invisible. The parent whose admiration and approval Frankie craved was the General's. On the day she graduated from Arcadia and gave the valedictory address, he had been in Washington, called there on business he didn't explain except to say that it was (he added "unfortunately" to soften the blow) more important than a high school graduation. Of course she said she understood because she had been brought up to understand and accept and be a good Marine. As young as Glory she had known to straighten her back and square her shoulders and do the right thing.

"I'm home to stay, Glory. I won't go away again." She licked her thumb and wiped away a smudge of toothpaste stuck to her daughter's cheek. "You're not going to be able to get rid of me, little kiddo."

"Are you okay too, Mommy? You didn't act okay. After. You didn't even know me. You asked me what my name was. Daddy says you were in shock."

"Maybe. A little bit."

"What if it was a gun, not a rock? What if it was a bullet from an M16 that hit Candace? She'd be dead now."

"How do you know about M16s?"

"I went online. I read a lot about the Marine Corps."

Sometimes Frankie wished there were a law banning computers.

"Glory, in this country people have a right to own guns but that doesn't mean they go around shooting them."

"Bad guys do."

"But there aren't many bad guys, Glory. I know it seems like there must be because they're always on television but this is a big country and most people are peaceful. You know television isn't the same as real life."

"The policeman at the clinic had a gun."

"It's his job to keep the peace. But police officers are just ordinary people. They don't want to shoot their guns. That cop at the clinic? He hopes he'll be a cop all his life and never have to shoot at anyone. That's what he hopes most of all."

"You didn't shoot anyone, did you?"

"No."

"But you could if you had to, right?"

"I know how to fire a weapon, I've been trained. But I went to Iraq to help the people, not kill them. I told you that we built a school."

Tried to, anyway.

Glory was quiet for a moment. "Candace took a bunch of crayons and put them in her pocket. I told her it was bad to steal but she said there were so many in the box it didn't matter. No one would notice. And they were old anyway."

"It is wrong to steal, Glory."

"But Candace isn't a bad person, is she?"

"No, honey. She's just poor."

"I don't think crayons are expensive."

"They are if you don't have any money for extras."

"Colette's got this gold bracelet she wears sometimes. Real gold, Mom. With real diamonds and rubies. That's like an extra, huh?"

"Glory, it's not real gold."

"No, Mom, it is. She says so."

"Maybe she thinks it's real but trust me, it's not."

"Everyone believes her." Glory rubbed Zee-Zee's head against her cheek. "I don't think crayons are extra. And I think sometimes it's okay to steal. Like if you were a kid and you were in Iraq and there was a suicide bomber who blew up your house and you didn't have any parents and you were starving. It'd be okay then."

Rick was right when he said that there was a lot going on in an eight-year-old head. It was a complicated age, a time of peering into the real world, of weighing options

154

and choosing paths. When Frankie left for Iraq Glory had been more concerned with extending her bedtime by thirty minutes than matters of right or wrong but now she was eight and morality weighed heavy.

Glory scooted farther down under her rainbow comforter. Zee-Zee's velvety chartreuse cobra hood peeked out from beside her. She said, "When the glass broke were you scared? Like you were in the war again? But I wasn't scared, Mommy. Maybe I'll be a Marine when I grow up. Like you and Grandpa."

Chapter 19

Downstairs Rick had loaded the dishwasher and started it going. There was a bottle of Johnnie Walker Blue open on the counter, a gift from a satisfied client.

"You?"

She nodded and watched him pour a long shot.

"Do I have a lot of catching up to do?"

"I'm one ahead."

She knew right then that she should tell him she wanted tea instead. But it had been *such* a day.

On the deck he had connected the heat lamp and arranged their chairs under its glow. Groaning he sank into one of them. After a few moments he asked, "Have you got everything ready for tomorrow?"

She had forgotten that they were hosting the weekly football party, the Chargers playing someone who would probably leave them in pieces on the field.

"I went to Whole Foods." She leaned back and closed her eyes. The Scotch eased her throat.

"I hope I feel more like a party tomorrow," he said.

"Couldn't we cancel? Everyone knows I just got home—"

"Two months. You've been home two months."

He said it like an accusation.

"We could blame the thing at the clinic."

"I suppose."

She knew the wifely thing to say—*we'll manage fine*—but there was no way she could make it sound convincing. Right now what she wanted was to get a middling buzz on and fall into bed for a long, deep sleep.

"I could do the calling. Everyone'd understand."

"We were supposed to host last month, Frankie. We can't keep putting them off. They're our friends."

These were the men Rick played poker with once a month as well as neighbors and business associates they'd known since they became a couple. Their wives and girlfriends had been friends of Frankie's before she went to Iraq. During football season they took turns hosting parties and where food was concerned, they were competitive. As the months went on the spread of appetizers and snacks became increasingly elaborate.

"I feel like I don't even know them anymore."

"Just try."

"You think I haven't been?" The scotch had made her a little belligerent. "You think I'm just taking it easy? You think this is fun for me?"

"No. I don't think it's fun."

"But?"

"Let's drop it, okay? You're in therapy, you're working on it."

"What's that mean?"

"Shit, Frankie, give me a break here, will you? If I say you have PTSD, you get insulted. If I say you've got 'issues,' you tell me I'm being evasive and to say what I really think. Well, here it is. I know you're working on your shit, but it's taking a long time." The energy went out of his voice. "Too long. I miss my wife and I'm getting tired of waiting for her."

She would have to be a tin soldier not to hear and feel the love mixed with his frustration. She didn't want to fight. "I miss me too." Reaching across the space between them, she took his hand, and for a while they spoke of other things, eventually coming around to the events of the afternoon.

"Harry said Glory might have some kind of delayed emotional reaction, but she seems okay to me." It occurred to Frankie as she said this that her brother might have been speaking of her when he said it. For a minute she was distracted, trying to recall exactly the words he used.

"If your brother would just close the damn clinic, set up somewhere else."

"You don't mean that. It's not the clinic's fault."

"I know it isn't. I know that he and Gaby are doing good down there, but if something had happened to Glory—"

"She's okay, Rick."

"I sure hope that mobile medical clinic thing comes through for them. It'd solve a lot of problems."

"They can park the clinic van in front of Mrs. Greenwoody's house."

It was good to hear Rick laugh, even if it took Johnnie Walker to make it happen. They watched the lights of Ocean Beach flicker at the bottom of the hill. Beyond them, the ocean was a dark line under a star-speckled sky.

"I wish it would rain," Frankie said.

"October's too soon."

"In Iraq I dreamed about rain."

Talking with her therapist the other day, she had realized that though she was home, water was still everywhere in her thinking and even in her dreams: sometimes she floated on a calm sea or stood beneath a waterfall, sometimes breakers crashed with the noise of mortar fire or she was in a bathtub filling and overflowing or a swimming pool too murky to see the bottom.

"You can't appreciate water until you live where it's so precious. Without it—"

Water and love. The world would die without them.

He said, "You shouldn't have gone. Everything out of your mouth just makes me more sure it was a mistake."

"You had Melanie to keep you company," she said, half teasing.

He looked at her sharply.

"Kidding." She waved her hand as if to erase the words

and then swallowed the last of her drink. There was something she had to say.

"Melanie's filled Glory's head with a lot of crap about homeless people and religion. I don't like it."

"Don't go off on Mel. She's a kid, a good kid with a big heart. And she's smart. My office has never been so organized." His voice grew husky. "And when you were gone she made me laugh. That's all. I needed that." He stared into his empty glass. "I was thinking about you all the time, wondered how you were getting along and if you were in danger. Having Melanie around just made it a little easier. But Glory always knew how I felt. I couldn't really fool her."

Quick as a whip.

"One time I was sitting in the living room and she came over and put her arms around me and told me not to worry. Just like that, out of nowhere, like she read my mind. She said, 'Mommy can take care of herself.' It was bizarre. I felt like I was being parented by my own child."

Another silence settled around them.

He said, "Did she tell you that Candace stole some crayons?"

"It wasn't a big deal."

"Little thieves grow into big thieves."

He sounded so pompous, she had to laugh. "You've had too much to drink."

And so had she. She should say good night then close her mouth and stagger upstairs, leave well enough alone.

But the words were out ahead of her and she couldn't catch up.

"Didn't you snitch stuff when you were a kid? I sure did. When I was in the fifth grade it was like a game to see how much we could get hold of without being caught. We dared each other."

Her mother had found all the lipsticks and unopened packages of false eyelashes in one of her sweater drawers and guessed how Frankie got them.

"She made me go down to Longs Drugs and hand it all back to the manager. I was mortified."

"I don't want my daughter playing with a girl who steals."

Hadn't he heard what she was saying?

He went into the kitchen and brought back the bottle and divided the last of the whiskey between them. Frankie stared at her glass and thought *what the hell* as she drank from it.

Down on Sunset Cliffs a siren screamed. Flame lifted her head and howled in mournful harmony.

"What happened to you over there, Frankie?"

Where? Oh, yeah, *there. The Big Suck.*

"I barely know you anymore."

She told herself that was Johnnie talking, but it hurt anyway.

"Like I said, it's Mad Max. The country, the war, it's all crap. Except the people."

In Damascus with her mother and brothers, rewarded for her silence by G4S or some anonymous arm of government, did Fatima remember that she and Frankie were a team? Did she think about Three Fountain Square? How could she not when they had been there together, and it took all Frankie's will and energy *not* to remember?

"You've got to help me here, Frankie. I want us to be the way we were before." His diction had grown sloshy. "I didn't sign up for this."

The before years were almost unreal to Frankie, a daydream she'd filled with so many sweet details that it couldn't possibly be true. She and Rick had been golden together and Glory's birth had only made them glow brighter. Frankie remembered thinking once that seeing Rick across the room for the first time had been all the proof she would ever need that the universe was powered by love. Once she had been certain that there would never be anything big enough or strong enough to hurt them.

Rick said, "I hate the Marine Corps."

She closed her eyes and felt the world lurch on its axis.

"Don't give up on me, Rick."

She opened her eyes. He'd gone inside.

Chapter 20

Late on Sunday morning Frankie stood in the mini-kitchen in the great room preparing food for the game day party. She had turned down breakfast and been sipping soda water for her upset stomach since she got up. Four Tylenol hadn't done a thing to her headache. She should have known better, should have heeded her instinct to turn down the Johnnie Walker. Her head hurt, and her stomach, and whatever interior gravity kept her organs in their right positions had stopped working. Only her skin held her intact this morning.

The vegetables bought at Whole Foods lay on the counter. Though fresh enough, they smelled faintly putrid to her. Crudités and dips had seemed like a good idea before she was actually faced with having to peel and cut things up. In the market everything had been irresistible as she pushed the cart around pyramids of apples and oranges, boxes of blackberries that only days before had ornamented mountainous bushes in the Northwest, cucumber and zucchini torpedoes, tomatoes as red as fast cars. The experience had been kaleidoscopic and pleasantly dizzying. The colors alone made her want to buy and buy. Now she stared at two glossy Japanese eggplants before her and tried to remember what she'd meant to do with them.

Across the room Glory sat on the floor with Barbie and her friends arranged around her, holding the new/used bear from the clinic toy box in her arms, Zee-Zee in attendance as always, observing everything with his hooded eyes. Flame had positioned herself, frog legs, her front paws and muzzle resting on the edge of the rug that defined the play area. Glory spoke seriously to the dog and dolls; sometimes the bear seemed to be talking back. Occasionally Flame thumped her feathered tail to show that she was doing her part. Every now and then Frankie heard a few words, enough to know that the topic was, not surprisingly, the events of the day before.

In the midst of solitary play Glory bore little resemblance to the precocious child she sometimes was in conversation with adults. She might have been an overgrown five- or six-year-old lost in make-believe. Thank goodness she had weathered the events of the day before without consequence, but Frankie couldn't say the same for herself. Added to the hangover she had earned the night before, something wormed under her skin, a feeling familiar as the apprehension she had felt as a student, waiting for a grade on an essay or theme on which she feared she hadn't worked hard enough.

For almost an hour Rick had been sweating out his hangover on the treadmill in the workout center that occupied another area of the great room. They'd spoken only a few words that morning. Variations on *never again*.

Stepping off the treadmill he came across the great room, shiny with sweat, smelling slightly sour. As he wiped himself with a towel he looked at the vegetables arranged on the countertop and started to laugh. Teasing he counted the cucumbers. "Ten? And all these carrots?" He counted again. "Who's going to eat all this? Jesus, Frankie, no one even likes raw zucchini."

She could have interrupted right then, laughed with him, told him to get back on the treadmill where he belonged and let her feed the troops. She should not have stood silently, letting his words abrade her like wind and sand.

"Did you just walk through the store, tossing in whatever you saw? 'Here's a nice cauliflower; the guys always go for cauliflower! Oh boy, eggplant!'"

He thought he was hilarious.

She could have thanked him for sharing and gone upstairs. Why hadn't she done that when all she really wanted was to lie down with a cool washcloth on her eyes?

"Frankie, can't you even buy food anymore?"

He wasn't teasing now. In his voice she heard disappointment and confusion and anger. Frankie sensed Glory listening from across the room.

"Here's what you do." He took charge. "Slice up a couple

of cucumbers, half a dozen carrots. Don't go overboard. Tomorrow you can put the rest in soup or something. Or toss 'em out, I don't care what you do."

As a child she had learned to stand still, feeling small, getting smaller as the General chastised her for coming second in a race or getting a B-plus grade on a test. She had not realized until now that buying food for the party had been a kind of test. She had shopped at Whole Foods and earned a B for her efforts. No, more like a C or even a D. Had she ever gotten a D on anything before? Never. But once a C, on a geography exam.

She turned on the tap and let a stream of cool water flow across her wrists.

She had enjoyed geography but the teacher insisted on rote memorization of everything—capital cities, rivers, principal mountain ranges. Lying in her rack on Redline, bone-weary but wakeful, she tried to bore herself to sleep by making alphabetical lists.

Rivers: *Amazon, Brahmaputra, Congo, Darling.*

"Are you listening to me, Frankie?"

Lakes: *Antigua, Baikal, Como.*

"What else did you get?"

"Hummus, pita bread. There's lots of cheese." *Asiago, brie, cheddar.*

"And wings? Did you get any of those? The kind you dip in ranch dressing? What about those little Chinese ribs?"

She shook her head.

"Frankie, this is a football party."

"Why didn't you say you wanted wings?"

"And maybe some garlic bread?"

"I'm not a mind reader. You should have given me a list." She drank from the tap. "Whatever you want, Rick. I'm sorry."

The sorry inside her went so deep and covered so many things, it overwhelmed her like the prospect of a forced march.

"I just don't feel like having a house full of company. I told you I didn't. I guess that makes me the wrong person to plan the menu, huh?" She hoped he would appreciate the irony. They would smile at each other and there would be peace.

"This has been planned for weeks, Frankie."

She drank again, letting the tepid water soothe her throat and wet her face.

"I don't like crowds anymore."

She'd gone to Bahrain on leave. A mistake. Except in the elegant shopping district (and how many designer bags could she look at without keeling over from boredom?), the streets were crowded with pedestrians, mostly men. The air stank of their sweat and the pomade they rubbed into their beards. They pushed her aside with their shoulders and their hands sometimes touched her, and there was nothing she could do or say to these surreptitious strokes and pokes that were clearly meant as insults. She could only cringe away from them and step a little faster and pretend she was somewhere else. There was a sound they made sometimes, seeing a Western woman on the street without an escort, a hissing hidden behind mustaches and beards and almost closed lips.

Maybe what she needed most was just to be alone. "Rick, I can't make small talk anymore."

"Try, Frankie." Weariness wounded his bloodshot eyes, and she saw that he was struggling to save the day.

She sliced into a cucumber, cut her finger, and swore loudly. As she raised the cut to her lips, it bled onto the cucumber wedges on the counter, each drop spreading a pink stain. Pretty, she thought, and was transfixed for a moment by the sight. Like watermelon.

Apple. Banana. Casaba.

She wound a towel around the finger. Rick took her hand and she pulled back. "It's nothing."

Glory came across the room and looked at the pink cucumber wedges. "That's so gross."

"Go back to your dolls," Frankie said. "I'll clean it up."

"No." Rick turned her so she faced the hall and guest bathroom. "There's Band-Aids and antibiotic ointment in the cabinet. Go."

When she came back the vegetables had disappeared and the countertop was wiped and shining.

"We don't need crudités," Rick said, wringing out a sponge. "I'll see what I can get at Vons."

He held her wrist and lifted her hand, looked at her bandaged finger, and kissed it lightly. "You have to be more careful."

I'm a Marine. Why is he talking to me like I'm eight years old?

She opened the refrigerator. The vegetables shoved into the crisper filled her with sadness and then an irrational protective anger, as if the carrots and cucumbers were refugees abandoned in steerage. She pulled them out and tossed them onto the counter. A carrot rolled to the floor but she didn't stoop to pick it up.

"What're you doing?"

She looked at him, picked up a zucchini, and dropped it at his feet. Then another carrot. Rick's expression widened with confusion and she had to look away from the damage she was doing. She dropped a handful of radishes, heard them roll, and felt herself begin to unravel like an old sweater gone to ruin. The backs of her eyelids stung and she pressed the heels of her hands hard against them until all she saw was blood red.

With a groan of something that sounded like sympathy but might have been despair, Rick dragged her into his arms, and as much as she wanted to shove him away, she wanted to stay until time ran backward and she could start all over again.

"I'll go to Vons," she said. "It's my job. I'll do it."

Chapter 21

Frankie sat for a moment in the market's vast parking lot and remembered what her therapist had told her. *Focus on your goals, but keep them simple.*

Today she was going into the market and she would buy food, he-man football food. Sandwich fixings from the deli, potato salad and fried chicken, quarts of ambrosia for the kids. She found paper in the glove compartment and made a list of a dozen items sure to please. Her goal was to go in, buy the food, and get out without a hitch. If she used the time efficiently she might even be able to nap before the company started to arrive.

The market was crowded, but she was prepared for this and not troubled by it, proving that when she thought things through in advance and had reasonable expectations, she could handle life as well as anyone. A woman pushing a cart full of kids and a few food items ran into her going in and Frankie only laughed and said *no problem* when the woman apologized.

In the frozen food section she found the last two boxes of hot wings and the baker was just setting out fresh loaves of garlic bread. She bought eight because everyone loved garlic bread. At a display of school supplies she stopped and stared at the varieties of notebooks, any one of which would serve as a journal. She moved on and then went back and grabbed the first her fingers touched. Black. Two hundred pages. *What a laugh that was.*

In the produce section she found plenty of avocados soft enough for guacamole and filled a plastic bag. She stopped to admire the season's first Satsuma tangerines and could not resist buying a few. As she was putting them in a bag she heard someone humming and looked up to see Mrs. Greenwoody across the aisle. Frankie recognized her from a newspaper photo.

She had been prepared for the possibility she would meet someone she knew at the market and been ready to make a few minutes of light conversation. But she wasn't ready to see, less than six feet away, Godzilla herself, Mrs. Greenwoody, examining yellow onions for soft spots. She didn't look anything like the part she played in Frankie's imagination: a witchy old broad with stinginess written in the lines of her face. Instead she reminded her of the fairy godmother in Disney's *Cinderella*.

Frankie and Glory had watched the movie just the other night.

Remembering her daughter brought Candace to mind and the moment when Frankie had seen her lying on the floor of the clinic waiting room, blood streaming from the side of her head. It could so easily have been Glory.

What if it was a gun and not a rock?

"Mrs. Greenwoody?"

She looked up, smiling. It was obvious that forty years before she had been a pretty girl. She still had a prom queen's harmless, welcoming expression.

"I'm Frankie Tennyson."

"Of course you are. If you hadn't spoken, I think I would have recognized you from the picture on your husband's desk. Did he tell you I was in the office last week? I've been trying to get him on the committee for months now but he keeps turning me down."

"My brother, Harry, runs the kids' clinic." Frankie put a tangerine in a bag. "I was down there yesterday." She waited for Mrs. Greenwoody to respond but she just smiled and tested another onion for softness. "I saw some of your people there. Demonstrating."

"Well, yes, it is a free country." She laughed lightly. "At least I think so. You have to wonder sometimes, don't you?"

Frankie wished she were wearing her uniform, even her cammies, instead of jeans and a T-shirt.

Mrs. Greenwoody said, "I hear through the grapevine that your brother and sister-in-law may shut down the clinic and go mobile."

A few nights earlier Frankie, Rick, and Glory had eaten dinner with her brother and sister-in-law. They lived in a remodeled beach bungalow on the flats not far from the clinic and a couple of blocks from the beach. On their tiny rooftop deck they had barbecued steaks and watched the pink and orange sunset. Gaby told them the results of her recent fund-raising. Two donors in Beverly Hills, television producers, wanted to fund a mobile unit and keep it running for a year, giving Gaby time to raise more support money. They'd all been excited about the future this opened up. They were debating whether to keep the Abbott Street clinic open.

"The kids' clinic does great good, Mrs. Greenwoody."

"I'm sure it does. I'm not opposed to helping the needy, believe me. But our community has to look toward the future. Just imagine what it would do for the Ocean Beach tax base if there were condominiums along Abbott Street and not that old hotel and the clinic."

"Why not a factory?" Frankie asked, dropping another tangerine in the plastic bag. "Wouldn't that make the town even more money?"

"With child labor perhaps?" Mrs. Greenwoody laughed. "I'm not the monster you think I am, Frankie. I love our little town just as much as you do."

"Yesterday someone threw a rock through the clinic's window."

"Don't I know that? The television people were after me for a comment last night. You'd think I'd thrown it myself."

"Children were hurt." A slight exaggeration.

"You must know I deplore that."

"There was glass everywhere."

"You were inside?"

"I volunteer there on Saturdays."

"Good for you!"

"I was there and so was my daughter."

"Goodness, no one told me *that*. She wasn't hurt, I hope."

"Her friend was."

"I heard there were no serious injuries."

"But it could have been very serious."

"Well, yes, but it wasn't. And surely you're not blaming me for it?"

"Your committee encourages violence."

She held up her hand. "Excuse me, Frankie. I just have to stop you there because you couldn't be farther from the truth. We're a property owners' association. That's it."

"Does that mean you will speak out against the violence?"

"Absolutely not." Mrs. Greenwoody shook her head, bouncing her faux blond curls. "You and I are both realists. We know that publicity only encourages the lunatic fringe. They want attention, but I'm not going to give it to them. I told the television people I had no comment, now or in the future."

Mrs. Greenwoody looked over at Frankie's grocery cart. "I'll bet you're having a party today. Football? I never liked the sport, even when my husband was alive. Too violent for my taste. But there's room for everyone in this world, isn't there? Have a lovely day, dear. Enjoy your friends and tell your handsome husband I'm going to keep after him until he joins my little committee."

Frankie watched Mrs. Greenwoody turn the corner toward the checkout stands. She looked down at the tangerine in her hand. She had put her nails through the skin and squeezed. Juice filled her palm and dripped onto the floor.

In the car she rolled up the windows and screamed until she had no voice left. Silenced, she dived deep into her imagination where nothing held her back and to herself she said the logical and persuasive things she should have said to Mrs. Greenwoody. She let her rage out and called her all the names she deserved. Hypocrite. Phony. Coward.

And then she just sat in the hot car and let the truth sink in. She should not have allowed Mrs. Greenwoody her pale excuses for not speaking out against the violence at the clinic. Frankie should have argued with her and not having done so made her just as bad as the woman she despised. Though their excuses were different, neither of them was willing to speak the truth. She closed her eyes, felt the drumming pulse of her headache at the base of her skull and the peculiar disconnection of her body parts. For some time she did not trust herself to drive.

Chapter 22

By two thirty the great room was full of guests, some watching the game, some enjoying the view from the deck on the flawlessly clear Sunday in October. Frankie retreated to the bar, going through the motions of washing glasses and serving drinks, arranging plates of wings and mini-pizzas, sliced ham and roast beef and chicken, tomatoes and lettuce and cheese and all the condiments in the world. Behind the bar she tried to appear busy because as long as she looked like there was a job she had to do, people pretty much ignored her after saying hello. The word had gone out that Rick's wife was having *a hard time*.

She watched the clock.

Glory seemed happy, relating to everyone her clinic adventure with both the bear and the bedraggled Zee-Zee tucked up under her arm. Her manners were impeccable and she remembered everyone's name and said please and thank you. She ate chips and guacamole as if she were ravenous. A dollop of clam or onion dip the size of a serving spoon landed on the front of her tee.

Frankie watched from behind the bar as Melanie cleaned her up.

Who is the real Glory? The chatty little girl who illustrated her adventures with three-syllable adjectives and bold gestures, the girl who colored butterflies with her friend, or the one who went to school and talked about shooting Colette?

For that matter who was the real Frankie? The Marine, the wife, the mother? The coward and failure? The basket case?

Neighbors from down the hill, the Langs, arrived with their two lanky boys who dug into the guacamole first thing, double dipping with pita chips the size of salad plates. Frankie made more and watched them go at it afresh. In the last few minutes of the game, the score was tied and overtime seemed a sure thing. Guests came in off the deck and perched on the arms of chairs and couches, wherever there was room. Glory sat on Melanie's lap.

You're too old for laps, Glory. You said it yourself to the General.

Frankie carried a chair out of the guest bedroom and put it next to Melanie's.

"You don't have to sit on anyone's lap."

"She's fine with me. We like to snuggle, don't we, Glo?"

"I brought you a chair."

"I'm watching football."

"You don't even know the rules."

"Yes, I do!"

"Up." She snapped her fingers and pointed to the chair in a perfect imitation of her father. "Sit." She saw on her daughter's face a look she recognized as her own.

"Honest to God," Melanie said, "we've got heaps of room, don't we, sweetie."

"Oh. Heaps. Really? *Sweetie?*"

"We don't want to miss this." Melanie had flawless skin as if she'd never stood in the sun and her round blue eyes, perfectly lined and mascaraed, had never seen anything ugly. She squeezed Glory's shoulder. "The Chargers could win this one, couldn't they?"

"Shut up, Melanie."

Someone gasped but Frankie didn't care.

"Shut up and leave. I don't want you around my daughter anymore." She almost added, *or my husband*, but managed not to. "And why are you here anyway? Don't you have a boyfriend somewhere?"

Melanie looked behind Frankie. Rick stood a few feet away.

"What do you want?" Frankie asked him. "You want to cuddle too, *sweetie?*"

No one in the room was watching football now.

Rick put his hand on her shoulder. "This doesn't matter, Frankie."

"What do you mean it doesn't matter? I see what I see.

178

Am I supposed to shut my mouth and pretend I don't see what's right in front of my eyes?"

"Let's go upstairs."

"I don't want to go anywhere. Didn't you hear what she said?" Frankie spoke sugary-sweet. "'The Chargers might win this one. *Wanna cuddle, sweetie?*'"

"Shut up." Glory leapt away from Melanie. "Shut up, shut up."

"What's that down the front of you?" Frankie poked Glory in the chest. "Is that onion dip? And guacamole? My God, you are disgusting."

Rick's hand tightened on her arm.

She jerked aside. "Go upstairs and take a shower. Don't come down until you're cleaned up."

"No."

"That's an order, Glory."

"I won't go. I don't have to. Do I, Daddy? Do I have to?"

"I'm speaking to you. Me, your mother. Do as I say."

"I don't want—"

"I don't care what you want." Frankie stopped and stared as Glory reached her whole hand into the bowl of clam dip and smeared it across the front of her T-shirt. As the room watched, she covered her face with smears of sour cream and clams and ran her fingers up into her hair and then tugged it down so it covered her face in sticky dreads.

The sour smell of clams overwhelmed Frankie's senses.

"My God," she cried. "You stink!"

No one spoke. No one moved. A voice in Frankie's

head began to wail and she grabbed Glory's arm, felt her skin give like the skin of a tangerine.

"I didn't mean that, honey. I'm having such a bad day." Glory tried to twist away but she couldn't let her go until the look on her face changed and she was Glory again. "I'll be better, I will, I promise."

"I hate you. I wish you were dead. I wish you got shot over there."

Except for the sound of the announcer talking overtime and coin toss and yard lines, the room was perfectly quiet. Convulsively Frankie tightened her grip. Glory's scream sounded like tires on a hairpin curve. She leaned forward and bit down hard on Frankie's wrist.

Frankie slapped her face.

Chapter 23

From her kitchen across the street Maryanne watched the cars parked in front of Frankie and Rick's house pull away and thought it strange that everyone was leaving at the same time.

Upstairs the General was watching the football game with the volume muted. In recent years he had lost most of his interest in football and preferred to take a long nap on Sunday afternoons; but as ever in his life, he was afraid of missing something so he kept the picture on. Deep under the covers and curled on his side like an old tomcat, the General slept more soundly in the afternoon than he ever did at night.

Maryanne was at the sink scouring the copper bottoms of her favorite pans with salt and lemon juice when Frankie rushed into the house, tears streaming down her face.

Maryanne started toward her. "Is it Glory?" It was a fear never far from a grandmother's heart.

In the living room Frankie fell on the couch, facedown

in a pile of rough wool pillows. For a moment Maryanne watched, letting the vision register. How odd, how unlikely, and how deeply disorienting it was to see her daughter break down in this way. She laid her hand between Frankie's shoulder blades.

"Stop this now and tell me what happened."

Frankie turned onto her back. Her round and even-featured face was the antonym of exotic, too homespun and prairie ever to be considered more than pretty. But at that moment Maryanne thought she was almost beautiful, an angel of misery with her fair hair half out of its braid, her cheeks flushed as roses and the tears still shining in the light of her frantic eyes.

Maryanne pulled a dark blue lap rug off the back of the couch and covered her shivering body. The kindness seemed to be too much. Covering her face with her hands, Frankie blurted out the story. The epic went on and on and Maryanne stopped trying to follow the chain of crises.

"And then I slapped her, I slapped her face."

This was the crux of it.

"I'll make us some tea."

Maryanne had been expecting trouble since Frankie came home from Iraq. At family meals and drop-ins, the many planned and unplanned interactions that occurred almost every day because they lived across the street from each other, she had observed her daughter and knew that she was unhappy. But, in spite of all she had gone through with the General, she had hoped that Frankie's problems would resolve themselves without catastrophe. The worst of it was, Maryanne had no better idea how to help her daughter than she'd had thirty years before when Harlan was chasing the dog around the house in the middle of the night, waving a loaded Beretta.

Frankie came into the kitchen.

"I want to sleep. I want to go under and never come up."

"Have some tea first." Maryanne pointed at one of the ladder-back chairs arranged at the round oak breakfast table.

Somewhere in the dark ages of childhood, even before Harry's accident had put him out of the running as successor to the General's glory, Frankie had set her heart on the impossible goal of pleasing her father, and she had never faltered in pursuit of it. It was like being the mother of Sisyphus, watching Frankie struggle and fail again and again.

Her efforts to balance the General's importance in Frankie's life had been clumsy failures. She and her daughter were just too different. Frankie had no enthusiasm for shopping or gardening or cooking, and, during the two days they'd spent at a spa in Ojai, Frankie's boredom had been embarrassingly apparent. For her part Maryanne never cared for sports though she faithfully attended all Frankie's matches and cheered appropriately. One year they had sung together in the choir at All Souls, but Maryanne was a soprano, Frankie an alto, and half the time they practiced on different nights of the week.

It was Harry whom she understood. Maybe that was

because they'd spent so much time on their own together in the years the General was deployed. In those days she had the patience for Tinkertoys and games of twenty questions and go fish. They'd gone to museums and aquariums, on road trips; and while she put in a vegetable garden, he excavated highways for his fleet of tiny cars and trucks. Even now, when Harry was almost forty, a husband and a doctor, they could sit at this table and talk all afternoon about not much of anything, laughing like friends. She had been the first to realize that his accident had been a disguised blessing, allowing him to find his true expression through medicine.

"Where did she bite you?"

Just above the small Semper Fi tattoo she and her Marine Corps friends had gotten after they finished Basic, the inside of Frankie's arm was fair and silken, faintly blued by the veins beneath the skin. Glory's teeth had left an ovoid imprint.

"Well, for goodness sake, of course you slapped her," Maryanne said, disgusted. "I would have done the same thing myself. My God, what's come over that child?"

"There's never any excuse for slapping a child, not on the face."

Apart from the shock and pain of it, a face slap was an insult intended to stomp out confidence and dignity and always a gross demonstration of power. Unlike Frankie, Maryanne didn't think that was necessarily a bad thing.

"Don't be so melodramatic." Maryanne held out a plate

of sugar cookies. "Have one of these. I made them yesterday. Children are adaptable creatures. If they weren't, the human race would have died off long ago. They can forgive far worse things than one slap." Maryanne did not romanticize childhood or believe it was meant to be one long romp in the park. "Think about it. She put her teeth in you. Like a dog. Your slap taught her a lesson she won't forget."

"If she's bratty it's my fault. I should have stayed home and done my job."

"Would a man ever say that? Stop blaming yourself."

"I was selfish—"

"Enough! You became a Marine Corps officer because you love this country and you went to Iraq because you believed it was the right thing to do. I never wanted you to go but once you made up your mind, I supported you. Feelings of patriotism and honor aren't restricted to men, you know."

"But I hurt her, Mom."

"I won't get on the pity pot with you, Francine." Maryanne could not take much more of this conversation. "It's called action and consequence and it's the way we learn what we can do in this world and what we can't."

The kitchen was hot and the fresh cookies smelled too sweet. Maryanne leaned across the sink and shoved up the window, letting in a gust of salt-smelling westerly wind.

She told Frankie to go into the room off the kitchen where there was a bed. Originally intended for a maid—though the Byrnes family had never had live-in help—it had been converted to a catch-all room for laundry, mending, and sometimes a quick nap.

"Whatever's on the bed, just push it off and lie down. When do you want me to wake you?"

"Rick'll worry. I should call him."

"Oh, I'm sure he can figure out where you are."

Maryanne returned to the living room where she folded the lap rug and fluffed the couch cushions. She remembered Harlan telling her when they were first married that she should keep the house in such order that if the base commander were to walk in without notice, she would have nothing to be ashamed of. Maryanne had taken his words to heart and, in retrospect, she knew that by such efforts—plus all the officers' wives' meetings she had attended, the committees she chaired and all the dinner parties she gave—she had contributed to her husband's success.

But she had failed Frankie by letting her believe that the General's impossible standards were the only ones that mattered. The truth was that the base commander was never going to drop in unannounced and perfection was overrated unless you were a sniper. Ease of mind and personal satisfaction counted much more, and Frankie had never had much of either.

Maryanne was standing at the kitchen counter thumbing through a cookbook trying to summon some interest in food when the clock at the top of the stairs struck six and Rick and Glory walked in.

"Is she here?" He looked haggard.

"Sit down, Rick. You too, Glory." Without asking if he wanted tea, she refilled the electric kettle. "Glory, get me two cups out of the dishwasher. They're clean."

Glory handed them to her. One second of eye contact with her grandmother and she began to cry an eight-year-old's galloping, gulping sobs, and Maryanne heard all over again the story of the vegetables, the stink, the bite, and the slap.

I'm too old for this.

She put tea bags and a teaspoon of sugar in the cups and poured boiling water over.

"Is she here?" Glory asked. "Where is she?"

Maryanne put a finger to her lips and then pointed at the closed door to the maid's room.

"I don't know what to do." Rick took his tea without looking at Maryanne. "I don't think there's anything I *can* do. She's been crazy all day."

Maryanne wanted to counter this statement with a few hard words, but now wasn't the time.

"What does her therapist say?"

He didn't know.

"Well, I think you'd better call her, Rick. Maybe she could suggest someone for *you* to see while this is going on."

"There's nothing wrong with me. I'm not the problem here, Maryanne."

"She's your wife, Rick. I'm her mother and that man upstairs is her father. We're all part of this and it's no good

187

pretending we're not. And I don't want to hear you say she's acting crazy. She's been through things you can't begin to imagine."

The little speech left her quite breathless.

"I never told her to go."

"Her conscience did. And you should be grateful you have a wife who's not afraid to do the right thing." She wanted to add *stop feeling sorry for yourself,* but that would be pushing too hard. She loved her son-in-law and did not wish to be unkind.

"What about me?" Glory asked. "She slapped me. That's child abuse."

"From what I hear you deserved what you got, young lady. You're not a German shepherd. You do not bite unless your life depends on it."

Glory shoved a sugar cookie into her mouth and sulked.

Rick said, "I want to take her home, but I'll leave her hear if she's sleeping—"

"She belongs at home. With you." Maryanne pointed to the closed maid's room door. "Go wake your mother."

Glory sucked in her lips and shook her head.

"Now."

She walked with her back straight, her shoulders squared like a T. It took only a slight blurring of Maryanne's vision to see Frankie at the same age, trudging off to do something she didn't want to do.

"Close the door behind you," Maryanne said. "Give yourselves some privacy."

WHEN SHE CAME HOME

It was warm in the maid's room, but Frankie had slept.

The door opened and the air freshened a little. Glory stood at the foot of the bed and details of the party came back to Frankie and there was nothing she could say that would change the stubborn and miserable look on her daughter's face. She sat up and opened her arms. She saw Glory flinch and her shoulders round in reflexive self-protection. And then she seemed to have a second thought. Water shimmered in her eyes and she dropped onto the bed and into Frankie's arms.

"I'm sorry, baby. So sorry."

Chapter 24

They sat at the table and picked at leftovers. To Mary-anne the moping and misery had begun to reek of self-indulgence and she wanted everyone out of the house. Admittedly it had been a bad day, a bad series of days, of weeks even. But she could tell Frankie and Rick about bad times.

The decades had vanished behind Maryanne, taking with them more than forty anniversaries and hundreds of orchestrated birthday parties, New Year's celebrations, and galas in aid of causes that had seemed worthy at the time. She had forgotten them all but the night when the General loaded his Beretta and threatened to shoot the dog for waking him out of his first sound sleep in a month, that she remembered in three dimensions and Technicolor. After she stood between him and the dog, crying *shoot me! shoot me!* he fled the house and was gone three days; and when he came home he never talked about where he went or what he did, and she was too angry and scared and relieved to ask him.

As if her thoughts had woken him from his nap, the General called to her as he came downstairs. At the sound of his voice the air in the kitchen stiffened and everyone around the table sat up straighter. He shambled into the room barefoot, wearing sweatpants and an ancient Marine Corps T-shirt. "...damn dream about that Belasco woman. General MacArthur was there. I haven't thought of that son of a bitch in at least ten years. Belasco had him in one of those old-fashioned witness boxes...." He stopped talking when he saw Frankie and her family around the table.

"I didn't know you were coming to dinner."

No one answered. He poked Frankie's shoulder with his index finger.

"I asked you a question."

"It's not important, Harlan. Go back upstairs." Maryanne ran scalding water into the sink and began noisily washing teacups by hand. If the hair on her head had stood up and sparked, she would not have been surprised. With her hands in the water, she could be electrocuted.

"I'll bring you some dinner on a tray."

"Am I sick? What's going on around here?"

"Mommy has PTSD," Glory said.

The General narrowed his eyes. "PMS?"

Glory giggled. She thought he was teasing, pretending not to hear correctly. Maryanne didn't know if he was playing or not. The General had never been a good listener and nowadays he was half deaf when he wanted to be.

"P. T. S. D," Glory said again, enunciating carefully. "She got it from Iraq."

The General appeared to think about this, turned, and left the room. Over his shoulder he told Maryanne, "You can bring me scrambled eggs. And some of those sugar cookies."

He was back on the bed watching 60 Minutes when she came in thirty minutes later.

She turned off the set and stood in front of it.

"Hey! Mike Wallace is going to talk about G4S. I want to see that."

"I don't care if he's talking about the Second Coming."

"You said you'd bring my dinner."

"That can wait."

She hadn't planned this and she might regret it; but Harlan, for all that she loved and respected him, had taxed her almost to the limits of her capacity. Until that afternoon she hadn't believed it was possible.

"I can't do this anymore."

"Can't do what? I don't know what you're talking about."

"I won't keep on stuffing my feelings so you can have the world the way you want it. I'm finished. I'm done. For the last forty plus years I have kept my mouth shut but tonight . . . tonight, I've had it. Your daughter is suffering, that whole family is in pain, and all you can think about is getting your dinner and watching *60 Minutes*." She gestured toward the house across the street. "You're either blind or you don't give a damn."

He looked as surprised by her outburst as if he'd been lassoed from behind.

"It's time for you to man-up, Harlan. You want to be the big shot in this family, start behaving like one."

"What the hell have I done to set you off *this* time?"

"You could help her if you wanted to."

"Is this about Frankie?"

"Damn you, Harlan, have I been talking to myself?"

"She's a grown girl. She can take care of herself. Or she should. Maybe Glory's right. Maybe she *is* crazy."

"PTSD isn't crazy. It's *normal*. War is a trauma, Harlan, and you know that better than most."

He talked right through her words. "Going off to Iraq like she had no responsibilities, if it wasn't crazy it was unnatural."

"Don't use that word." She clenched her teeth to keep from screaming at him. "I swear, if I hear you use that word to describe Frankie again, I will stop cooking for you. I mean it. You will have to exist on Cheerios and toast."

Now he looked like Glory. Pouting.

"Can't you see how much she loves you? Can't you *feel* it?"

"She wanted to be a Marine so I treat her like one."

"That's bullshit and we both know it. You've been hard on her since she was a toddler. You've never missed an opportunity to criticize her."

"Be fair, Maryanne. You make me sound like a monster."

He wasn't that, nothing like it. And he was right, it wasn't fair to take off on him after letting him get away with egregious behavior for so many years. They should have had this conversation years ago.

"She's brave, Harlan. And strong. She listened to everything you ever said about honor and duty, she sucked it all in."

He leaned against the headboard and picked at a tiny hole in his T-shirt. Once he had a dozen identical to this one, but over the years they had grown holey and been consigned to the rag bag. This was the last one, washed so many times it felt like silk under Maryanne's hand when she folded it. She would be sad to see it go.

She sat beside him and tried to hold his hands but like a bad-tempered child he pulled them out of reach.

"You are a fool, Harlan Byrne."

He gave her his little boy look, equal parts endearing and maddening. "But I'm your fool, right?"

"You don't deserve Frankie or me either. We're both way too good for you."

"That may be."

She grabbed his hands, he pulled, there was a tug-of-war, and he gave in.

"I'm just the way I am, Maryanne." He looked away. "I can't change."

In profile he was as handsome as he had been when they met. His jaw was still strong, his nose still straight. Against the light from the window she could see his eyelashes. Still long.

"Do you remember the worst night we ever had?"

"You don't have to remind me."

"Frankie's where you were then, Harlan. Different, but the same."

He picked at his T-shirt.

"What was that dog's name?"

"Pax." The ironically named Doberman. "You went after him with the Beretta. And then you left in the middle of the night and were gone for three days and I never knew where you went and I never asked. Afterward you just said you were sorry and you couldn't ever make it up to me, for leaving like that."

"Ah, Maryanne, it was a long time ago."

"Do you remember saying that?"

"I suppose I do."

"Well, this is your chance. To make it up to me."

"I love her. She's my daughter, for christsake. She knows the way I am."

"She doesn't know you love her."

"Well, I can't just come out and say it." As if love were the language of another species.

"You must, Harlan."

She had never loved him more than she did at that moment when he was trying to understand what was expected of him, when he wanted so earnestly to do the right thing. "Stop being a stubborn leatherneck. Stop being a general. Just be Frankie's father."

Chapter 25

Frankie spent most of her Monday morning appointment with her therapist talking about the day before. Afterward she was sure the Marines in the financial office took note of her red and puffy eyes. Complaining of an allergy only made matters worse so she said nothing and went right to work.

Colonel Olvedo's office door was open and she felt him watching her. She dropped pencils and hit her knee on an open desk drawer, she dribbled coffee down the front of her cammies.

All she could think of was Glory and Rick.

He had said almost nothing to her when they came home from across the street. He took his computer to bed and played solitaire, which she interpreted as passive aggression. She was too unhappy and ashamed of herself to try to break through his frigid reserve. The truth was she was just as happy not to talk—about the scene in the kitchen or the game day party. By Monday morning he still wasn't talking, but by then her self-defense system had gone to work; she was still ashamed and full of regret, but now she was also angry and told herself she didn't care if he never spoke to her again. As always Glory did not want to go to school and screamed at Frankie when she told her to get in the car. Sadly the moments in the maid's room had been less a reconciliation than a time-out between hostilities.

Rick's last words to her on Monday as she hurried out of the house struck her with equal parts fear and rage.

"I can't go on like this," he said. "I won't live this way."

She had ignored the elevator to White's office and took the stairs, two at a time, arriving on the fourth floor with aching quads and still angry. She told her therapist the story of the weekend, front to end, without pausing. White's response was much like her mother's.

"I'm sorry you slapped her, Frankie. But she'll survive. I'm more concerned about your father."

"Why? No one slapped him. Who'd dare?"

"You say Glory told him you have PTSD. And he just walked away? Without saying anything?"

Not a word.

"How did that make you feel?"

"I'm used to the way he is."

"You weren't angry?"

"What's the point? He's a mean s.o.b." She had spoken without thinking. "Not really."

"Would your mother agree? Would Rick?"

"The General loves Glory. He treats her like his little princess."

"Well, that must be hard to take."

"The other night she told me she might be a Marine when she grew up. He'd probably go with her to sign up and then have a parade in her honor."

She spent most of her lunch hour running on the treadmill in the gym but even six fast miles couldn't pacify her. She was angry with everyone including herself. At the same time she sensed another emotion beneath her anger and knew that she would rather rage at the whole world than feel whatever that was, simmering below.

She was going through a second batch of mail when a call came from Trelawny Scott at Arcadia.

"There's been an incident, Frankie. I think you should come."

It took Frankie five minutes to explain to Olvedo, thirteen more to drive up Washington Street running every yellow light. She was standing in the school's front office twenty-one minutes after the call.

"Go right in, Captain Tennyson." Dory Maddox followed her into the headmistress's office, shutting the door behind her.

Bad sign.

"What did she do? Is she hurt?"

Scott gestured Dory to the couch and Frankie to the chair across the desk. "Your daughter is fine."

Your daughter.

"Where is she?"

"Please, can we talk first?" Behind her glasses the head-mistress's eyes were kind but tired. "Glory left school without permission today."

"Right after early recess," Dory said. "She passed me in the hall and when I said hello, it was like she didn't hear me. I came into the office and then I thought about the way she looked, upset and all, and I thought I better go after her. She was off the grounds by the time I caught up." Dory looked genuinely unhappy as she told her story. "She said she was leaving school and never coming back."

It was possible to walk from East Mission Hills to Ocean Beach, but it was a distance of several miles, hilly and indirect.

"I told her she didn't have to walk. I said we'd call you, you'd come and get her. But she was so upset, I doubt she even heard me." Dory pulled a wadded tissue from her sleeve and patted her lips with it.

Scott said, "There was quite a struggle."

"She bit me." Dory held out her arm.

Without thinking, Frankie's fingers touched her own wrist. One bite could be excused, put down to impulse. Two was a pattern.

Dory said, "I guess I screamed when she did it. A gardener came running and nabbed her before she got to the end of the block. She fought all the way back to school."

"I don't know what to say, Ms. Maddox. I'm so sorry. She'll apologize, of course." Frankie remembered Colette. "She's been tormenting Glory for weeks. Ever since school started. She must have done something to set her off. Did you ask her what happened? She's turned all the girls in the class against Glory. Colette's the teacher's pet."

The headmistress sat back. "That's what she told you."

"I know when Glory's telling the truth, ma'am. If she says her teacher plays favorites, then she does." Frankie told the story of the overflowing toilet, and as she did she wondered why she had not come to Scott as soon as she learned of the bullying. She had been too focused on her own problems to take the proper course of action. Thinking back she saw that she had been not only distracted but negligent as well.

Scott looked at Dory. "Do you know anything about this?"

The secretary shrugged. "I hear things, Trelawny, but you know—" She crossed her legs. "There's always chatter."

"Chatter about what?"

"Well, Ms. Peters does seem to like a particular kind of girl especially. The pretty, uncomplicated ones. Not that Glory isn't pretty, you understand."

"But she's complicated."

"There's lots going on inside her." Dory squirmed a little. "She's a deep child, Captain."

Frankie couldn't argue with that.

"She threw her history book at Colette." Dory folded her arms across her chest, unfolded them, and added, "Missed, thank God."

"Why wasn't I told?"

"I was getting to it, Trelawny. It's been quite a morning."

"She bit me too." Frankie held out her wrist.

Scott frowned and thought a moment. "This puts a new light on the situation. The biting. We know that when a child as old as Glory resorts to biting, it is almost always an act of pure frustration. She wouldn't be biting and throwing things if she knew another way to deal with her issues. This has been building for a while, I think."

"What do you mean?"

"I think Glory's unhappiness probably started back when you deployed."

My fault. Again my fault.

"We talked a lot before I left. She understood that it was something I had to do and she knew how long I'd be away and we talked on the phone several times a week. She and her father are very close and my parents live right across the street.... She had a strong support system. I wouldn't have gone if she hadn't."

"I'm not being critical, my dear. She could have all the love and care in the world and still it wouldn't be easy. You're her mother, after all. Probably the most important person in her world."

Frankie wondered if this would make more sense if she and her own mother had been close.

"It's not like I abandoned her."

"Nevertheless, it might have felt that way. To her."

"Rick says she was fine until I came home."

"And that's no surprise. While you were in harm's way she didn't dare let herself feel angry. But now you're home, it's safe to let all the bad feelings out. She loves you but at the same time she's angry. Think about it, Frankie. Adults don't deal well with contradictory feelings. Imagine how hard it is for a child. That's where the frustration comes in. The throwing and biting."

"After she bit me, I slapped her face."

As recently as a week ago Frankie could not have confessed something so shameful. No doubt her therapist would consider her candor as some kind of progress. From being shut down, sealed off, battened, and bolted, she was on the verge of becoming a compulsive blurter and weeper.

Anger. Road rage. Slapping. Hitting. Biting. Throwing. PTSD and secondary PTSD: Frankie saw how inextricably her troubles and Glory's braided together and how far beyond her the challenge to untwist them was. In her therapist's office the moment was never right to make a direct plea for help. There she thought she was supposed to learn to help herself; but learning took time, and it seemed to Frankie as she sat across from Dr. Scott that for her family, the sand in the hourglass was almost gone.

"I don't know what to do."

"Frankie, you're not alone in this. We all want what's best for Glory."

Dory stood up to leave. As she passed Frankie's chair she laid a comforting hand on her shoulder. "She's a good girl."

Frankie sniffed and Dr. Scott handed her a tissue box.

"Is there another class she could go to? Away from Colette?"

"There's Mrs. Barber but a transfer would just be a Band-Aid. And Ms. Peters is a good teacher. She cares for her girls."

"But not mine. And you've said yourself, she's young."

"So are you, Frankie. Does that make you incompetent?"

Could she blame her behavior at Three Fountain Square on youth and inexperience? Would an older Marine, familiar with the sights and sounds of death, have behaved differently? Would another Marine have brought her guilt and regret home with her?

"What are you going to do?" she asked the headmistress.

"A number of things. First, I'm going to suspend Glory from school for a week. She needs some time to cool off."

"That's so unfair." Frankie knew she was transparent, unable to conceal her anger and—worse—how perilously close to tears she was. "I'm not going to deny that I've had some problems since I came home, but this Colette person is a bully and that's something else entirely."

She swallowed to relax her throat and took a deep

breath. Her voice wouldn't ripple if she could breathe properly.

"She and Ms. Peters's favoritism are both school problems." Another swallow. Another breath. "Dr. Scott, I'm doing the best I can. I've made some mistakes, but this is your job, not mine."

If she was aware of Frankie's struggle to get the words out, the headmistress gave no sign. "I promise you, I will deal with the bullying once I've managed today's events. I will also have words with Ms. Peters. Believe me, I take bullying very seriously."

"Please, don't suspend her, ma'am. You know the girls will talk. They'll say—"

"I know, the rumors will fly. But I can't stop gossip. Never mind what happens when the girls are in school. Most of them have cell phones and they text all the time. I think the best thing we can do is let the dirty laundry hang out until they lose interest in it. The suspension has to happen. For one thing Colette's parents are going to want—they will *demand*—some kind of consequence. Before I can address the bullying, I have to take care of that."

"But Colette started it." Frankie stopped. "You do believe me?"

"I do, I do." The headmistress paused, staring thoughtfully into the middle distance. "Now I don't want you to misinterpret what I'm saying. When it comes to the bullying, I'm not blaming Glory one bit. But the fact is that not all children get bullied. You must try to understand this. There's a type of girl, a 'Colette,' if you will, who senses vulnerability in others. It's as if their emotional radar is particularly attuned to it. Glory's pain and anger are something for Colette to exploit."

If Frankie had not gone to Iraq, Glory would not be in pain, nor would she be angry. Colette would be bullying another girl instead. Frankie could not deny she was the first cause. The Big Bang.

"I'll do anything. Whatever it takes."

She would keep a journal.

She would join a group—for therapy, for support.

"I love her so much." Frankie blinked hard to stop the tears. "She's the dearest thing in the world to me."

Dr. Scott turned her chair and looked out the bank of windows facing onto the playing fields. They watched the girls practicing kicks into the goal. The goalkeeper, a redhead with long skinny arms and legs, stopped about half of them. Frankie was again grateful for the headmistress's kindness, for how generously she gave space to her feelings. Not just her anger and sadness but the humiliation of tears and helplessness as well.

"You were always such a high achiever, Frankie. I was thinking about that before you got here today. I was wondering if you were a National Merit Scholar because you were smarter than other girls, or if you just worked harder than anyone else."

At Stanford Frankie had been surprised to discover that the work was not terribly difficult. She had labored over her books so long and hard at Arcadia that the effort required to maintain her scholarship was just more of the same.

"We sometimes mislead our star students and athletes when we heap rewards on them for their achievements." Scott faced across the desk again. "A girl like you with nothing but success behind her—Frankie, I know how hard it is to admit you don't know what to do. But that's often the way it is in real life. Being a mother or father can't be learned like grammar or algebra. You can't stay up until two a.m. mastering the art of parenting."

"But she's so angry."

"She'll get over it."

"And she won't talk to me."

"Tell her the truth about how it feels to be home. About what you're going through."

"I want to protect her. She's too young to understand."

"Don't be too sure. Glory is a sensitive child. Deep. She'll take in what she can and forget the rest and then she might want to do her own talking. If you're lucky. Listen to her. That's what we all want, Frankie. To be heard, to be known."

Late in the day, mother and daughter sat at the end of the OB pier on a bench that was rough and salt sticky to the touch. Somewhere over the horizon there was weather brewing, a storm and maybe rain. The brisk air was blowy and salt stung the corners of their eyes and settled on their tongues, seasoning the ice cream they'd bought at the Koreans'. The bright white of the gulls' immaculate wings and the sunlight flashing on waves made Frankie's eyes water. They talked and the wind broke their words into a code each understood. A clear channel opened up between them and they seemed, for a few minutes at least, to understand each other soul to soul.

"Colette told everybody you went to Iraq because you didn't want to be around me." Glory licked her spoon. "She said I smell bad and that's why you don't—didn't—love me."

"And you believed her."

The wind carried Glory's sigh toward shore.

"When you hear something over and over, it's hard not to believe it."

"That's why I threw the book at her. I knew she was lying but I got so mad and I couldn't think."

Glory stirred her chocolate chip and peppermint ice cream together, making a soup of it.

She said, "You know in the blackbird song you used to sing to me, when the words say *no one here can love or understand me?*"

"That's how you felt when I was gone?"

"Sorta. Not really, but...yeah."

They watched the gulls slipping along the drafts over the choppy water.

"How come you don't sing anymore?"

"My voice can't find the melody."

"I used to like it when you sang, Mommy." Glory leaned into her. Not a lot, but enough to mean something. "Is that part of the PTSD? Not singing?"

"Maybe."

"So when you're better you can sing again?"

Frankie lifted Glory's chin and looked into her eyes. "There's lots of stuff I don't know yet and it's going to take a while for me to figure it all out. But I have a doctor who's helping me. And I'm going to go to a special group with other people who are having problems."

"Like Domino?"

Frankie nodded. "My doctor wants me to keep a journal. About what happens and how I feel. Do you want to keep one too?"

Glory shook her head.

"No one will read it, Glory. It's just a way to sort things out."

Glory's eyes held the sea and the sky. "I wish we could be a normal family."

The words hurt despite the matter-of-fact tone in which they were spoken.

"I'm sorry I bit you, Mommy. Did it hurt?"

"Did it hurt when I slapped you?"

Glory nodded.

Frankie slipped her arm around her. "Me too."

Chapter 26

Frankie and Glory brought home fish and chips from Crusty's, and they stopped at the French bakery for half a dozen chocolate-filled cornucopias. Rick raised his eyebrows when he saw these because they always meant a celebration of some kind. He didn't ask questions, however, and went ahead and made a salad while Frankie changed into pajama bottoms and a T-shirt. In the kitchen she hummed as she warmed the fish and chips in the microwave. They ate on the deck.

"What's up with you two?"

An uncommon hopefulness, a lightness of spirit.

"And don't say it's nothing."

Frankie lifted Glory's hair and whispered in her ear. "Start at the beginning."

Glory went through all the eight-year-old tics that meant she was nervous and stalling the moment when she would have to confess to her father that she'd been suspended from school for a week. She puffed out her cheeks and petted Flame, she folded her arms across her chest, and pretzeled her legs one way and then another.

Observing this Rick didn't smile.

"I got suspended cuz I threw a book at Colette."

In fits and starts she told the story of the backed-up toilet and Rick listened without asking questions or showing emotion, but when she finished he immediately looked around for his cell phone. "We pay a bloody fortune for you to go to that school. I expect better—"

"You can't call, Daddy. It's too late. The school's closed."

"Then I'm going over there tomorrow morning, first thing. Who is this Colette anyway? Do we know anything about her?"

"Last year I went to her house for a party. Remember, Daddy? Someone came from the zoo and brought a wolf puppy we could pet?"

"That's the girl who's done this to you? I thought you were buddies." The instability of eight-year-olds' friendships confused him. "Now she says you stink?"

"You don't have to go to school, Rick. Dr. Scott's on it and if it's not settled, I'll handle it."

"You?" he looked at Frankie, disbelieving. "You can barely take care of yourself. Yesterday—"

Glory stepped between them. "Daddy, it was my fault."

"Colette called you names."

"No, I mean yesterday, when Mommy slapped me. She only did it because I bit her."

Frankie was both ashamed and grateful that Glory

211

wanted to defend her, but in that instant there was a mother-daughter connection as if both recalled the conversation on the pier and the promises they had made to each other: to be a better mother, to be a girl who didn't bite or throw things, to work together to put this bad time behind them.

She dipped a fry in ketchup and held it out to Rick, a peace offering. "A week away from school won't hurt her."

"It'll go on her record."

"So? Arcadia's not the Marine Corps."

"I guess we can all be thankful for that."

They ate cornucopias for dessert and played a few rounds of Boggle before Glory's bedtime. But as soon as Glory was asleep Rick shut down. Frankie couldn't see him doing sit-ups on the far side of the bed, but she heard the huffing and straining.

"Is it me?" she asked, looking down at him. "Are you mad at the school or Colette or me?" Determined not to argue again, she tried to keep her voice light. "We had a good time tonight, didn't we? Why won't you talk to me?"

With a groan he stopped exercising and lay on his back, his forearm covering his face. "You can't slap your daughter and act like it never happened. You can't insult Melanie, who's never done anything but be generous and helpful. You can't throw a fit in front of our friends and pretend it doesn't matter and today's just another ordinary Monday. Glory's been suspended from school for violence. You've got to take responsibility for that and for all the other shit that's happening in this family."

Generations of Byrnes rose up in her defense and she struggled against the instinct to fight that was programmed by her genes. Behind her back she made a fist so tight her nails carved scimitars into her palm.

"Did you go to your therapist? Did you tell her what you did yesterday?"

"Of course."

"You say that like I should know. How should I know, Frankie? How should I know what you do there or anywhere else? You're a big unknown to me most of the time." He turned over and balanced in the plank position until his arms trembled and sweat glistened on the fair hairs at the small of his back.

She had always loved his body, the flat belly and narrow waist and broad shoulders he'd kept since college when he'd been a distance swimmer. She remembered long ago, straddling his thighs, facing him, both of them naked after sex. To sit there so exposed and to know that it was safe to touch and be touched, that this man would never hurt her no matter how vulnerable she allowed herself to be: such intimacy had been a wonder to her and she swore in her heart that she would never do or say anything to jeopardize it. But now he was slipping away and how could she blame him? Why would he want her when she barely wanted herself?

"This morning you and Glory weren't speaking and now all of a sudden, life's a bubble bath. Only it's not. For me it's not."

"We told you. We went to the pier and talked. She gets how it is with me."

"How can she? I'm a fucking grown man, I'm your husband, and *I* don't get you."

"Yes, you do, you always have." Frankie stretched out on the floor beside him. "I was awful yesterday. I know I was way out of line. I know it. But you do get me, Rick." She choked back a growing panic. "You're the only person who's ever understood me."

All day long she had been fighting a terrible thought and now it skewered its way to the front of her mind. Maybe she had exhausted his capacity to forgive and understand; the loyalty she had loved in him from the beginning had worn too thin to depend upon.

They had always talked so well in the dark, but that night, nothing. Frankie stared at the ceiling and though she knew it would only make her more miserable, she remembered the night they met, calling up each detail as if by hurting herself she could prove that the memories were strong enough to hold them together.

In her parents' house the living and dining rooms had been decorated for Christmas in red and green and gold. On the dining room table surrounded by plates of sizzling canapés, the centerpiece was Great-grandmother Byrne's gleaming silver service surrounded by red glass balls and tiers of candy-striped tapers. Candlelight. The glow of Navy and Marine brass. She and Rick had seen each other across the room. He was the tallest man there, she the tallest woman. They came together like pages in a book. As soon as they could politely escape, he had walked her across the street and up through the three levels of his partially constructed house.

Frankie already knew from her mother that neighbors up and down the street had not been happy when wreckers demolished the midcentury house on the property and the new structure began to rise, bigger than any other on the street. But none of them had seen it as Frankie did that night by cold Christmas moonlight. Rick pointed out the rooms, the decks, the wide windows; and Frankie knew that Rick's house would be beautiful, not garish or ostentatious as the neighbors whispered.

On the third floor where the bedrooms would be, he found a pile of old blankets and they sat on the plywood subfloor wrapped in them and talked until almost four a.m. He had been less of a mystery at the end of that first night than he was now, lying in bed beside her. He had escorted her back across the street to the house where she had grown up, and they sat on the porch and talked some more, and when the sky in the east turned yellow they went inside and she fixed them both coffee and breakfast and they kept talking. Frankie had believed they would never run out of conversation.

"Talk to me, Rick."

"I'm past talking, Frankie."

"Tell me what you're thinking."

"You don't want to know." He half laughed. "Or maybe you do. Maybe the suspense is killing us both."

She wasn't sure what this meant, and she didn't want him to explain.

"Don't give up on me, Rick."

He propped his pillow against the headboard.

"Before you went to Iraq, if Glory was having trouble at school, if this Colette had been giving her a bad time, you would have been on the phone to me right off. And mad as hell, I know it. I would have had to calm you down just so I could understand what you were saying. But I barely heard one word about this before she was suspended. The other night you made it sound like some nothing problem. When you told me about the camera in the playground, all that, I distinctly remember you telling me it wasn't a big deal. That was a lie, right?"

"I didn't want to worry you."

"Bullshit. You don't know what matters anymore. Before, you never would have done that. I could have counted on you—"

"You still can."

"No. No, I can't. Not anymore. You're different. You're not Frankie anymore."

She had to say something but a boulder had lodged in her throat.

I'll do everything. I'll never miss therapy. I'll fill a dozen journals and I'll go to group, I swear I'll be the way I was.

Except she knew that no matter what she did, there was no going back. The war had changed her in the same way a dose of radiation alters a person's atomic structure and causes a mutation. That's what she was, a mutated version of her old self. The old Frankie was gone, another person she could not save.

Next morning Rick and Glory concocted a villainous breakfast of pancakes layered with blueberries and whipped cream. Glory was ebullient.

"We know you don't like sweet stuff, Mommy, so I made you a soft-boiled egg and soldiers." Soldiers were what Frankie's mother called the buttered toast cut in strips for dunking in the soft yolk.

Frankie corrected her. "Egg and Marines."

Glory's smiled widened. "Right, Mom." She rolled her eyes. "Sorry, Mom." High five. "*Semper Fi,* Mom."

The moment freeze framed: Glory sweet and spunky and dressed for suspension in shorts and a tee, no shoes on her feet, whipped cream at the corners of her mouth. Rick, handsome in his white shirt with sharp laundry folds, a red silk tie, his springy ginger and silver hair still damp from the shower, lying flat as it never would when it dried. If this was the end she wanted to remember everything.

Glory didn't seem to have noticed that her parents weren't speaking to each other. "Can we go to the beach? I

217

heard on the radio that this is the hottest October in nine years. We could go to Dogs' Beach and take Flame. She'd love that."

"No way," Rick said. "Check your dictionary. *Suspension* and *vacation* aren't synonyms."

"You're going across the street for the day. Grandma's going to put you to work polishing silver."

"I hate that job."

"Too bad," Rick said.

"I can stay home alone. I'm eight. I know the rules."

Glory had been angling for more independence and sooner or later they would have to begin to grant it. But trusting Glory alone for those first few hours was a momentous step. Like learning to walk in the first place, there would be no undoing it.

"Absolutely not," Rick said.

"How come you're mad at me, Daddy?"

"I'm not mad at you."

"Yes, you are. I can tell."

"Leave it alone," Frankie said.

Glory flopped onto a chair dramatically. "Can I at least write my Christmas list today? I want a wet suit this year so I can surf in January."

"I thought you wanted to be a kickboxer."

"Daddy, I can do both."

Frankie looked at Rick, ready to take her cue from him; if he smiled, so would she. But he had tuned out his family.

218

He stood in front of the microwave studying his stern reflection in the glass door, tying his tie. She wanted to stand behind him and rest her cheek on his shoulder but she knew that if she did, he would move away, and that would break her heart.

Chapter 27

The MCRD was fifteen minutes from home on a good day, just over the hill off the Pacific Highway. Somewhere between Ocean Beach and work, Frankie's Nissan developed a rattle. A finger-snapping click that twitched under her skin, telling her hurry-hurry, busy-busy to a rap beat. Stuck in a line of cars at the light at the bottom of Nimitz, she swore at a driver trying to make a U-turn in rush hour traffic. She was late getting to the shop, and once there she rushed to catch up, and her day careened downhill.

The office troops were slower and more careless than usual. She had to explain the limitations of spell check to one young recruit who took the inability of the software to second guess his thinking as a personal betrayal. He seemed younger than the legal age for military service, and she wondered who had sent him to her, what malign deity had thought it would be amusing to watch him mess up the finances of the United States Marine Corps. Probably the same one that deleted a document she needed, forcing her to waste an hour getting it back. Her staff sergeant, Donovan, was hungover, taciturn and uncooperative, and when she didn't have a chance to eat lunch and it was almost two in the afternoon, she couldn't take his scowls and self-importance anymore and laid into him. Immediately she regretted losing her cool. Under the best circumstances he resented having to take orders from a woman. As payback he or one of his buddies would feed something unflattering, maybe downright insulting, about her into the rumor mill.

In some ways the Marine Corps was as bad as Ms. Peters's third grade.

Olvedo called her into his office and told her to sit down.

"You getting a cold, Captain Tennyson?"

"No, sir."

"Lately you've been sounding like a frog."

"Thank you, sir." She focused her eyes on his graying buzz cut.

"I heard you reaming out Donovan."

"You know how he is, Colonel. He's insolent and he's a gossip and I got tired of putting up with it."

"Something worrying you?"

"No, sir." She was aware of sounding like ninety-day wonder in a recruitment video. *Yes, sir. No, sir.*

"What happened at your kid's school yesterday?"

"She got suspended." Quickly she filled him in, an abridged version that omitted stinky butts and biting.

"So she's home now? Who's taking care of her?"

"My folks."

"You need time off?"

"I don't want leave, sir." Her struggling sanity required the distraction of work. She welcomed the order it imposed on her life when everything else was falling apart.

"I didn't ask you if you want it. I asked if you need it."

Frankie had known Olvedo since before she deployed, and they had always worked well together. He was a devoutly religious man and devoted to his wife and sons. It made no sense to go on pretending to him. He knew her. He saw through her.

"I'm a wreck."

"It shows." He pulled out a bottom drawer of his desk and used it as a footrest. "Frankie, finance isn't an easy MOS. There's no glamour, no heroics. To work here takes an eye for detail and precision and you've got to like structure to do it well. Come the day you're out, we're gonna be in big trouble around here because I don't think you can be replaced."

She blushed. "Thank you, Colonel."

"It's not a compliment. It's a fact." He heaved his large body into a new position. "But lately—the last couple of weeks especially—you're making mistakes. Like that dustup with Donovan this morning. So he's a jerk, we all know that, but he's been around the corps since you were Glory's age. A guy like him's never going to accept you. You know that as well as I do."

"I'm sorry, sir, but the look on his face—he's got a permanent scowl."

"Oh, yeah? Look who's talking."

She managed a weak smile. "I think I laughed last week."

"Happy to hear it. Take the rest of the week off and see if you can do it again. Then come back ready and do the job right. Understood?"

"Sir, I don't—"

"Tennyson, you can take your kid to the beach or drink a bottle of NyQuil and sleep for four days, I don't care. But next Monday I want you in your boots, healthy and focused. Are we clear?"

Master Sergeant Donovan didn't look at her as she left, nobody did. She told herself not to care.

The recently resurfaced parking lot smelled of asphalt and gave beneath her boot heels like a wet sponge. Walking toward where she could see her car cooking in the sun, she scanned her cell phone messages and saw two calls from Harry. She was about to key in her brother's number when she heard a car behind her and stepped aside to give it room to pass. She heard the hum of a window going down and turned as the charcoal-tinted back window of a Lincoln Town Car dropped out of sight.

"Good afternoon, Captain Tennyson."

The New York accent was familiar but the thin, lined face and large sensual features weren't immediately identifiable. It was a matter of context. Senator Susan

Belasco did not belong in the parking lot of the San Diego MCRD.

Frankie spoke automatically. "No."

"Am I such a monster we can't even talk?"

"I told your guy. Jared Whatever. I told him, I don't want any part of your hearings."

"And I'm delighted to meet you as well."

"You're wasting your time."

"I suspect you don't want to be seen with me. Especially here. May I suggest we drive around the corner and meet in the post office parking lot? My driver tells me there's usually a shady spot there."

Frankie walked toward her car and the Lincoln kept pace with her.

"I made this trip down from Los Angeles especially to see you. You're curious, aren't you? Just a little?" The senator's teeth were square and even and professionally white.

"I want to be left alone, Senator."

"Ah, well, who can blame you for that? It may surprise you to know that, from time to time, I share your desire. But I'm afraid that's not possible. This matter is too important."

"I have nothing to say."

"Oh, you have a lot to say. Let's at least agree on that."

Frankie stared at her boots. Sweat prickled at the back of her neck.

"I can subpoena you, Captain. But let me be clear, I really don't want to do that. I would like you to come forth of your own volition and tell the committee what you saw."

"I don't know what I saw." The words had fingernails that scratched her throat.

"That can't be true. Your memory was perfectly clear when you spoke to the chaplain and your CO on Redline."

Did everyone over the rank of private know that she had gone to the chaplain and then her CO for advice?

"Why don't you subpoena them?"

"I will. The chaplain would claim privilege so there's no point there. But the fact that you went to them both with your story is one of the things that makes you a most credible witness." Senator Belasco removed her dark glasses, blinking in the bright autumn light. "I would also like to speak to your interpreter, Fatima, but she is, unfortunately, out of my jurisdiction."

"Is she all right?"

"She's been paid well for her silence."

"You don't know that."

"If you mean I haven't seen the actual cash, you're right. But we both know that for her to have gotten out of Iraq safely with her family, to find good work and a place to live—"

Sunlight ricocheted off the Town Car's polished chrome and bull's-eyed Frankie's right eye. She pressed the ball of her thumb against the eye socket.

In Iraq a Mercedes sedan had been the car of choice for diplomats and dignitaries. In the Green Zone everyone drove an SUV, most often a Suburban, and almost always white. Halliburton ran a car wash that was busy night and day. But the vehicles that tore into Three Fountain Square weren't Mercedes or white Suburbans. They were Escalades, fat black beetles lined up end-to-end and surrounded by armed men in uniforms that identified them as G4S.

Frankie drove her Nissan around the corner to the post office. Now, sitting in the dark gray leather interior of Senator Belasco's Town Car, she felt as if she were closed in a luxurious cell where the air smelled of Chanel No. 5.

"Ellis," the senator leaned forward to address her driver, "would you take Captain Tennyson's car and find us some coffee?"

Ellis looked at Frankie. "Ma'am?"

Belasco said, "We'll both have one of those frozen coffee drinks, the largest size, whatever they call it. And an extra shot of espresso in mine. Do you want an extra shot, Captain?"

"I don't want coffee."

"Please. Don't make me drink alone."

"All due respect, Senator, but I don't know Mr. Ellis and I'm not giving him my car keys."

Senator Belasco sighed, and removed her glasses again. She pressed her fingertips against her large lids, taking care not to smear her mascara or eyeliner. "I have had an extremely difficult several days, so you will forgive me if I'm a little abrupt. Here is your choice. You may give Ellis your keys and he will return in twenty minutes with or without a coffee for you. Your vehicle will be safe with him. He's been my driver for many years and I can attest to his excellent record. Or, if you prefer, he will sit in the front seat and listen to our conversation. Your choice."

Paranoid riffs played Frankie's imagination. Ellis was going to search her car or hide something on it—a GPS of some kind, a microphone. She didn't believe any of this, but it all crossed her mind.

"Stay out of the trunk," she said, mostly joking. "It's full of guns and top secret docs."

Ellis left the post office parking lot in Frankie's car and Senator Belasco relaxed into the corner of the Lincoln's generous backseat, her hands folded in her lap like those of a proper schoolgirl, ready to learn.

"I may never have served in the military, Captain, but over the course of my years in the House and Senate I have probably talked to more of our fighting men and women than you have. And I have considerable empathy. I think I know what you're going through. I suspect you've spent the last several months reliving what you saw at the square and agonizing over what to do about it. Conflicting loyalties and all that. I imagine it's pretty much destroyed your personal life. I don't blame you for not wanting to revisit the scene with microphones rearing at you like snake heads."

Rick was ready to walk away from her, Glory was suspended from school, her voice was failing, and she could barely breathe. "I can't deal with this. Not now." *Maybe never.*

"I've visited the square," the senator said. "It's an important part of that neighborhood's life. If you were to go there today, it would appear to be quite an ordinary place—apart from the rubble. Untidy by our standards, disorderly, but the square itself is crowded and busy most days. There are, of course, the government buildings or what remains of them. If you were there I think you might feel as I did, a certain undercurrent, something painful about the place. It's in the air, so to speak. As if an unreconciled ghost is lurking around, poisoning the atmosphere. Demanding satisfaction. I've been told that fifty years ago it was a lovely spot. There actually were three fountains once upon a time. And date palms. But between Saddam, the insurgents, and the coalition—and G4S, of course—it's lost its charm."

The senator spoke like a person who enjoyed words and was accustomed to being listened to. She didn't stammer or register even a whisper of doubt that what she thought and said was important.

"Hearings like mine aren't popular, in case you didn't know. Most of my colleagues on both sides of the aisle don't want anything to do with them. And getting witnesses to appear willingly is always difficult. In the case of incidents involving G4S, it's almost impossible. Particularly now, in 2008 in the middle of the surge, the company has many powerful friends."

"I'm not afraid."

"I didn't mean to imply that you are. I think you agree with me that those people and that place deserve justice. Isn't that why you left your family and went to Iraq in the first place? Because you believe in justice and because you know that despite our faults, and they are many, America is still the world's brightest and best hope?"

Senator Belasco was right about her gifts of empathy.

"You believe that a child has the right to walk down the street without being gunned in the back. Yes or no, Frankie?"

"It's so much more complicated."

"Tell me. Help me to understand."

It was easier to talk about the General.

"My father would consider my testimony a betrayal."

"Are you sure? Have you asked him? No, of course not. But you and I know that the only real betrayal will come if you deny your conscience. Might he agree? And what do you think G4S has to do with the Marine Corps anyway?"

"Many of the employees are former Marines."

Belasco arched one precisely drawn eyebrow. "Including your godfather, Bunny Bunson."

Frankie's throat squeezed shut and the drilling behind her eye became a laser.

"You didn't know that?"

Someone would have told me. Unless. Was it possible her mother and the General didn't know?

"Have you spoken to your godfather about testifying? You have, of course. And I'm sure he's told you there will be terrible consequences if you do it."

She thought of Bunny's beautiful shirts and ties and

the diamonds encircling the black face of his watch and something he said to her when he ambushed her at Jamba Juice on her lunch break. She'd asked him about his Chanel watch.

"I wasn't like your dad, I didn't come up through Culver and the academy. Before I became a Marine, I was an Army grunt. You could say I gave my life to the service. So when I came into a little cash, I thought maybe it was time I treated myself to something special. A little reward for hard work."

The senator placed her hand on Frankie's knee, gently calling her back from the drift. "Captain, I know you feel loyalty to your godfather and, of course, to the general. These feelings speak well of you. But there is an important issue of national security here. Throughout our country's history the loyalty of our military has been one of America's great strengths. Fully armed and trained private security companies threaten that strength because their loyalty is first to their paychecks, then to their employers, and maybe then—for those who are US citizens, anyway—maybe then their loyalty is to America."

The senator had experience with unwilling listeners. Her unwavering eye contact, her syntax and precise diction, the careful pauses between words and phrases demanded Frankie's attention.

"I'm not against private security companies. My critics say I am, but they never really pay attention to what I'm saying. They're more interested in trying to make me look foolish. The draft is not coming back and for this reason, like it or not, companies like G4S have their place. Ours is a professional military force now, and no one is conscripted against his or her will. But while ours is a large army, it's not big enough to provide security for every tinhorn sheik who feels threatened. Nor do we have the manpower to peel potatoes or clean up the mess hall and the latrines. So let's agree that private security companies are an unfortunate necessity. The question is, should they be free to operate outside the scope of the law?"

"It's a military matter," Frankie said, parroting the General.

"I might agree if the military were inclined to do anything much with transgressors. But they are not. There was a recent incident, perhaps you followed it. A security company employee was accused of wounding an Iraqi man and raping his daughter. Unlike most such incidents, it got a lot of press. But the Pentagon did nothing. DOD? Almost nothing. Both trivialized the event. The security company paid the Iraqi man five thousand dollars for his shattered collar bone and his daughter's virtue, his family's good name and future. The security employee was sent back to the United States and given a pension and a payoff of an undisclosed amount."

Frankie knew all of this and agreed it was a scandal.

"We are either an honorable nation of law and morals, or we are not. You decide, Frankie. You saw what happened at Three Fountain Square that day. It's up to you to tell the truth. It would be an act of heroism. Different from your father's, of course, but no less heroic."

Heroic? The idea was so absurd, it worked to clarify everything.

"I can't, I won't do it."

The senator sighed. "In that case you will receive a subpoena to appear. I will make you testify. I will make you tell the truth."

Get home, Frankie thought. Close the doors, lock the doors, all the doors.

She parked the car in the garage, collected the day's mail, and went upstairs. In the kitchen Flame danced around her, demanding either attention or a biscuit, preferably a lot of both. Frankie tossed her a Milk-Bone. She was casting third-class mail into the blue recycling bin when she remembered to listen to Harry's message on her cell phone.

"Frankie, can you find Domino? We did some blood work on Candace the other day and turns out she's got hep A. Not a huge thing but super contagious so we can't let her go to school until it's treated. Domino's probably got it too and she works with food. Not good. Can you find them?"

Chapter 28

It wasn't quite three o'clock. Glory could stay with her grandmother a while longer.

Frankie sped back over Point Loma, almost exactly retracing her earlier route to the Pacific Coast Highway. Traffic lights and gridlock, drivers who did not signal their turns, an off-road vehicle with tires four feet wide, all pulled at the strings of her fraying nerves. Her heart kept time with the Nissan's hip-hop beat.

Finding Domino and getting her to accept help would be difficult, but of all the problems Frankie faced, this was one she felt competent to solve. The rest of her life was advanced calculus by comparison. She had helped no one, saved no one in Iraq. She had broken her promises to Fatima. When she met Mrs. Greenwoody over the onions and tangerines, she'd been half tongue-tied, unable to defend the kids' clinic or condemn the violence. At home—she wouldn't think about Rick and Glory, couldn't face the facts and their complications. Right now helping

Domino was not only her desire but imperative if she was to save any of her self-respect. But she couldn't do it alone.

It was after four and still unseasonably warm when she parked under the sign of the blue nude and walked across the street and into the veterans' complex. A large rectangular corkboard on wheels had been positioned in the middle of the entrance, blocking the interior patio. A sign stuck in with pushpins directed her to the left for information.

The woman behind the counter in the office looked up, her expression equal parts defensive and accusatory, determined to give nothing away. For a time Frankie had traveled with a team out of FOB Redline made up of Army recruits who were nineteen and twenty years old, many of them women. They drove the trucks and Humvees and turned a tough face to the world in a way she came to believe was both learned on the job and carried over from their lives before they chose the uniform. They did as they were ordered and protected themselves. Frankie understood how it was. Even when there was no threat showing, a woman in the military had to be ready for it.

Her name tag said she was Josie.

"Help you?"

"I'm looking for a guy who works here sometimes. His name's Dekker!"

"You mean Bo. He's on the patio, but he's got a group now."

Frankie said she would wait.

She stood in the shade of the open arcade and looked out into the courtyard, bright and hot in the late afternoon sun. The table umbrellas were up, red and green like decor for a sunny Christmas, and each round table was occupied by men and women talking quietly or, more often, reading or writing. No cell phones. No music. In the far corner eight or so men had gathered at two tables, pulled together. They were an odd assortment. Long-haired, skinhead, or scruffy, tattooed, neatly dressed and not, they sat backward on metal folding chairs or right-way around, tipped forward, hunched over the table. The focal point of the group was Dekker. She recognized him from the support group she had looked in on a week ago.

Discreet in the shadows of the covered walkway, she watched and saw immediately that like Dr. White, he was a listener by nature. The men responded positively to his concentrated attention. Sometimes he nodded or asked a question but mostly he just listened. Once he threw back his head and laughed hard and the sound carried across the courtyard to Frankie. She wanted to run.

That's the kind of group Dr. White wants me to join. The words that popped into Frankie's mind were *undignified* and *embarrassing.* Which was pretty funny when she recalled how dignified she'd been just fifteen minutes earlier, snarling like a junkyard dog at the drivers on Rosecrans. This group might not be right for her but for the first time she realized that somewhere there must be one that was.

All the tables were occupied. Frankie approached one

where a woman sat alone, reading a book with her feet propped up on a chair. A notebook—of course—lay open beside her and Frankie saw a few scribbled lines written in pencil.

"Mind if I sit here?"

"Be my guest." She gave the footrest chair a little kick in Frankie's direction.

Frankie wanted to send Harry a text, telling him what she was doing, and she thought about texting Rick but there was nothing she could say that wouldn't take thousands of words and hours of time. She put her hand into her purse for a mint and her fingertips touched the spiral binding of the notebook she had bought on Sunday at Vons. Thus far all she had written in it was that first day's date. She stared at her nails and wished she had an emery board. Eventually she withdrew the notebook. Opening it to the first page, she wrote the day's date right under the previous date.

I'm sitting in Veterans' Villa waiting to talk to some guy Domino trusts.

She imagined Dr. White asking her why.

Candace is sick.

In some populations hepatitis A was as common as a head cold and just as contagious. Even so this didn't explain why Frankie was sitting in Veterans' Villa waiting for Dekker when for weeks she had been avoiding his group.

This isn't about me, she wrote and then crossed out the

words and ran her pen over and over them so she wouldn't have to look at the lie.

Candace was Domino's daughter and Domino was like a sister to Frankie. Although they hadn't literally fought together, the specifics didn't matter because Mosul, Fallujah, the Green Zone, and FOB Redline were the same in more ways than they were different. At its heart war was all the same.

I need to make something work out right for a change.

She looked at the words she had written and wanted to scratch them out too. She heard her therapist asking *why?* Frankie drummed her pen on the metal table.

"Do you mind? That's really irritating."

"Sorry." Shifting her chair away from the table and into a patch of October sunlight, Frankie tilted her head to the warm light and closed her eyes and drifted, letting the tangled spool of time unwind, freeing the memory of Three Fountain Square. She saw the Iraqi boy only a few feet away, running toward his father. He wore soiled khaki pants and an orange T-shirt. She saw the terror in his dark eyes, the sweat cutting rivulets down his grimy cheeks, his young arms pumping. Within Frankie, a wound tore open. The pen dropped from her trembling hand and rolled across the uneven paving stones, coming to rest against the toe of a boot, scuffed down to the color of mustard.

"Josie said you were looking for me." Bo Dekker picked up the pen and handed it to her.

Lost for a moment, she stared at him.

"You're Captain…"

When she managed to speak her voice was as rough as the old wood bench on the Ocean Beach pier. "Frankie Tennyson. Domino's my friend."

Dekker wore his gray hair, thin at the front, combed straight back from his high forehead. Frankie could see that decades ago he had been handsome in the roguish fashion of an eighteenth-century highwayman, but time had eroded all softness from his face, leaving only angles and crags. His eyes were slits of bright blue.

"My brother runs the kids' clinic in OB. Do you know it?"

"I do."

"He did a blood test on Candace and found out she's got hepatitis A. He wants to see her and Domino needs to be checked too. She works—"

"She doesn't work there anymore."

The woman at the table said, "You guys want to take it somewhere else? I'm trying to read."

Dekker said, "Come on inside."

Frankie followed him down the hall to the room where she had briefly observed his group. At the time she hadn't noticed a gray metal desk shoved against the far wall. He got her a folding chair from the group circle.

"Domino never said your name."

She was surprised by how much this hurt.

"But Candace talks about your kid all the time. Can't shut up about her best friend. Glory, right?"

238

Frankie wondered if it had always and only been about the little girls.

"You were going to find her a place to live," she said. "Did you?"

He studied her, chewing his lower lip thoughtfully. "I don't want to be rude here, but I gotta be honest with you. I'm not comfortable talking about Domino."

Her reaction was immediately defensive. "What am I, some kind of enemy all of a sudden?" And then she understood. "You're protecting her from Jason."

"You know him?"

"Has there been more trouble?"

"Do you know him?"

"No. Of course not. How would I? Why would you ask me that? I told you, I know Domino. We met at the clinic and we're friends. Even if she never told you my name." Her voice rose. "Where is she? What's happened?"

"I'll take a message."

"No. I want to see her."

The drawn-down weariness in Dekker's expression called forth a physical reaction inside Frankie. Her body felt sluggish, as if she had absorbed through her pores the weight of the stories told in this room, Domino's story multiplied hundreds of times over.

"My therapist, Dr. White in La Jolla? She wanted me to join one of your groups. Do you know her? She says you're...good. At what you do."

"But I haven't seen you around here. Just that one time."

She was a scholar and star athlete, the General's daughter. What was it Harry said? *Born to be a hero.*

"I thought I was different."

"Terminal uniqueness." He smiled a little. "We all think the same."

If she wasn't special, what was she?

"I'll drive around until I find her."

"Don't waste the gas. I'll talk to her. Give me your number. If she wants to see you, I'll call and we'll do it."

Chapter 29

That night Frankie made a picnic dinner of ham sandwiches and salad and they ate on a blanket at Dogs' Beach. Glory hit tennis balls for Flame, who was a frustratingly indifferent fetcher, preferring to visit with other dogs and chase birds. During the meal Frankie and Rick played their roles: happy mom and dad.

If Frankie thought about how she and Rick had come to this point and if she allowed herself to wonder what lay ahead and what it would all mean to Glory's future, she dropped into a reality too depressing to bear.

"There's a few grapes left. Wanna split them?"

He shook his head.

Rick had never clammed up this way, never refused to look at her. When they disagreed their way was to tangle and argue back and forth until they reached a compromise or one of them waved a white flag. This wasn't the Rick she knew.

Running her fingers through the sand, she stared out to

sea, remembering a story from Iraq. It might not even be true but it had dug its claws into her memory.

A soldier found a runty dog, a poor starving creature with three legs and half its teeth gone and, defying regulations, kept it as a pet, feeding it hamburgers and chicken he carefully picked off the drumsticks served in the mess. Regulations against keeping animals were often ignored in Iraq. War was a lonely business even if you were in a noisy crowd all day. It was comforting to pet a dog and look into its worshipful eyes. One day when the soldier went out in a convoy, there was a sandstorm and an explosion, and he never came back. The dog, left chained to the tent, had been buried alive in the sand. When she thought about breaking up the family, Frankie felt like that dog.

At home Glory wanted to watch a video in the great room. Rick disapproved.

"You aren't on a holiday."

Glory's face wilted. "Please don't be mad at me anymore, Daddy."

It's me he's mad at, not you.

"I don't think you realize how serious it is, to be suspended from school."

She stomped upstairs to her room.

"And no computer," he yelled after her.

Frankie asked him, "Would you like some tea? And a cornucopia? There are two left over." *From last night when I thought we could be happy again.* "It's cool tonight. Maybe the weather's changing. Finally, huh? Shall we have a fire?"

"I'm going to work out."

She was reading in bed when he came in later, dripping sweat.

"How far did you go?"

"Not far enough." He went into the bathroom and closed the door.

She tried to pay attention to the mystery open on her lap: Los Angeles, murder, mayhem, and an angsty cop with a fondness for jazz; but her feet were cold, and her mind would not settle. She closed the book and let it drop off the side of the bed. Pulling the comforter around her shoulders, she waited to see what would happen next.

Rick came out of the bathroom, releasing a whoosh of steamy air into the bedroom as he did. Wearing a towel slung low on his hips, he moved about the room picking his clothes up from the floor and lobbing them into his closet. He stopped at the foot of the bed.

"Melanie gave her notice today."

For a moment Frankie could not remember who this was.

"She said she was too embarrassed to stay. Apparently everyone in the office thinks there's been something going on between us. Thanks to you."

"What's she going to do?"

"Is that all you've got to say?"

"I'll call her. I'll apologize."

"Don't bother. She doesn't even blame you. She's too nice for that. She says she knows you're not well."

243

At Rick's feet, Flame rolled over, wanting her tummy rubbed. He obliged her though he probably didn't even know he was doing it. He needed to keep moving, doing something, anything to stay out of bed, away from her. In the same way she wanted to keep talking because so long as they were talking about everyday matters, she didn't have to say what was most important.

"I heard from Harry today. Candace has hepatitis."

"The thief."

"He asked me if I knew where to find her. I went down to the Veterans' Villa. There's a man there she knows, but he wouldn't tell me where she is. Not right off anyway. He's protecting her from her ex." She talked on, filling the emptiness with people and lives Rick didn't care about. She knew better but she couldn't stand the silence.

Rick sat in one of the easy chairs that faced the television. His back to her.

"Are you going to watch TV?"

He turned it on and then immediately off again. "I don't know what I'm going to do," he said and left the room.

He did not come back to bed and was out of the house before she awoke the next morning.

Frankie relented to Glory's logic and let her stay home alone while she went to La Jolla for her appointment with Dr. White. Before leaving she reviewed the rules. Glory was not to leave the house or use the stove or microwave oven. She could go in the back garden but not on the decks.

"Keep Flame with you."

"Why? She'd just lick a robber to death."

"Don't let anybody in. Don't even answer the phone."

"Even if you call me? Even if I see your name on caller ID?"

"Okay. Me or Dad."

"What about Gramma or Uncle Harry?"

"You know what I mean, Glory. Use your good sense."

"Why is everyone so mad at me?"

She found a parking space on Herschel, next to the most beautiful automobile she had ever seen. Before going up to the office, she stood on the sidewalk and admired the sea-green Bentley convertible as if it were a piece of sculpture in a gallery. The car gave her something to talk about during the warm-up minutes of her appointment when there was always a slight awkwardness; but her therapist wasn't a car enthusiast and, really, neither was Frankie so the small talk got smaller and eventually vanished.

She stared out the window at the palm trees. When the wind blew the fronds brushed against each other and made a sound like rain.

She burst into tears. "He's given up."

"Frankie, I'm so sorry. Things must have gotten much worse."

Light danced off the palm fronds.

"Talk to me, Frankie."

"He's cold now. He's never been cold before."

"What does that mean?"

"He won't look at me. Or talk to me. He slept downstairs last night."

Once sex might have been a bridge over a stressful time, but they had not been intimate in six weeks. Frankie's choice. She couldn't relax in his arms and lying beside him, not touching, his desire was like an unpredictable animal. At first he had been patiently understanding. Twice she'd forced herself to have sex out of guilt, both times were disasters worse than abstinence. The rejections hurt him, she knew, but she couldn't keep saying she was sorry all the time.

Dr. White handed her the tissue box and she remembered Trelawny Scott doing the same thing a few days earlier. She had cried more since she came home than in the previous two years, five years, maybe her whole life. Tears came when words were inadequate. Tears came gushing out of sorrow and resignation, out of hopelessness.

"He's given up on me and I don't blame him. How can I? Talking to Glory's headmistress, I realized it's all my fault. Everything. Glory's problems, Rick's and mine. I've asked him to be patient and give me more time, but I really haven't done anything to make things better."

"You come here twice a week. I think that's something."

"Why? I sit in your office and cry."

"Therapy's a new language, Frankie. It takes time to learn how to talk about all the things you don't want to talk about. In the meantime, you cry."

This was the nut of it: *All the things you don't want to talk about.* This was what closed her throat and killed the songs, sent the black crows flying through her thoughts and into the past, circling over Three Fountain Square, the forbidden territory.

"I met that guy you recommended. Bo Dekker?"

"You went to his group?" There was no missing the hope in White's question.

"Because of Domino. I thought we were friends, but he didn't even know my name."

"That hurt you."

She began crying again. "Damn, I hate this."

"Catharsis is real, not just something the Greeks invented to make their plays more interesting. Even a general's daughter needs it."

Frankie sneaked a look at the clock. Thirty minutes remaining. She blotted her tears and began shredding the tissue.

"What are you thinking?"

"Nothing. Everything."

Dr. White laughed. "Sometimes they can feel like the same thing."

"I left Glory home alone."

"And you're nervous about this."

"Wouldn't you be?"

"Are you?"

"She's a good girl and she knows not to talk to strangers. Besides my mother's across the street."

"But something still bothers you."

Tears again. "I don't want her to grow up. She's on her way out the door before I even had a chance to be her mother."

"Did you want to be a mother?"

"You know the answer to that." Rick had been the one eager to begin a family. "But now that she's going—"

"Frankie, you left her home alone for two hours. There's a long way between that and 'going.'"

"You don't have children. You don't know how the time flies. He'll be gone and so will she and I'll be alone."

"You could have another baby. Have you thought of that?"

"I just told you. He's finished." And so cold, he chilled the house.

"Has he told you he wants out of the marriage?"

"I know, I can tell. He's already gone."

She imagined their divorce. At first they would make every effort to keep it amicable, but it couldn't stay that way because Rick would want Glory. He would argue for her in court. A judge would determine that Frankie was an unfit mother.

"I left her and went to Iraq."

"Men do it all the time."

"A judge wouldn't care." A judge would feel as the General did. She was *unnatural*.

"It strikes me that you're spending a lot of time looking ahead to what might happen in the future. Maybe there's somewhere else you can put your attention. Something you can deal with right now."

She told her about Domino. "I'm just waiting to hear from Dekker."

"I agree that it would be good if you could help your friend. I think it might boost your confidence. But I was thinking of something closer to home, Frankie."

"Like what?"

"Well." Dr. White settled herself. "You could ask Rick straight out if he wants a divorce."

Chapter 30

Bunny's dark blue BMW was in the driveway, blocking the garage door. Frankie parked on the hill and rushed up the stairs onto the deck. Through the wall of windows she saw into the living room. Glory sat cross-legged on the floor, Bunny on the couch. Between them on the glass-topped coffee table was a Monopoly board.

As Frankie let herself in Glory bragged, "I've got three hotels on Park Place."

"What are you doing here?"

"And good morning to you, Captain Tennyson."

She knew her godfather's expressions and could distinguish a true smile from the one he used as camouflage.

"Glory, you weren't supposed to open the door. We talked about this—"

"But it was Uncle Bunny, Mom."

"Go and clean your room. I'll be up in a little while."

"But, Mom, we're—"

"You heard what I said."

Glory threw down her token. "What're you mad at me for? What did I do?" She flounced from the room, and a second later Frankie heard her bedroom door slam.

Bunny said, "I'm getting ready to go back to DC and I thought I'd stop over and say good-bye. I've only been here a few minutes." He shrugged as if to underscore how natural a thing this parting visit was. "Don't be too hard on the kid."

She could not stand to look at him and she hated the way he sweetened his voice. How was it that this lying and cajoling man was part of her family?

"I've been worried about you."

"Senator Belasco came to the MCRD."

"Susan can be a very clever and persuasive woman."

"You call her Susan?"

"Washington's a small town."

Especially for a lobbyist, Frankie thought.

"She's going to subpoena me."

He laughed shortly. "I wouldn't be too worried. Just be patient. She'll find other witnesses, either that or the whole mess'll burn out."

"Does my father know you're a lobbyist? Does Mom?"

He sat back down on the couch and patted the cushion beside him. "You're upset and I guess I shouldn't blame you. But you've got to get a grip before you do something you regret."

251

"Just tell me." She would not sit. "Do they know?"

"Your mom and dad believe what they want to believe." He said. "And what does it matter, Frankie, when we're all after the same thing? G4S, the corps, and everyone else in uniform just want to make the world a safer place. Let's not quibble about the details."

There had never been a time in Frankie's life when she did not know this man. He held her in his arms when she was baptized, he took her out to Fiesta Island and taught her how to drive because it made her parents too nervous. Now she couldn't look at him.

"Ride it out. A few more weeks and you'll be in blue skies."

"What if I don't want to ride it out? What if riding it out is making me crazy? Have you ever been to the Green Zone, Bunny?" She laughed at her own silly question. "Sure you have. I bet you loved it. Right? Fatima and I were there once. You remember her? My interpreter? The one G4S paid off and sent to Damascus?" She did not know this for sure, but it made more sense than any other explanation. "Maybe you made the arrangements. I bet you're more a fixer than a lobbyist. You'd be good at that. Not that I blame her for taking the offer, by the way. She needed to get out of Iraq."

"Calm down, Frankie."

"Do you know what I do down at the shop? I process invoices transferring millions of dollars from Defense through the corps to companies I've never heard of who supposedly provide the military with support services. And for what? Another fleet of Chevy Suburbans, regulation white? More razor wire and car washes? So guys who dress like Mormons on a mission can eat at Burger King in the exact spot where Saddam's sons fucked their bimbos?"

Bunny winced.

"So they can shoot innocent children?"

"In a war, even children can be dangerous. I've seen—"

"That boy wasn't much older than Glory."

Her words might carry upstairs but she didn't care. She remembered the feeling of freedom when she tipped over her shopping cart and walked away. This noisy, righteous, from-the-gut anger wasn't so different, not so different at all.

"We worked for ten months to make a school and when I left Redline it still had no running water or reliable power. But they had Girl Scout cookies. Cases of them, compliments of the Department of Defense." She pressed her palm against her charging heart.

"Get a grip, Frankie. You're right, it is a crazy war. We don't have to argue about that." She had once overheard the General telling someone that what made Bunny Bunson a superior sergeant major was his ability to stay calm while Shit City blew up. "We made a lot of mistakes in the beginning but now we've got the surge going and we're turning it around. At this point in time talking to the committee would be a mistake."

She folded her arms across her chest to keep her heart from beating its way out of her body.

"Your father loves you, goddaughter. You're the world to him."

She did not know if this was true. At the best of times she had been barely good enough to satisfy his demands. After more than thirty years of effort she had never won the approval she so wanted.

Bunny's voice was a soothing monotone like the purr of a cat. "He's seventy-five years old and just because you spent ten months in Iraq doesn't mean you know anything about what he went through in 'Nam. He might look pretty good to you, but believe me, those years age you double. Inside that tough old hide he's held together with paperclips. You talk about what you saw and you might as well pull the plug on him. He's proud and the shame of his daughter—"

"No Marine would ever do what I saw that contractor do."

"It's a war, Frankie. Bad things happen."

"I saw his face. I'd recognize him in a crowd of people."

"That's what you say now, but think about the pressure if you testify. You'll be sitting at the witness table with all those microphones poking at you and the photographers in the hole snapping pictures and you'll try to talk and you know how your throat's gonna get. Like it is now. Like a stretch of dirt road. Senator Delaware'll pick you apart with his questions. You'll make a fool of yourself."

She heard footsteps on the stairs up from the street. Rick came through the door.

She asked, "What's wrong? Why aren't you at work?"

"We need to talk. I haven't been able to think straight all morning." He stopped, looked at her and then at Bunny, seeing him for the first time. "What's going on? Frankie, you look like someone kicked you."

"Bunny's just leaving."

He heaved himself up off the couch. "I guess I am." He lifted his wrist to look at his watch and the diamonds sparkled in the bright room.

She told Rick, "He works for G4S. He lobbies for them. Or something. That's how he can afford a watch like that."

"Good to see you, buddy. Take care of my god-daughter—"

"Tell him why you're here."

"I'd like to stay longer, but I'm flying out—"

"I saw a boy killed by a G4S contractor and Senator Belasco wants me to testify."

Rick stared at her.

"You think I'm lying, Rick? You think I'm an unreliable witness?"

"No, no, of course not. You never said—"

"But now I am. Now I'm saying. I saw an innocent boy shot dead by a contractor and Bunny wants me to pretend it never happened. He thinks I'd make a fool of myself in front of the committee. Shame the corps." She added, swallowing hard, "He thinks it would kill the General."

Glory spoke from the foot of the stairs. "What's gonna kill Grandpa?"

Chapter 31

At FOB Redline the women's showers were a city block away from the can where she slept. Under her feet, the stall was always gritty with sand and in the corners it piled up in tiny dunes. The hot water ran out fast. Stepping out into the desert air she had never felt really clean.

Frankie left Glory and Rick and went upstairs. In the bathroom she stepped into the shower fully clothed and raised her face to the chilly needles, letting the water tattoo her eyelids and cheeks as she undressed, kicking her sodden jeans and shirt and underwear into the corner of the shower. Achingly cold she pulled her braid apart and ran her shaking fingers up through her hair. Gradually she increased the hot water until the shower steamed. Like a farm worker or a coal miner at the end of a buried day, she lathered herself and rinsed and lathered again. She washed her hair, stood bent at the waist for five minutes letting the water pour through it. She twisted the knob and gradually the water chilled again.

She was shaking when Rick opened the door and reached in to turn off the tap.

"Frankie, don't do this to yourself."

He stood with a towel stretched wide, and she walked into his arms and he wrapped it around her. She stood still, letting him towel her dry and help her into her terry-cloth robe and tie the sash. With her hair turbaned in a towel, she followed him into the bedroom. She felt as numb as if she'd been anesthetized.

"Where's Glory?"

"Downstairs. Watching TV."

"What did you tell her?"

"I said it was just a figure of speech. Like saying '*I'm dying for an ice cream cone*' doesn't really mean I'm dying. She got it." Rick pulled her down beside him on the bed and drew the bedclothes over them. They lay on their sides, face to face.

"What am I going to do with you?"

"Throw me out with the trash."

"I need to get a bigger barrel."

"I'm sorry, Rick." She didn't know what she was apologizing for but it was all she could think to say.

"Why didn't you tell me what you saw? I would have listened. You don't need to hold that nightmare inside you. It's like poison."

"There's more . . . I did something terrible."

"Tell me."

Instead she talked about the journal she had begun to

keep. At least she'd written the date and a few words. They were the first steps through the maze. "I can't say the words."

"Belasco really came to see you? You must be a very important person. I'm impressed."

"I won't testify."

"If you can't say the words—"

"I can't."

"It's up to you, Frankie."

"You think I should." Telling the truth for all the world to hear, the shame would be too great. "Don't ask me to do it."

"I'm not asking. But whatever you do, you have to be sure it's for the right reasons. Put yourself first, not the general."

"Bunny said it would kill him."

"Bunny Bunson's the king of the bullshitters. You know that. After all your old man's been through, I don't think hearing the truth would hurt him."

Holding her face in his warm hands, he kissed her eyelids and, lightly, her lips.

"It's not even noon," Frankie murmured. "Why are you here? You came home in the middle of the day. Why?"

"Jesus, honey, figure it out. I was having a crappy day. I didn't sleep last night. I lay on the couch in the great room and watched TV. My eyes feel like fried eggs."

"You could have come upstairs."

"I knew if I stayed in the bedroom I was going to say things I'd be sorry for later."

"Like what?"

"Ah, babe, I felt so helpless, so done in. I wanted to walk. I got to work before seven and left a message on Tom Courtney's machine." Tom was their lawyer. "I told him we were splitting up. I thought, after I said that, I'd feel something. Maybe not better but at least relieved. Only I didn't, I felt worse."

"Are you still—?"

"What would be the point, Frankie?" He held her more tightly. "With you or without you, I'd still be miserable. This family is everything to me."

"It's my fault."

For some reason, her words made him chuckle to himself. "Maybe it is. A lot of it. But when I'm not feeling sorry for myself, I know that as bad as these last weeks have been, it's gotta be worse for you and I feel like a shit for giving up."

"I might get worse. I might get worse and worse until I go crazy. It happens sometimes. Not everyone gets better."

"If that happens, I guess we'll figure something out."

"You could build me a little house in the backyard. Lock the door."

"Nah, the planning commission wouldn't give me a permit." His arms tightened around her. "I guess I'm basically an optimist. I tried being a pessimist for a few hours but it didn't work for me." He unwound the towel turban around her hair and dropped it onto the floor. He combed his fingers through her damp and tangled hair. "I love you, Frankie. When it comes down to it, I'd rather be unhappy with you than without. I can stick it out if you can."

Glory came into the bedroom, holding Zee-Zee. "Are we ever gonna eat lunch?"

Frankie made a space beside her. "Want to cuddle?"

Glory scooted up and snuggled down under the comforter between her mother and father, a pleased look on her face. At the foot of the bed, Flame eyed them longingly.

"Can she come up too?"

The setter, fluent in human body language, jumped and found a spot at Glory's feet.

Rick grabbed the remote off the bedside table and clicked on the television. "Let's see what the leisure class watches in the middle of the day."

"Can we have pizza for lunch?"

"Sure." How easy life was when she stopped fighting it.

"Can we eat it on the bed and watch a movie?"

Frankie looked at Rick. It was a relief to laugh together.

"I know how to order on the phone, Mom. When you were in Iraq I did it lots of times."

It wasn't that Frankie's problems had gone away or that she'd forgotten them. Belasco and her hearings were a question mark, the General was still the General, Glory had been suspended from school, and Domino had vanished. But for an afternoon none of these seemed material and she was going to sit on the bed, eat pizza, and watch a movie with her husband and daughter and dog. Today was an oasis where the caravan could stop for a while before heading back into the desert.

Chapter 32

At a little before ten that night as Frankie was in the great room folding laundry, Dekker called.

"You still want to see Domino?"

"I said I did."

"Okay, then. I'll meet you up at the Jack around eleven."

When she put down her phone, Rick was looking at her.

"I have to do this."

"Can't this guy give her a message about the hepatitis?"

"You're right. He could."

She held Rick's hands against her heart, aware that this moment was, in its way, as important to their future as their talk on the bed that morning. If Rick could understand why she had to see and talk to Domino, it would mean that his words—*I can stick it out*—stemmed from something more substantial than hope and wishful thinking.

"I've done so many things wrong or only half right, Rick. I have to try to make up for it. I mean, I never can,

not really, but this is something. Helping Domino. I can't
fail this time."

She ordered coffee and a churro at Jack in the Box. The
night manager recognized her and asked if she had seen
Domino.

"She don't work here no more. Her crazy husband,
though, he's still here most nights. I see him in his car.
Waiting."

"If her ex wasn't a problem would you hire her again?
She was a good employee, you told me so."

"Too much trouble. I got a kid works now. College kid.
No ex-husband."

The Jack in the Box on Washington Street dated from a
time when fast food was a bare bones operation without an
inside dining room because almost no one cared to eat on
the premises. Frankie took her coffee and churro around
the building to where four picnic tables were bolted to a
cement slab, under a wide roof of corrugated steel. Though
the October days had been warm enough for shorts and
picnics at the beach, after sunset the temperature dropped
quickly. She buttoned her down vest and sat, leaning
against the wall with her legs stretched out along the bench.
She was alone except for a couple seated one table away,
a man wearing a grayed T-shirt and a jittery woman with
small fox-like features who reminded Frankie of Shawna
Montoya, the soldier who had been driving the Humvee

when they came to a stop on the edge of Three Fountain Square. She had the same sharp nose and pointed chin as this woman clutching her coffee cup like a hand-warmer, hunched over and talking urgently. Occasionally Frankie picked up a word or two, but she was on the lookout for Dekker and not paying close attention. Several times the woman looked up at Frankie and then quickly away.

After a while a primered panel truck pulled into the lot and Dekker got out. Seeing him away from Veterans' Villa where he had some authority, she had a moment of doubt about trusting him. He was older than she had realized and his face showed every day of the hard life he must have led.

He stopped at Frankie's table. "I have to talk to my friends over there. It might be a while. You okay with that?"

"If you'd give me her address—"

He stepped back.

Resigned she said, "I'm not going anywhere."

He went inside and came back out with a large bag of food. He dealt out hamburgers and French fries to the man and the fox-faced woman who grabbed up the food and ate quickly, without speaking. Her movements were jerky and she almost knocked her coffee off the table, but Dekker caught the cup before it went over the edge. In response the woman crossed her arms over her chest and rocked from side to side, her eyes squeezed shut. They popped open and she saw Frankie watching her.

"What do you want?" She had a deep rolling voice. "What you lookin' at?"

264

"You almost spilled your coffee." Frankie didn't know what else to say.

"So?"

"I just noticed, that's all."

Dekker took several folded sheets of paper from the back pocket of his jeans and opened them out in front of the woman, smoothing them with the palm of his hand. From where Frankie sat she saw that they were forms of some kind. He spoke quietly, using the point of his pen to indicate particular lines.

"I don't know any of that crap." The woman shoved the papers away.

Dekker remained calm, talking and smoothing the papers again, and gradually, she settled down and began nodding her head as if she understood what he was saying. Frankie watched, trying not to be obvious, but curious about the woman and the forms and about Dekker, who spent his days counseling at the villa and his nights apparently doing the same thing.

Suddenly the woman pointed at Frankie. "Stop lookin' at me!"

Dekker turned around. "You may as well come over here and sit with us."

"Her? Who she?"

"Dawny, she's a friend of Domino. Her name's Frankie."

"She's a lyin' maggot."

The young man at the table was tattooed with brightly colored serpentine shapes, like a vine growing up his arms and peeking out from under the neck of his shirt. He shoved the remains of a bag of French fries across the table at Frankie. As she reached for one, he grabbed her hand and turned her arm to reveal the small *Semper Fi* tattoo.

"In or out?"

"In."

"How long?"

"Nine-eleven." The date was shorthand that explained a lot.

Dawny said, "Assholes."

Frankie steeled herself not to look away as the young man peered at her from under his thick eyebrows, like an animal hidden in the brush.

"How you know Dom?"

Frankie looked at Dekker for a cue how to proceed. He nodded and she talked about meeting Domino at the clinic and about Candace and Glory being friends.

Dawny still wasn't happy. She jabbed her index finger on the papers. "So we gonna do this or what?"

Dekker said, "I told you, Dawny, you have to find some kind of ID that shows your date of birth and all. A library card won't cut it."

Dekker's voice was kind, but watching him Frankie sensed that he had not always possessed this self-control. She wondered how long it had taken him to make peace with his demons.

"What about your discharge papers? Can you remember where they are?"

266

Dawny wasn't listening to him.

"You got a house?" she asked Frankie. "Where's your house?"

"Go easy, Dawny."

"She makes my head hurt."

"I'm sorry, I don't mean to hurt you." Frankie looked at Dekker. Should I say more? she wondered. *Should I leave?* He shrugged and shook his head as if to say that—stay or go—it probably wouldn't make much difference. Frankie recognized Dawny's suspicion, her headaches and despondency and pointless anger, as first and second cousins of her own disturbed thinking. Her mind spun away and drifted off down Washington Street searching for somewhere safe, a doorway or a patch of ground behind a bush, against a wall.

It might rain. I'll need shelter if it rains.

Dawny was talking about bad dreams and Dekker asked her if she had stopped taking her meds.

"Fuck you and the horse you rode in on."

The tattooed boy's laugh brought Frankie back. He said, "Dawny was in the Army. She worked in a prison."

"Why you telling her that? It's none of her business."

"She's waiting to go on disability but it's hard to get all the documents together. Plus she mostly don't make it to her appointments."

Dawny stood up, her body rigid. "Shut up, bigmouth."

"Sit down now, Dawny. No one wants to fight."

"Make her go away."

267

"I will." Frankie scrambled off the bench. "I'll go over there, I'll sit. I won't look at you, Dawny. I promise."

"Why? You think I'm ugly?"

Dekker's vivid blue eyes crinkled. He found humor in all this. Maybe that was part of his secret. Without humor how could he face another day of other people's pain?

"I'll wait in my car."

Sitting in her car Frankie thought about Dawny and then of Shawna Montoya. They had ridden together several times. What made Shawna memorable was the way she talked to herself as she skillfully maneuvered the big Humvee. Approaching Three Fountain Square, the road they were on made an abrupt dogleg turn, and just like that, it wasn't much wider than an alley. *Holy shit and what the fuck, we've got us a problemo aquí.* Frankie wondered what had happened to Shawna, if she might be in trouble like Dawny or homeless like Domino or just screwed up like she was. She wondered if any of them had come out of Iraq with their lives together.

Dekker surprised her when he said her name at the car window.

"We have to get out of here before Jason shows." He looked up and down Washington Street. "He's a smart guy. He could be hiding, watching now."

"Where is that?"

"You'll never find it on your own. Just follow me. If you lose me, I'm not coming back for you."

At first it was easy to keep Dekker's clunky primered

panel truck in sight on the neighborhood streets of Hillcrest, but after a mile or so, paralleling Washington on Robinson, it turned right, into an area of irregular residential blocks close to Balboa Park where there were sudden canyons and stop signs at every cross street. He took to the alleys, making so many turns that Frankie lost track of where they were until an old and poorly marked freeway entrance appeared and the truck darted down it and into the stream of traffic merging onto Interstate 8.

The AstroLuxe was an old motel situated far up Mission Valley, well out of the area popular with tourists where the motels advertised free shuttles to the zoo and Sea World and two-for-one breakfast vouchers. It was a dozen units, single story in an L-shaped configuration built back against the valley wall facing south toward the rear of a nondescript office building. In front of the motel, secured by a chain-link fence, there was an aboveground circular swimming pool surrounded by warning signs. No lifeguard, no diving, no responsibility. A red plastic float bobbed on its surface.

The AstroLuxe didn't feel like San Diego. It belonged in a dead-end corner of the country that had given up hope when the mills closed or the factories outsourced. Frankie did not want to get out of her clean and comfortable car, but Dekker stood on the narrow sidewalk that ran in front of the rooms and gestured for her to hurry. The motel made Domino's desperate plight real to Frankie in a way that the van never had.

Despite its size, the van had been a homey space fitted out like a tiny one-room apartment with a bed and shelves for cups and plates and plastic cutlery taken from Jack in the Box. Domino and Candace had kept it clean and tidy with hooks to hang clothes on and a plastic bin that was a table at the same time that it stored a loaf of bread, a box of cereal and another of powdered milk, cans of soup, and a bag full of sugar packets, again compliments of Jack. More than knowing Domino and Candace used a one-pound coffee can and plastic bags for a bathroom and that Priest Martha let them shower in the All Souls' parish hall, the AstroLuxe told Frankie that her friend had come to the end of her possibilities.

"I had no idea."

"Why would you?"

And yet Domino would not accept Frankie's offer of a loan to help her until she could help herself. Her refusal had seemed like blind pride. Until now Frankie had not appreciated the depths of her humiliation.

"Where's the van?"

"Near the Dumpsters." He pointed at one of the doors. "That's it. Number eight. We better get inside."

Chapter 33

She looked around at the dark parking lot. There were two or three other vehicles parked in the unmarked spaces, nondescript cars and a truck that had traveled a long way. With the office building between them and the freeway roar, it was quiet enough to hear a dog bark in the backyard of one of the houses above the valley.

"I'm sure we weren't followed. I almost lost you myself."

"Never underestimate the enemy, Captain. Didn't they teach you that?"

The caged light over the door cast a burned caramel glow, and both blinds and curtains were drawn across the window. Frankie heard the sound of a canned television laugh track.

Dekker knocked and the corner of the blind moved. The door opened a crack and Frankie felt a whoosh of cold stale air on her face. Candace let out a cry of joy and grabbed her around the waist, pulling her into the room.

"I knew you'd come. I said it and said it and I knew I was

271

right. Mom said we wouldn't see you again but I knew we would."

Domino sat on the bed with several pillows propped behind her. By the light of the TV her transformation was grotesque. Her lustrous dark hair had been dyed a shrieky orange, accentuating the damage done to her beautiful face. The orbits of both her eyes were bruised purple and the lid of one had swollen shut. One side of her jaw stuck out like a cartoon character with a toothache. She had used a towel to make a sling for her right arm.

Frankie tried to keep her expression neutral, but her arms around Candace tightened as if to protect her. Really it was she who needed support.

Dekker said, "He found her two nights ago."

"Has she seen a doctor?" Emergency room doctors were required to report beatings to the police. "Has anybody helped her?"

"I called Mr. Dekker. Mama had his telephone number on a card."

"I'm pretty good at first aid," Dekker said. "I've had some experience."

"You're a good man to know." She spoke to Candace, "And you were smart to call him. I guess you're a good person to know too." She tried hard to put some lightness into her scratchy voice.

Fresh-faced and hopeful as she always seemed to be, Candace smiled at the praise; but in the cramped room at the AstroLuxe Frankie interpreted her cheerful resil-

272

ience and Domino's stubborn independence, as she hadn't before. These were their default attitudes and assured that no one would ever pity them. With a pang she understood that she had never seen either of them in a truly unguarded moment.

"He said he loves me," Candace said and leaned into Frankie's hip. "But I don't want him to love me."

"Enough," Domino said. Her engorged lips barely moved.

Two suitcases stood at the end of the bed.

"Where are you going?"

"Santa Maria," Dekker said.

"Tell me how I can help."

"Don't . . . help."

Candace stood beside her mother. "We're doin' okay."

"Go home," Domino said.

In the cramped room Frankie felt huge and awkward, all dangling arms and big feet. She had imagined that she and Domino were friends, that they had a particular connection. Whether or not this was an accurate description of their relationship didn't matter anymore.

"I'm not going anywhere."

Domino squinted in the effort to speak, drawing her brows together, cutting two deep creases above her nose. "Stay away . . . Jason."

"I don't even know what he looks like. I wouldn't know the man if I tripped over him."

Candace laughed. The tightness in Frankie's shoulders

and back eased a little. She sat beside Domino and carefully, tenderly, drew her into her arms. For an instant Domino resisted and then Frankie felt the starch wash out of her.

Brave soldier. Brave girl.

War was a terrible thing. It didn't matter that the statement was a cliché. It needed to be said and said again in every language until all the world accepted the truth in the same way it was known around the planet that battery acid wasn't for drinking. Good war, bad war: Frankie knew there was a difference, but the wounding was the same. Mind and body, brain and bone, no one came away unmarked. Even Glory and Rick, who had stayed in San Diego and waited for her to come home, even they had their hidden scars.

"Going. Morning."

"Without saying good-bye?"

Domino looked at Dekker, asking him to explain.

"She was going to call you when she got to Santa Maria. I know some folks up there connected with the VA. They'll help her get a job and she can park the van on their property until she finds an apartment."

"And I'm gonna go to school. For really. And the beach isn't far away."

"Before they go, they both have to see a doctor, My brother."

"We've got someone we trust up in Santa Maria."

"How will they get up there?"

"'rive," Domino said.

"That's ridiculous. It's almost three hundred miles. You can't drive in your condition. I won't let you." Frankie had rarely felt so sure of anything. "You're coming to my house until you're better. I have plenty of room and you can stay as long as you need to."

Domino shook her head.

"Don't argue with me, Domino." Frankie looked at Candace. "Tell her. You know she shouldn't drive."

"She gets dizzy."

"I'm sure she does."

"Frankie's right, Mama."

"In your condition you wouldn't make it to Orange County." Frankie stood up. "We're not going to negotiate on this, Dekker. I have a room with two beds already made up. She can leave the van where it is now and we'll come and get it tomorrow. As soon as I get home, I'll call Harry. Domino needs to be looked at by a doctor." Frankie thought about telling Domino that Candace had hepatitis, but that could come later. "If we were in Iraq, Domino, and you were hurt, I'd pick you up and carry you to safety. You wouldn't fight me there. Don't fight me now."

Dekker said, "It's your call, Domino."

"Please, Mama."

Domino seemed to fold in the middle and her head dropped forward onto her knees.

They loaded the Nissan's trunk and Frankie helped Domino into the backseat. Driving back to Ocean Beach with Dekker following them, she wondered what Rick's reaction would be. She feared a setback in the détente of the afternoon. The fair thing to do was to call him and give him a little time to prepare, but she didn't want to hear his objections so she left her phone in her purse.

It was after two when Frankie pulled into the garage with Candace and Domino and a portion of their worldly goods. Rick didn't seem as surprised as she had expected him to be. And not put out either. He was politely welcoming, and while they drank a beer in the kitchen Dekker told him some of Domino's story. Frankie settled her and Candace in the guest room on the first level. Glory had awakened when Flame barked at the strangers, but her initial excitement at having her best friend in the house vanished the moment she saw what Jason's fists had done to Domino's face. Subdued, she stayed near Rick with her hand locked in his.

Harry came through the front door without knocking and went downstairs to examine Domino. He dressed her injuries and gave her pain meds, assuring her a sound sleep that night.

In the kitchen he told Frankie, Dekker, and Rick that he would be back the next day. He wanted to see Candace in the office for a complete physical, much more thorough than the one required for school enrollment.

"I don't feel sick," Candace said.

"Well, that's good, that's what a doctor likes to hear. But hepatitis is sneaky. Tomorrow we'll get you checked out and give you some medicine and you'll be good as new. Ready for school up in Santa Maria."

Harry looked at Frankie. "Sis, you're a wreck." He dug in his bag for a sample pack of sleep medication. "Eat something, take one of these, and go to bed."

Eventually, the house settled for what remained of the night.

"I never saw anything like what happened to her face," Glory said as Frankie tucked her into bed. "On TV it doesn't look so bad when someone gets in a fight."

"It wasn't a fight, honey. It was a beating."

"Did she do something bad?"

"No, but even if she had, Glory, there's never any reason to beat someone up like that."

"I'd never do that. Not even to Colette."

"I know you wouldn't."

"Will she be okay?"

"She'll heal."

"Was it like that in the war? Did people look bad like that?"

Frankie pulled her daughter into her arms and let her cry. Poor eight-year-old girl, bullied and abandoned and exposed to violence. How had this happened when all Frankie had ever wanted was to protect her?

In the bedroom that still smelled faintly of garlic and pepperoni, Frankie lay still and waited for Harry's wonder pill to put her to sleep. Rick slept like a boy without a trouble in the world. He had accepted Domino and Candace into their home as graciously as if they were old friends.

He loved her. He was going to stick. They both were.

She didn't feel at all sleepy and would not put it past her brother to have given her a placebo. Either that or she was too wired by the day's events. After staring at the ceiling for thirty minutes, she got out of bed and in her warm robe with down slippers on her feet, she curled in the chair by the television and wrote in her journal.

She began by writing about Domino and Candace and without planning to she transitioned into a recollection of Three Fountain Square. She wrote for more than an hour, and her right hand, unaccustomed to holding a pen for so long, cramped in the claw position. As she massaged it she read over the pages covered in large looping script, sometimes adding a detail or a name. Just a few weeks ago she had told her therapist that she would never be able to find the words to describe what happened that day; and now, while it was true that a part of her wanted to tear the pages out and bury them in the garbage under the old vegetables and dribbly coffee filters in a sodden and stinking place where no one would ever look for the truth, she knew she would let her writing stand.

She felt a great emptying relief.

She closed the book and put it on Rick's dresser where he would find it and returned to bed, fitting herself against the curve of his back and the bend of his legs. He murmured something from the depths of a dream and reached around to pat her thigh.

He would learn that she had gone to Iraq to make the world a safer, better place for all children, and how badly she had failed. It was all there in the journal. Evidence of murder and cowardice and dereliction of the duty. But writing her story wouldn't be enough for Senator Belasco. She wanted her to stand before Senator Delaware, the cameras, and the whole world.

Make my bed and light the light
I'll arrive late tonight
Blackbird, bye-bye.

Chapter 34

The morning started slowly with Frankie up first. She felt surprisingly good despite little sleep. She was making oatmeal and a pile of toast when Candace peered into the kitchen, uncharacteristically tentative.

"Is it okay?"

Frankie was so pleased to see her that for a moment all she could do was smile.

"Can I help?" Candace pulled a stool up to the stove where Frankie was stirring the oatmeal. "My grandmother used to make oatmeal. Do you have real milk or do you use the powdered kind?"

Rick came downstairs and while he settled the girls for breakfast, Frankie took a tray to Domino and found her sitting up in bed, staring at the opposite wall. When Frankie walked in, she covered her battered face with her hands.

"Don't be embarrassed. Please."

"...can't stay."

"How do you feel? You sound a little better."

"...don't want to make work..."

She made a place for the tray on the bed. "A couple of days, Domino. That's all."

"Your husband?"

"He's forming a posse to go after Jason. You can stay as long as you want as far as he's concerned."

Domino looked as if she did not quite believe this, but she let it pass. "Candace?"

"She's having oatmeal with Glory and Rick."

"...don't want you to wait...us."

"Can't you for five minutes stop being so damn defensive and just say thank you?"

"Did Candace? Manners?"

"She's happy, Domino. That's what I noticed."

Frankie pulled a Tylenol bottle from her pants pocket and tossed it onto the bed. "You need a couple of these, I bet."

Domino swallowed four with orange juice.

"Do you want to tell me what happened?"

They had been parked at the Frye's lot off Interstate 15. Jason must have been cruising all the big lots that night.

Domino leaned back, closing her eyes.

It was after midnight and she was dozing in the front seat when suddenly the van started to move. It was in park and the brake was on, but Jason had rammed his big truck against the bumper and was ready to do it again.

"I had to get out...make him stop."

He did not believe that they were truly divorced. He

claimed that he had never signed the papers, that he was being railroaded. Frustrated beyond reason, he had begun to hit her and her cries had awakened Candace. She screamed at her father to stop what he was doing and when he seemed not to hear her, she pulled the card with Dekker's number from inside the van's ashtray and lit out across the Frye's parking lot to the back of the store where men worked nights, unloading and unpacking electronic goods. She begged to use one of their cell phones. By the time Dekker got to them, Jason had fled. Domino lay on the asphalt, half conscious.

Frankie sat, letting the story sink in.

"Don't hate him."

"He'd kill you if he could. You know that."

"...doesn't think right. His head's full of—" Domino shrugged. They both knew what his head was full of.

Across the street Maryanne Byrne had arranged travel brochures in two piles on the dining room table. One she called His and the other Hers with room between them for the Both pile. A few galleries for her, soccer or polo or even cricket for him to watch. It didn't really matter what the game was. He enjoyed competition. A beach would please them both if there was a cabana or umbrella, a shady spot where he could snooze all afternoon.

In the middle of the night her arthritic knees had woken her from a sound sleep to announce that the weather in

San Diego was about to change. She'd heard Frankie come home late. Yesterday she'd been in the mood for New York but this morning she leaned toward something tropical.

First married, she and Harlan had lived in military housing in Honolulu, a bland apartment without so much as a palm tree in view. Whenever they could, they retreated to a shacky community off Kalanianole Highway and rented a bungalow on a rise of land overlooking the beach. Pineapple for breakfast, sun and snacks and naps and then fresh fish for dinner. They made love early in the morning when the air was fresh.

"You're daydreaming, Mom." Frankie came through the screen door.

"Why aren't you at work?"

"I told you yesterday. I've got a few days' leave."

Maryanne didn't care for surprises, but she sensed a lift in Frankie's spirits and so forgave her for jolting her out of a pleasant memory.

"Is Dad around?"

"The gopher ate all the daffodil bulbs. Your father's staging a major water strike."

"What kind of mood's he in?"

"Good. If you're not Ho Chi Gopher." Maryanne looked at her daughter, trying to figure out what was different about her. "What're you up to anyway?"

"Are you going on vacation?"

"I asked you a question, Francine."

283

She pulled out a dining room chair and sat down. "I saw Bunny yesterday. Glory let him in when I was at my therapist. She thinks he's family."

"Poor child."

"Do you like him, Mom?"

"I thought no one would ever ask. I loathe him. I always have."

"You hide it really well."

Maryanne sighed. "He's your father's friend."

"Maybe. When it suits his purposes."

Maryanne's eyes narrowed. "Don't get between them, Francine."

"Why are they so close anyway? Do you know the story?"

"I don't. Whatever it was happened on their last tour. Before that they were just ordinary friends. I asked your father to tell me what it was, but he said some things are best not talked about."

Maryanne wished she still smoked. She had broken the habit years ago, but there was a type of conversation that always roused a craving for nicotine.

"I'll tell you something I'm sure of, Frankie. Bunny Bunson is no hero. He didn't save your father's life or anything conventional like that. It's not gratitude your father feels." Maryanne straightened the piles of brochures, knocking them against the tabletop like decks of cards. "I think something happened in 'Nam that revealed a part of Bunny that you and I will never see, and whatever it was, it made your father feel protective. I don't think the General likes him as much as he feels sorry for him."

"He never wanted to protect me. As far as he was concerned, I was on my own out at the end of the gangplank."

"But you never fell in. If you had, he would have dived in after you. He would have fought sharks for you, Frankie. But you never needed him to."

Frankie looked as if she were trying to believe this.

"So yesterday. What did Bunny have to say for himself?"

"He implied that Dad's sick. Is it true?"

"He's fine except for the fact that he's seventy-five years old and spent three tours in hell."

"I need to talk to him, Mom."

"About what?" Frankie didn't answer right away. "Well, never mind, I don't need to know. He'll listen." At least she hoped he would. A thought occurred to Maryanne. "Unless . . . You haven't reenlisted? Tell me you haven't done that."

"No."

"Well, that's good news because I don't think he'd take that well at all."

"Actually I can't wait to be a civilian again."

Maryanne began gathering the brochures in a pile. "I hate to disappoint you, Frankie, but you're every inch a Byrne and that means you'll always be a Marine. It's not just that little tattoo on your wrist. It's part of your DNA."

Chapter 35

The General was in the shade house washing his hands. "Got him this time." He dried his hands on the old-fashioned roller towel beside the sink. "The bastard can't live forever."

Every autumn the same ritual was enacted in different parts of the garden. The General planted daffodil bulbs, choosing a spot far from the previous year's failed effort, and every year a gopher found and ate most of them. He would never admit it, but hungry bugs and caterpillars and gophers were what he enjoyed about gardening. They made it a competition.

"What brings you across the street this morning?" He narrowed his eyes. "You don't look so good, Francine."

"I didn't sleep."

"Well, if that's all it is. Nobody ever died from lack of sleep."

"I need to talk to you, sir."

There were two well-used Adirondack chairs on a

square of grass at the highest point of the garden. From there they had a glimpse through the neighbors' rooftops to the horizon where the sea and cloudy sky met.

The General said, settling into the chair, "Better enjoy the last of the warm weather while we can." Before Frankie could say anything, he added, "Go on down to the fridge in the shade house and bring me up a Heineken. Have one yourself, if you want to."

He talked about the gopher, about the weather, about anything to avoid a serious conversation.

"Listen to me, sir. Please. Senator Belasco wants me to testify about something I saw in Baghdad. She came to see me specially. To ask me to do it."

"You?" He waited for her to say more. "Just tell her you won't."

"I don't think I have a choice, not really, Dad." She seldom called him Dad. *Sir* came more comfortably, *Daddy* never. "I have to tell you what happened over there. Will you listen?"

"Between you and your mother, I don't think I have a choice."

At one time the school in an outlying district of Baghdad had educated both boys and girls in two separate buildings with an office between them. The school had been a source of pride for the community, but when Frankie saw it, almost nothing remained of the classrooms. She and Fatima had met with the principal of the school and several of the teachers and elders of the community, listened to their accusations and complaints. It might be true that coalition forces had inadvertently destroyed the school. There was no way to prove the truth of the accusations. What mattered, Frankie kept repeating, was the new school they were all going to build together. These had been Frankie's first close encounters with Iraqi women and what had struck her about the conversations was their profound fatalism. Frankie had a vision for the destroyed school and their inability to believe in it with her made the meetings exhausting.

"You must understand," Fatima told her after one particularly frustrating encounter, "these women have lived through Saddam and embargo and invasion and now the people who were their neighbors a few years ago are their enemies and why should they believe you when you promise books and paper and glass on the windows? Promises are cheap to these people. Promises are the back side of lies to them."

At the end of the day Frankie went to her rack worn out not from work but from the challenge of believing in the new school enough for all of them. In her mind she began referring to the project as Sad Sack School and then just Sad Sack.

They always left Redline for Sad Sack before dawn, a convoy of three or four vehicles. Generally Frankie and Fatima rode in a Humvee second in line, their driver a soldier, often a female. The first trip Frankie had been so scared that she couldn't breathe normally; and she never became blasé about the trips outside the wire, but she learned to compartmentalize her fear and to identify it as a good thing when it was a motivation and kept her vigilant. They never traveled the same route twice in a row. Insurgents were always on the lookout for patterns of behavior they could exploit. Sometimes they moved at a crawl along the littered streets. Occasionally soldiers walked ahead of the first truck watching for trip wires and booby traps.

Over the months Frankie came to understand the Iraqi women who operated the school. But their fatalism could be contagious if she let it be, especially since progress on rebuilding moved glacially. The men required to clear the ruins were unavailable. Soldiers were needed elsewhere. It was too hot to lug rubble and the labor was considered beneath the dignity of most of the Iraqi men and so it had to be done by boys from Arkansas, Montana, New York. Some in the community were completely against building another school, and they blocked the way however they could. From the beginning all the men, Iraqi and American, resented being told anything by Frankie.

Along the way she lost her sense of humor and then found it again.

Eventually the rubble was cleared away and a new building began to take shape, constructed of locally fired bricks. Halfway through the kiln broke down and there was no one who knew how to fix it, so bricks had to be trucked in from somewhere else and half the time the loads never made it to Sad Sack or they were the wrong size or they were badly made and crumbled under pressure.

In her rack, in her can, standing in a cold shower with sand between her toes, Frankie despaired. Her CO told her to take it easy. He said she was too involved. "Ease up, Tennyson, you'll give yourself a hernia."

Eventually the school had a cement floor, walls, and half of a new roof, and she began to believe in the window glass and screens she had promised the women on the first day. Then came a Tuesday. She was in a room in all that remained of the original school, a ten-foot-square office of some kind, when a soldier outside smoking a cigarette was hit by sniper fire. After that Frankie was told it was too dangerous for her at Sad Sack. She was stuck pushing paper while soldiers and a handful of Marines went house to house, rousting the inhabitants and going through their possessions. Several weeks passed before Frankie could return to Sad Sack and then it was with a special contingent of soldiers who, like guardian angels, quickly spread out around the community, taking up surveillance positions on rooftops surrounding the school, their weapons at the ready. Frankie felt a surge of something like love for these men who were willing to risk their lives for her and for the school.

But after the sniper attack the atmosphere in the community was even less cooperative than before. The women and the few men she had counted on to keep the project going were reluctant to speak to her now. Or they were absent altogether. While Frankie was gone the school had been cannibalized for repairs to homes in the neighborhood. A section of wall was gone and a third of the roof tiles.

They were returning to Redline in a convoy of three—a truck, a Humvee, and a third truck. Over the last week there had been an uptick in insurgent activity and the day before there had been a mortar attack and a suicide bombing along two of the possible routes to the base. They were headed home through a busy neighborhood, a way no one wanted to go because it was always thronged and they were vulnerable from dozens of compass points but the obvious risks and inconveniences made it an unlikely choice and possibly safer for that reason. Frankie was in the front seat riding shotgun, Fatima behind her. A half-dozen soldiers rode in the first truck and more in the rear. The Humvee driver was Shawna Montoya.

The street they were traveling had been hit by IEDs several months back. The many destroyed buildings were proof of that and occasionally opened up wide sight lines from where Frankie sat. Suddenly the street did a dogleg and she heard Montoya mutter to herself. *Holy shit and what the fuck, we've got us a problemo aquí.*

The street was barely wider than an alley. The rear truck was out of sight, around the corner. The Humvee straddled the dogleg.

Fuck and frijoles.

The lead truck stopped where the narrow street entered a busy square. The squawk of Montoya's radio filled the Humvee.

Frankie was the only person with a clear view of what lay ahead. On her side of the street, a building lay in ruins, and she could see through to the square crowded with activity. Directly across it, partially obscured by the busy marketplace, was an ornate building that appeared to be some kind of government office.

Prayers were over and the men had gone from the mosques to cafés where they would drink coffee and smoke while women, veiled or wearing scarves, shopped at the stalls. Frankie couldn't see what was for sale off the backs of dilapidated trucks, spread on rugs opened on the dust, or in tarp-covered stalls, but she had been in souks similar to this one. The vendors sold DVDs and Iraqi flags, bolts of cloth, kids' clothes and cooking implements, and produce: onions and beans, figs, dates and oranges and tomatoes when they were available. In all such open-air marketplaces there were brightly colored spices sold from bins by the scoop. In the café the men were watching television, probably soccer. Frankie saw the flicker of the screen. Inside the gritty air would be dense with cigarette smoke.

This square in Baghdad was as far from San Diego as Frankie could imagine being. She had to keep reminding herself that the people she saw were essentially like her despite the obvious cultural differences. It was too easy to think of them as another species when she knew they loved their children, ate meals together, enjoyed sports, and gossiped just as Americans did. She thought about the school they were building and told herself not to stop believing in the mission.

Inside the Humvee the air was hot and rank and she felt sweat running down her side.

The convoy could not just charge ahead through the marketplace, expecting people and animals to move aside. The previous week a truck had run down a family's goat and there'd been hell to pay. But parked where they were, Frankie felt like a duck wearing a "shoot me" sign in a fairground shooting gallery. She wondered why the US military didn't travel in rattletraps like ordinary Iraqis. No one would notice them then.

A headache bloomed in the hollows of her eyes. The radio crackled and she heard the convoy officer in the forward truck tell them to hold where they were. Something was happening. Montoya kept on swearing to herself in Spanish and English.

"This is not good," Fatima said.

Things happened quickly after that.

Three black Escalades sped into the square from the northeast corner, at Frankie's ten o'clock position. Immediately the square began to clear. The men drinking and smoking outdoors left their coffee and cigarettes and fled into the café. The vendors slapped together their tables and chairs and awnings and disappeared with their cash boxes, leaving their goods unattended. Frankie saw a generic dog sniff at the table where something savory must have been displayed, but even it sensed trouble and skulked away with its tail between its legs. Frankie heard someone yell in Arabic, an answering yell, and then silence.

Heavy with armoring the Escalades careened into the square and wallowed to a stop, forming a black line in front of the civic building.

From the radio Frankie heard the convoy officer tell them again to stay where they were. *Nobody move.*

Frankie reached behind her and grabbed a pair of powerful binoculars.

"What's happening out there?" Montoya's view was blocked by the truck ahead. "What can you see, Captain?"

"It's G4S."

Frankie could read the insignia on the car doors, a sword and saber beneath an olive branch. Some of the men formed a perimeter around the vehicles, others entered the building.

Frankie had met a few G4S contractors. She refocused her binoculars to get a better look at the men around the SUVs on the chance she might see a familiar face. One figure held her attention. He had silver-blond hair, worn rather long, and his skin was startlingly white. In Iraq the man's pallor was freakish. She thought of him carefully applying sunscreen every hour to protect his skin from the sun and of the ribbing his crew must give him for this. She named him Whitey in her mind.

Montoya hit the steering wheel impatiently. "What the fuck is going on?"

They were all thinking about snipers and IEDs. To Frankie the tension was like an article of clothing, a bra many sizes too small.

Two Arab men in Western dress emerged from the civic building surrounded by G4S personnel. At the same moment, only a few yards from Frankie, a bearded man in a flowing white dishdasha darted out from the ruins on her right, a shopping bag swinging from his hand. Behind him came a woman, her face covered, gripping the hand of a child, a boy around Glory's age. The woman tripped on a chunk of brick at the edge of the road a few steps ahead of the Humvee's front right fender. She let go of the boy's hand just before she hit the ground. The man, behind the Humvee now, ran on, and as he did he dropped the bag he was carrying, spilling onions and beans under the vehicle's tires. The boy stopped and Frankie thought she could feel his indecision. Should he pick up the food, help the woman, or run ahead? Across the square someone yelled. Frankie lifted her binoculars, and in that second she saw Whitey take aim. She saw the flash from the muzzle of his M16.

Four feet from where she sat Frankie saw first the boy go down and then the woman hit, the bounce of her body as bullets ripped into her, the snap of her head as her chin hit the dirt. Blood geysered from her throat. The boy's body was so light, the bullets lifted him off the ground and he seemed to flutter for an instant before he flipped onto his back. The shooting stopped. Frankie was vaguely aware of the Escalades speeding out of the square as she tried to open the door of the Humvee. She saw the boy blink, saw his hands grab at the air.

"He's alive," she screamed and struggled but Montoya held her back.

Alive. Alive.

"Look away." From behind, Fatima tried to cover Frankie's eyes. "You cannot help him. Look away."

For Frankie to touch a Muslim boy, even to save his life, was taboo. Still she fought against Montoya's strength and tore at Fatima's hands until she had no more strength left and all she could do was rest her forehead against the dusty window and watch the boy blink. And blink and die.

As Frankie told the General her story, a line of crows had come to perch on the ridge of the house. She thought of them as jurors in a silent line.

"I went to the chaplain and he advised me to go to my CO. He told me it was awful what happened, the child and all, but he was sure the contractor had a good reason to fire. I told him they were coming from the market with beans and onions, but he said it didn't matter and I should put it out of my mind."

"Your CO was right. It could have been beans or onions or it could have been grenades." The General took her hand and held it between his own. "Terrible things happen in war, Frankie. Things I never wanted you to see."

"You say that, sir, and so did the CO, and Bunny. It's what people always say. But it's not an excuse. It doesn't make it okay. I could have saved that boy."

"It's reality." The General's hold on her hand tightened. "I never wanted you to go—"

"But I did! And what I was doing, working with people, trying to build a school, I was good at that, and I was a good officer, my Marines respected me and they knew I had their backs."

The General scuffed his shoe at a line of ants.

"I was, I am, a good Marine. But that day? I wasn't a good human being."

"And now you want to go in front of cameras and air that dirty laundry? Make a public confession and bring shame on the military?"

"This is about G4S, sir. My story? I don't know if I'll talk about that or not. Probably. Maybe. I will if I have to. I just don't know yet. Right now, I'm talking about one man wearing a G4S uniform who shot down two people in cold blood. I'm not saying they're all bad because I know they're not. I honor the good ones, sir. But this guy was dirty. I saw him take aim at that boy and his mother."

"He saw the bag in the man's hand, Frankie."

"So he shot the mother and child? After the man had dropped the bag of groceries? It went down fast, but I saw it all." They had been no more than target practice for the blond-haired man. "They were killed for a paycheck, sir. Most of us, we believe in something more important than that."

The General had no response.

"Bunny said that if I told you the truth, it would kill you. Well, I'll be honest, holding it inside is killing *me*. I don't want to lose my husband over this, sir. Or Glory."

"Is it that bad?"

She knew only this for certain, that she could not go on as she had been. She would rather be dead than face the same memory and shame every morning for the next forty or fifty years. "You taught Harry and me to do the right thing even when it wasn't easy. Well, this isn't easy. I don't want to testify but I've thought about it a lot and I know it's the right thing to do. I've known it from the beginning. That's why I went to the chaplain."

"What about the interpreter. Or the driver. You weren't the only person there."

"But I'm the only one who saw it all." She pulled her hands away from his and folded them in her lap. Her voice was thin and clear, trembling. "I have to do this, sir. With or without your blessing."

She waited, not knowing what he would say.

The General stood up and she knew he was going to walk away as he had the other night when Glory announced she had PTSD, as he had done when she told him she was going to Iraq. He stared up at the crows staring down at him.

He said, "You'll wear your uniform, of course. And you'll stand tall and you'll answer every question." He turned, his back as straight and strong as it had ever been. "Senator Delaware'll give you a hard time but you won't dodge around and you won't cry. He'll eat you for lunch if you cry."

"I won't cry, sir."

"You'll tell it to the committee just the way you told me?"

"I will."

"And you won't forget who you are?"

"Never."

"You're my daughter and you're a Byrne, never forget that."

"I won't, sir."

"Then I'll be proud of you." His blue eyes filled with tears as he saluted her. "*Semper fi*, Francine. *Semper fi*."

Discussion Questions

1. In the prologue of *When She Came Home* we are introduced to Frankie as a child, and we see the way her family interacts during a very important moment. What does this tell us about the Byrne family and how does it prepare us for the rest of the novel?

2. Frankie attributes her desire to enlist in the Marines to the attack on September 11. She says she imagined that her own child could have lost her life, and she wanted to help ensure that kind of violent tragedy would never happen again. Do you think this truly was her motivation, or was there another desire driving her? Could she have had more than one motivation?

3. General Byrne has clear feelings regarding the roles men and women should play both in the military and at home. How do you feel about his position? When it comes to women serving in the armed forces, is there a double standard? Is there a difference for a child when her mother deploys rather than her father?

4. What do you think about Rick's relationship with Melanie? Do you believe they were just friends? Is this friendship understandable and acceptable given the circumstances?

5. Rick suggests that the problems in their marriage are more Frankie's fault than his, and she seems to agree with that assessment. Do you agree that Frankie is more at fault than Rick? If so, why? If not, is Rick more to blame, are they equally at fault, or is there another factor to consider?

6. Should Rick have done more to help Frankie readjust to life after Iraq? What more could he have done to help her? Is two months an acceptable amount of time for a person to adjust after coming home?

7. How do you feel about the way Frankie handles Glory's troubles at school? Should she have gotten Rick involved sooner? Should she have punished Glory in some way? Do you think she gave her sound advice for how to deal with the problem? What might you have done differently if you were Glory's parent? How common do you think bullying really is? Did you ever experience bullying in school?

8. Compare the relationship Glory has with Rick to the relationship Frankie has with the General. What positive influence might a father have on his daughter when she is Glory's age (eight) or older? What were Rick's strengths as a father? What were the General's?

DISCUSSION QUESTIONS

9. Frankie is sometimes jealous of Glory's relationship with the General. Why is that? Is it a normal response, for a mother to envy a daughter? What other circumstances might give rise to this feeling? Is the General a bully? If you accused him of this, how would he react? How does bullying in the family compare to that which goes on in schools?

10. Maryanne has seen two generations of Byrne Marines come home from war and knows how difficult the readjustment process can be. Do you think she was right to stay quiet about what she saw in Frankie? Should she have gotten more involved in Frankie's problems? If so, what could she have done? Or conversely, was Maryanne wrong to speak to Rick and Glory as she did after the football game incident? How would you have handled that situation in her position?

11. Maryanne and the General were very much in love when they were young. How has this love changed with the years? How does their forty-year marriage compare to others you might know? Why have they stuck together?

12. Why is Domino so important to Frankie? Should Frankie have ignored Domino's protests and called the police to go after Jason? Do you think Frankie did the right thing by bringing Domino into her home, or by doing so was she putting her own family in danger? What is the significance of Frankie's meeting with

Dawny at the Jack in the Box? With Mrs. Greenwoody at the supermarket?

13. In some ways Frankie seems like her own worst enemy. She initially didn't want to go to therapy and is reluctant to write in her journal or attend group sessions. She keeps secrets from her husband and won't see a doctor about her throat. Are Frankie's actions understandable, given the circumstances? Why or why not?

Drusilla Campbell presents a gripping
story of three generations of women
who must overcome a legacy of
violence, secrecy, and lies...

Please turn this page for an excerpt from

THE GOOD SISTER

Chapter 1

San Diego, California
The State of California v. Simone Duran
March 2010

On the first day of Simone Duran's trial for the attempted murder of her children, the elements conspired to throw their worst at Southern California. Arctic storms that had all winter stalled or washed out north of Los Angeles chose the second week of March to break for the south and were now lined up, a phalanx of wind and rain stretching north into Alaska. In San Diego a timid sprinkle began after midnight, gathered force around dawn, and now, with a hard northwest wind behind it, deluged the city with a driving rain. Roxanne Callahan had lived in San Diego all her life and she'd never seen weather like this.

In the stuffy courtroom a draft found the nape of her neck, driving a shudder down her spine to the small of her back: she feared that if the temperature dropped just one degree she'd start shaking and wouldn't be able to stop. Behind her, someone in the gallery had a persistent, bronchial cough. Roxanne had a vision of germs floating like pollen on the air. She wondered if hostile people—the gawkers and jackals, the ghoulishly curious, the home-grown experts and lurid trial junkies—carried germs more virulent than those of friends and allies. Not that there were many well-wishers in the crowd. Most of the men and women in the courtroom represented the millions of people who hated Simone Duran; and if their germs were half as lethal as their thinking, Simone would be dead by dinnertime.

Roxanne and her brother-in-law, Johnny Duran, sat in the first row of the gallery, directly behind the defense table. As always Johnny was impeccably groomed and sleekly handsome; but new gray rimed his black hair, and there were lines engraved around his eyes and mouth that had not been there six months earlier. He was the owner and president of a multimillion-dollar construction company specializing in hotels and office complexes, a man with many friends, including the mayor and chief of police; but since the attempted murder of his children he had become reclusive, spending all his free time with his daughters. He and Roxanne had everything to say to each other and at the same time nothing. She knew the same question filled his mind as hers and each knew it was pointless to ask: what could or should they have done differently?

Following her arraignment on multiple counts of attempted murder, Simone had been sent to St. Anne's Psychiatric Hospital for ninety days' observation. Bail was set at a million dollars, and Johnny put the lake house up as collateral. He leased a condo on a canyon where Simone and her mother, Ellen Vadis, lived after her release from St. Anne's. Her bail had come with heavy restrictions. She was forbidden contact with her daughters and confined to the condo, tethered by an electronic ankle bracelet and permitted to leave only with her attorney on matters pertaining to the case and with her mother for meetings with her doctor.

Like Johnny, Roxanne visited Simone several times a week. These tense interludes did nothing to lift anyone's spirits as far as she could tell. They spent hours on the couch watching television, sometimes holding hands; and while Roxanne often talked about her life, her work, her friends, any subject that might help the illusion that they were sisters like other sisters, Simone rarely spoke. Sometimes she asked Roxanne to read to her from a book of fairy tales she'd had since childhood. Stories of dancing princesses and enchanted swans soothed Simone much as a lullaby might a baby; and more than once Roxanne had left her, covered by a cashmere throw, asleep on the couch with the book beside her. Lately she had begun to suck her thumb as she had when she was a child. Roxanne faced the truth: the old Simone, the silly girl with her secrets and demands, her narcissism, the manic highs and the black holes where the meany-men lived, even her love, might be gone forever.

A medicine chest of pharmaceuticals taken morning and night kept her awake and put her to sleep, eased her down from mania toward catatonia and then half up again to something like normal balance. She took drugs that elevated her mood, focused her attention, flattened her enthusiasm, stifled her anxiety, curbed her imagination, cut back her paranoia, and put a plug in her curiosity. The atmosphere in the condo was almost unbearably artificial.

Across the nation newspapers, magazines, and blogs were filled with Simone stories passing as truth. Her picture was often on television screens, usually behind an outraged talking head. Sometimes it was the mug shot taken the day she was booked, occasionally one of the posed photos from the Judge Roy Price Dinner when she looked so beautiful but was dying inside. The radio blab-meisters could not stop ranting about her, about what a monster she was. Spinning know-it-alls jammed the call-in lines. Weekly articles in the supermarket tabloids claimed to know and tell the whole story.

The whole story! If Roxanne had had any sense of humor left she would have cackled at such a preposterous claim. Simone's story was also Roxanne's. And Ellen's and Johnny's. They were all of them responsible for what happened that September afternoon.

Roxanne's husband, Ty Callahan, had offered to put his work at the Salk Institute on hold so he could attend the trial with her, but she didn't want him there. He and her friend Elizabeth were links to the world of hopeful, optimistic, ordinary people. The courtroom would taint that.

The night before, Roxanne and Ty had eaten Chinese takeout; and afterward, while he read, she lay with her head on his lap searching for the blank space in her mind where repose hid. They went to bed early and made love with surprising urgency, as if time pressed in upon them, and before it was too late they had to establish their connection in the most basic way. Roxanne should have slept afterward; instead she got up and watched late-night infomercials for computer careers and miraculous skin products, finally falling asleep on the couch, where Ty found her in the morning with Chowder, their yellow Labrador, snoring on the floor beside her, a ball between his front paws.

"Don't look at me," she said, sitting up. "I'm a mess."

"You are." Ty handed her a mug of coffee, his smile breaking over her like sunlight. "The worst-looking woman I've seen this morning."

She rested her forehead against his chest and closed her eyes. "Tell me I don't have to do this today."

He drew her to him. "We'll get through it, Rox."

"But who'll we be? When it's over?"

"I guess we just have to wait and see."

"And you'll be here?"

"If I think about leaving, I'll come get you first."

In the courtroom she closed her eyes and pictured Ty with his postdocs gathered around him, the earnest young men and women who looked up to him in a way that Roxanne had found sweet and faintly amusing back when she could still laugh. She knew how her husband worked, the care he took and the careful notations he made in his lab notebooks in his precise draftsman's hand. With life falling apart and nothing certain from one day to the next, it was calming—a meditation of sorts—to think of Ty at work across the city in a lab overlooking the Pacific.

Attorney David Cabot and Simone entered the courtroom and took their places at the defense table. Cabot had been Johnny's first choice to defend Simone. Once the quarterback for the San Diego Chargers, he had not won many games but was widely admired for qualities of leadership and character. His win-loss statistics were much better in law than in football. He had made his name trying controversial cases, and Simone's was definitely that.

Simone, small and thin, her back as narrow as a child's, sat beside Cabot, conservatively dressed in a black-and-white wool dress with a matching jacket and serious shoes in which she could have hiked Cowles Mountain. In her ears she wore the silver-and-turquoise studs Johnny had given her when they became engaged. As intended, she looked mild and calm, too sweet to commit a crime worse than jaywalking.

Conversation in the gallery hushed as the jurors entered and took their seats. One, a college student, looked sideways at Simone; but the others directed their gazes across the courtroom to the wall of rain-beaten windows. Among the twelve there were two Hispanic women in their mid-twenties, one of them a college student; three men and a woman, all retired professionals; a Vietnamese manicurist; and one middle-aged black woman, the co-owner of a copy shop. Roxanne tried to see intelligence and tolerance and wisdom in their faces, but all she saw was an ordinary sampling of San Diego residents. For them to be a true jury of Simone's peers at least one should be a deep depressive, one extravagantly rich, and another pathologically helpless.

Just let them be good people, Roxanne prayed. Good and sensitive and clear-thinking. Let them be honest. Let them see into my sister and know that she is not a monster.

In this provocative story, Drusilla Campbell explores the fears that drive good people to do bad things—and the courage it takes to make things right.

Please turn this page for an excerpt from

LITTLE GIRL GONE

Chapter 1

Madora Welles was twelve when she learned that some girls are lucky in life, others not so much. On the day her father walked into the desert, she learned that luck can run out in a single day. After that, there's no more Daddy telling the whole story of "Jack and the Beanstalk," start to finish, in one minute flat. No more laughing Mommy standing by with a stopwatch to make sure he doesn't cheat. Lucky girls did not have fathers who changed from happy to sad, easy to angry to tears in the space of an hour, locked themselves in the shed and banged on things with a hammer. No lucky girl ever had a father who walked into the desert and put a bullet in his brain.

Yuma, Arizona: the town is laid out like a grid on the desert flats. Single-story buildings, fast-food joints on every corner, dust and heat and wind, lots of military, and a pretty good baseball team. That's about it.

Madora's mother, Rachel, said Yuma killed her husband, said it was killing her too. To save herself she turned on the television, stepped into other people's stories, and got lost. For a long time she forgot to care about her daughter. Failing in school, drinking, and wading into the river of drugs that ran through the middle of Yuma, Madora was seventeen when she met Willis Brock.

Madora's best friend was Kay-Kay, a girl from a family with slightly better luck than her own. Instead of using a gun, Kay-Kay's father had been drinking himself to death for a few years when she and Madora latched on to each other like twins separated at birth. Rachel recognized trouble when she saw it come through the door chewing gum and smelling of tobacco, but Madora had stopped listening to her by then. Rachel fell asleep in front of the television, in the old La-Z-Boy lounger that still smelled like Old Spice.

Madora and Kay-Kay and a boy named Randy who knew someone who knew someone else who had a car drove south of Yuma, into the desert near the border, where they had heard there was a party house and big action. Rachel had told Madora a thousand times to stay away from the border, but in the years after her father's suicide, Madora's life was all about escape and rebellion; and the drugs and remote setting excited her. Until the bikers came she was having a good time drinking bourbon from a bottle and smoking grass, taking her social cues from Kay-Kay. Unconsciously, she copied Kay-Kay's slope-shouldered, world-wary posture, and she was careful not to smile too much or laugh too loudly. Not that there was ever much humor at parties like this; and what passed for conversation was dissing and one-upping, arguments and aimless, convoluted complaints and comparisons of this night to others, this weed to the stuff they smoked the week before.

At seventeen, Madora's thinking was neither introspective nor analytical, but she was conscious of being different from Kay-Kay and the slackers around her and of wishing she were not. She wanted to eradicate the part of herself that was like her father: a dreamer, a hoper, a wisher upon first stars. At the party that night in the desert she kept to herself the resilient romantic notions that floated in the back of her mind. Never mind the odds against it: a handsome boy would come through the door, and he would look at her the way her father once had and she would feel as she once did, like the luckiest girl in the world.

Instead the bikers came. Voices rose and the air snapped; the music got louder and the run-down old house vibrated to the bass beat.

Kay-Kay put her mouth close to Madora's ear, her breath an oily whiskey ribbon. "I'm gonna do it." It was so noisy, she had to say it twice. "Those guys, they brought crank. I'm gonna try it."

Madora had been drinking and toking all night. Kay-Kay's words didn't really sink in, but what her friend did, she wanted to do as well. "Me too."

In a room at the back of the house, they sat on the floor

opposite a bearded man with a gold front tooth who said his name was Jammer. Men and girls—long-haired and skin-head, pierced and tattooed and leather jacketed, all strangers to Madora—leaned against each other, stood or squatted with their backs to the wall. Jammer wore a black tank top so tight it cut into the muscles of his overdeveloped arms and shoulders and chest, and his hands were spotted with burn scabs. He held a six-inch pipe with a bulb at the end and played the flame of a lighter under the glass taking care not to touch it with the fire, rolling the pipe as he did.

Madora watched in fascination as the pale amber cube in the bulb dissolved. Her lip hurt and she realized she was biting down on it. *I shouldn't be here,* she thought, and looked at Kay-Kay. One sign that her friend wanted to leave and Madora would have popped to her feet in an instant. But Kay-Kay was mesmerized by the pipe in Jammer's hand. She leaned forward, watching avidly as he turned and rolled it. A drop of saliva hung suspended from her lower lip.

The others in the room passed a joint and spoke softly; occasionally Madora heard someone laugh. The door to the rest of the house was shut, but beneath her Madora felt the beat of the music. In the smoky room her eyes watered and blurred. A man crouched behind her, pressing his knees into her back. He held her shoulders and urged her to lean back.

"Relax, chicky, you're gonna love this."

Jammer held out the pipe to Madora, and Kay-Kay

elbowed her gently and grinned encouragement. Madora thought of a birthday party, the expectant moment just before the lighted cake and the singing began.

The man behind her stroked her arm, running his fingers along her shoulder and up into her hair. He whispered, "Don't be afraid. I'll take care of you."

She took the pipe between her fingers and put her lips around the tube. She started to inhale, but just as she did, the image of the birthday party came back to her, and she saw her father holding the cake; and she was six again, and no matter what, Daddy would always take care of her. Her throat closed; her hand came up and dashed the pipe onto the floor. Someone yelled and her head exploded in white light and there was no yelling or talking, no music anywhere, just a burning pain as if her head were an egg and someone had thrown it against the wall.

She struggled to her feet, fell to her knees, and stood up again. Someone grabbed her and pushed her against the wall. Hands groped at the front of her T-shirt and she flailed and tried to scream but her throat and her lungs had frozen shut. More hands grabbed her arms and dragged her across the floor; her ballerina slippers came off her feet, and her bare heels tore on the broken linoleum. A door opened and she fell forward into a wall of fresh air. Someone shoved her into a chair and she sat down hard, gagging for air.

A voice growled. "Stay with her."

Kay-Kay's voice came from far away. "Holy shit, are you all right?"

Madora's left cheek jerked as her eye blinked crazily.

"You want me to call your mom? Oh, Jesus, Madora, I can't get her to come out here."

Madora wanted to stop the twitching, but her hand couldn't find her face.

"No one's gonna stop partying to drive you home."

Her hands and feet and head were attached by strings. She bobbled like a puppet.

"Jammer said you only got a whiff. Lucky, huh? Are you listening, Mad? He says like only one in a trillion people react bad like you. It might've killed you. I can't believe how lucky you were."

Someone was stirring her brain with a wooden spoon.

"No one wants to leave yet, and anyway, Jammer says you'll feel better."

Then she was alone on the porch outside the house. A coyote padding across the yard stopped to look at her, moonlight reflected in its yellow eyes. Kay-Kay returned and sat beside her for a few moments, holding her sweating hands, and then she went back in the house.

The desert temperature dropped, and the air, cold and dry, lay over everything. The sweat dried on Madora's body and she shivered, and her teeth rattled like bones in a paper bag. She dragged her feet up onto the chair and wrapped her arms around her knees. She rested her face on her knees and tried to close her eyes, but the lids bounced as if on springs. In the house someone had turned up a CD of an old Doors recording. The keyboard riffs scored her senses and the beat got down inside her, deep. Her muscles ached with it.

Car lights streaked across the cholla and prickly pear. For a moment she was sightless, then bleary-eyed, and the figure coming toward her seemed to emerge out of water like something blessed, a holy vision. Without knowing why, she tried to rise from the chair where she'd been cowering. Her legs wobbled under her and he reached out, helping her to balance.

"Hey, little girl, you better stay down."

She saw two of him, sometimes three, floating like a mirage, but his voice was clear and strong. Under it, the pounding beat and the keyboard riffs grew fainter until they seemed to come from far out in the desert, where she knew there must be a party going on but nothing that concerned her anymore.

"Don't be afraid, little girl. Willis won't let anything bad happen to you."